# Praise for Joe R. Lansdale

"The most consistently original and originally visceral writer the great state of Texas (or any other state for that matter) has seen in a score of flashpoint summers."  —*The Austin Chronicle*

"A folklorist's eye for telling detail and front porch raconteur's sense of pace."
—*The New York Times Book Review*

"Lansdale's prose, both laconic and sarcastic, is so thick with slang and regional accent that it's as tasty as a well-cured piece of beef jerky. Readers will want to savor each bite."
—*Milwaukee Journal Sentinel*

"Lansdale reaches the reader on a gut level. . . . A terrific writer."
—*Ellery Queen's Mystery Magazine*

"Lansdale is an exceptional storyteller."
—*Rocky Mountain News*

# Books by Joe R. Lansdale

## In the Hap and Leonard Series

*Savage Season*
*Mucho Mojo*
*The Two-Bear Mambo*
*Bad Chili*
*Rumble Tumble*
*Captains Outrageous*
*Vanilla Ride*

## Other Novels

*Sunset and Sawdust*
*Lost Echoes*
*Leather Maiden*

Joe R. Lansdale

# *Bad Chili*

Joe R. Lansdale is the author of more than a dozen novels, including *Sunset and Sawdust* and *Leather Maiden*. He has received the British Fantasy Award, the American Mystery Award, the Edgar Award, the Grinzane Cavour Prize for Literature, and seven Bram Stoker Awards. He lives with his family in Nacogdoches, Texas.

www.joerlansdale.com

# *Bad Chili*

## A Hap and Leonard Novel

## Joe R. Lansdale

**Vintage Crime/Black Lizard**
Vintage Books
A Division of Random House, Inc.
New York

FIRST VINTAGE CRIME/BLACK LIZARD EDITION, MAY 2009

*Copyright © 1997 by Joe R. Lansdale*

Library of Congress Cataloging-in-Publication Data:
Lansdale, Joe R., 1951–
Bad chili : a Hap and Leonard novel / Joe R. Lansdale.
—1st Vintage Crime/Black Lizard ed.
p. cm.
ISBN 978-0-307-45550-5
1. Collins, Hap (Fictitious character)—Fiction. 2. Pine, Leonard
(Fictitious character)—Fiction. 3. Texas, East—Fiction. I. Title.
PS3562.A557B33 2008
813'.54—dc22
2009002065

www.vintagebooks.com

Printed in the United States of America
10  9  8  7  6  5  4  3  2

This one's for my brother, Andrew Vachss, warrior.

Life's like a bowl of chili in a strange cafe. Sometimes it's pretty tasty and spicy. Other times, it tastes like shit.

—Jim Bob Luke

# *Bad Chili*

# 1

It was mid-April when I got home from the offshore rig and discovered my good friend Leonard Pine had lost his job bouncing drunks at the Hot Cat Club because, in a moment of anger, when he had a bad ass on the ground out back of the place, he'd flopped his tool and pissed on the rowdy's head.

Since a large percentage of the club was outside watching Leonard pop this would-be troublemaker like a Ping-Pong ball, and since Leonard hadn't been discreet enough to turn to a less visible angle when he decided to water the punk's head, the management was inclined to believe Leonard had overreacted.

Leonard couldn't see this. In fact, he thought it was good business. He told management if word of this got around, potential troublemakers would be sayin', "You

1

start some shit at the Hot Cat Club, you get that mean queer nigger on your ass, and he'll piss on your head."

Leonard, taking into account the general homophobia and racism of the local population, considered this a deterrent possibly even more effective than the death penalty. The management disagreed, said they hated to do it, but they had to let him go.

That wasn't enough of a heartbreak, about this same time Leonard lost his true love, Raul, again, and was in the mood to tell me about it. We drove out to a friend's pasture in Leonard's latest wreck, an ancient white Rambler with a loose spring under the passenger's ass, set up some cans on a rotting log and took pot shots at them with a revolver while we talked beneath a bright blue, cloudless sky.

Way it happened was Leonard knocked a row of cans down with a few good shots, and as we walked over to put them up again, he was beginning to tell me how he and Raul had been arguing a lot—which was nothing new—and how Raul had walked out. This was not new either. But this time Raul hadn't come back. That was new.

Few days later Leonard discovered Raul had taken up with a leather-clad fella with a beard and a Harley, and had been seen riding around LaBorde on the back of the bike, pushed up tight against Leather Boy. So tight, Leonard said, "He must have had his dick up the fucker's ass."

We had one revolver between us, and as Leonard talked, he handed the revolver to me and I started to load it. I had placed four shells in the chambers when out of the woods, bounding as if on a Pogo stick, came a frenzied squirrel.

Let me tell you, if you have never seen an agitated squirrel you have seen very little, nor have you heard much, because the sound of an angry squirrel is not to be forgotten. It is high-pitched and shrill enough to twist your jockeys up your crack.

For a moment, Leonard and I were frozen with amazement, stunned by the shrieking. Both of us have been in and around the woods all our lives, and as a youngster I had hunted squirrel and our family had fried and stewed and eaten them with poke salad and mustard greens on many occasions, but in all my born days, and I'm sure in Leonard's, we had never seen anything quite like this.

I suddenly wondered if my taste in meat had been passed down through generations of squirrels by word of mouth, and here, finally, was old Beebo come to avenge the death of a relative. That rascal was bouncing four feet high at a leap, and after about four leaps it was totally clear of the woods and was springing directly toward us.

We broke and ran. The squirrel, however, was not a quitter. Glancing over my shoulder, I saw that it was in fact gaining on us, and Leonard's cussing was having absolutely no effect, other than to perhaps further enrage the animal, who might have had Baptist leanings.

We made the car just ahead of the squirrel, but we didn't make the doors. We jumped onto the hood and then the roof of the car, which was, of course, useless. The squirrel sprang to the hood effortlessly and, with a chatter and a spray of froth, leaped onto the roof and directly at me.

Leonard rescued me. He swatted it aside with the back of his hand, knocked it twisting to the ground, where it did a kind of dance on two legs, regained its footing, then began to run hysterically about in a circle. A heart-beat later it broke the circle and charged the car again.

I opened up on the fucker. Three shots in quick succession, but the way it was moving—all those battlefield tactics, zigzagging and whatnot—I succeeded only in throwing up some pasture dirt.

Next moment, the squirrel regained the hood and the roof, and the little bastard made clear I had been his intended all along. It latched onto my right forearm with its teeth and it didn't let go, and let me tell you, squirrels have some serious goddamn teeth. It may not be lion or tiger stuff, but when they latch on to you the difference seems minimal.

I was off the roof of the car and running, the squirrel hanging on to my arm as if it were a dog tick. I swatted it with the revolver and it still wouldn't let go. I held it out at arm's length and shot it through the chest, but it wasn't going to let a little thing like a bullet make it give in. I ran about the pasture hopping and jerking my arm, and after what seemed an eternity the squirrel finally lost its hold, taking flesh with it. It hit the ground and rolled, and even with a bullet hole in its small chest, it began to chase me willy-nilly about the pasture, bleeding and chattering all over the place.

I wheeled and tried to fire again, but the revolver was empty. I threw it at the squirrel and missed. I ran every which way but the squirrel was not deterred. It came leaping and biting at my ass as I darted, bobbed, and weaved, and surely would have overtaken me had not Leonard run over the disgruntled critter with his car. Another thirty seconds and my lungs would have burst and the squirrel's intended plans for me would have been moot.

I first realized what had happened when Leonard hit his horn, and I looked over my shoulder to see the squirrel get his. It was a nasty thing, this squirrel destruction. The car banged the squirrel as it leaped, making it a kind of temporary hood ornament. When the squirrel hit the dirt, Leonard slammed on the brakes, backed up, took sight of the injured beast and ran over it, then reversed over it, got out, found a stick and poked at the parts of the squirrel that were sticking out from under the tire. The damn thing was still alive and shrieking. Leonard had to finish it with the stick and his boot heel.

On the way to the doctor, me dripping blood all over the Rambler, Leonard said, "I was wondering, Hap. Did you know that squirrel? And if so, could it have been something you said?"

# 2

"Rabid would be my guess," said Dr. Sylvan.

"Oh, shit," I said.

"That about puts it into perspective. Rabies is making a big comeback these days. The woods are thick with foam-mouthed critters."

Me and the doc were in one of his examining rooms and I was sitting on the examining table, and he had just finished sewing up my arm and fastening a bandage around it. He was a sloppy-looking silver-haired man in his sixties, wearing a blood-specked white smock (my blood), rubber gloves, and an expression like someone waiting for a brain transplant. This expression was misleading.

Sylvan put his foot on the trash-can lid lever and pressed. The lid came up, and very carefully he removed his gloves and dropped them into the can and let the lid close. He washed his hands in the sink, fumbled inside his smock, got out a cigarette and lit it.

"Isn't that bad for your health?" I said.

"Yeah," said Dr. Sylvan, "but I do it anyway."

"In your examination room?"

"It's my examination room."

"But that seems like a bad idea. Patients will smell it."

"I spray a little Lysol around."

"You sure the squirrel had rabies? Could he have just been pissed off about something?"

"Was he frothing at the mouth?"

"Either that or he had been eating whipped cream."

"And you said he was running about in an erratic manner?"

"I don't know it was so erratic. He came right for me. He seemed to have a mission."

"You ever seen a squirrel do this before?"

"Well, no."

"Did he leave a note? Some indication that it might not have been rabies?"

"That's funny, Doc."

"Rabies. That's what it is. You bring the squirrel's head in?"

"It's not in my pocket or anything. Leonard threw the squirrel, still attached to its head, into the trunk of the car. He thought it might be rabid too."

"Then you're the only one that doesn't think so."

"I don't want to think so."

"What we need to do is cut off the squirrel's head, send it to a lab in Austin, let them do some research, see it's rabid or not. In the meantime, you could go to the house and wait for symptoms. But I don't think that's a good idea. Let me tell you a little story, and let me warn you

7

up front that this one doesn't have a happy ending. My mother told me this story. In the twenties, when she was a girl, a boy she knew got bit by a raccoon. Kid was playing in the woods, some such thing. I don't remember exactly. Doesn't matter. He got bit by this raccoon. He got sick. He couldn't eat, and he couldn't drink water. He wanted water, but his body couldn't take it. The doctor couldn't do a thing for him. They didn't have the medicine for rabies we have now. The boy got worse. They ended up tying him to a bed and waiting for him to die, and it was not a pretty thing. Think about it. Watching your son suffer from something like this, and it just goes on and on. Kid got so he didn't know anybody. Laid there and messed on and wet himself, bit and snapped at them like a wild animal. Chewed off his tongue. The father finally smothered him with a pillow and everybody in the family knew it and didn't say a goddamn word."

"Why are you tellin' me this?"

"Because you have been bitten by a rabid animal, and beginning right now we have to start shots. Rabies is pumping through your system, and believe me, it will not be denied. Way I see it in my head is all these little microscopic rabid dogs foaming and snapping at the air, dog-paddling through your bloodstream, heading for the brain, where they intend to devour it."

"That's a very interesting picture, Doc."

"I came up with that when I was a kid and was told the rabies story. First I imagined raccoons, but since I was always hearing about dogs being the carriers, it changed to dogs."

"What kind of dogs?"

"I don't know. Brown ones. We haven't got time to fuck around here, Hap. Bottom line is we don't start shots, you go the same way as the kid, only maybe without the pillow. Right to life, all that."

"All right. You got me convinced. You take rabies shots in the stomach, don't you?"

"Not anymore. That's changed. In fact, it isn't so bad. But this is serious, my man, and we don't want to make too light of it."

"Couldn't we wait until we get the results off the squirrel head? I hate shots."

"I just gave you one."

"Yeah, and I didn't like it."

"You'd have liked it less, me sewing up that wound without deadener. Listen up, Hap. We wait until the results come back, it'll be too late. You'll be running around on all fours and bouncing and biting the air. Trust me on this. I'm a doctor. I'll make arrangements at the hospital."

"Can't we do it here?"

"I could, but they also have what I need there. And since I know you don't have any money and I'd like to get paid, you go to the hospital I can get something out of your insurance. You do have insurance?"

"Yeah. I even overlap a bit. I've got insurance from the offshore work that'll be good for a while, and I have a kind of penny-ante insurance that I've been managing to pay for the last few years. I don't know it'll do much."

"Most of this shit insurance, which is what I figure you have, does better you go to the hospital. So give the information to my secretary when you go out, and if it's anything we're familiar with, we may be able to get policy information right away. If not, it'll take a while. I want to check Leonard over too, see if he got scratched or bit. He might have and not even know it. He's got a bite, you'll both go to the hospital. Step on out and tell him to step on in."

"Doc, if we got to send the squirrel's head in for dissecting, and I'm going to take the shots before we get results, why bother?"

"Could be an epidemic. Squirrels aren't usually the carriers. Raccoons, foxes—they're the main culprits. But somehow it may have gotten into the squirrel population. People ought to know. Step on out and send Leonard in. We got to get this show on the road. Oh, before you go, here's a trash bag. Get the squirrel and put it in the bag and leave it behind the reception desk. I'll have someone pick it up."

I gave the insurance information to the receptionist, borrowed Leonard's car keys, got old Beebo out of the trunk and bagged him and put him in a cooler they had behind the desk. Then I sat in the waiting room and tried to read a nature magazine, but at the moment I wasn't feeling all that kindly toward nature.

I wasn't feeling all that kindly toward the brat that was waiting there either. His mother, a harried woman in lace-up shoes designed by the Inquisition, a long black dress, and a Pentecostal hairdo—which was a mound of brown hair tied up in a bun that looked as if it had been baked into place to contain an alien life form—was pretending to be asleep in a waiting-room chair.

Couldn't say as I blamed her. This kid, who had torn up three magazines and drank out of all the paper cups at the water cooler and stuck his gum on the doorknob leading out of the office, wasn't someone you wanted to look at much.

He was about eleven, and spent a lot of time scratching his red head as if it were full of lice. He had a nose that ran like an open faucet, and he was eyeing me with an intense look that reminded me of the squirrel's expression just before it clamped its teeth on my arm. I wanted to ignore him, but I feared if I looked away he might spring.

He asked me some questions about this and that and I tried to answer politely, and in such a way as not to encourage conversation, but the kid had a knack of turning a nod into an invitation. He told me, without my asking, that he didn't go to school, and that his parents taught him at home, and would continue to do so until LaBorde "built a Christian school."

"A Christian school?" I said.

"You know," said the boy, "one without niggers and atheists."

"What about nigger atheists?" Leonard said, coming into the waiting room.

The kid eyed Leonard's black skin as if he were trying to decide if it were real or paint. "Them's the worst kind," the kid said.

The Pentecostal mother opened one eye, then closed it quickly.

"How would you like me to kick your nasty little ass?" Leonard said.

"That's child abuse," said the little boy. "And you used a naughty word."

"Yep," Leonard said.

The boy studied Leonard a moment, fled to a chair next to his mother, sat there and glared at us. His mother seemed not to be breathing.

"Come on, Hap," Leonard said. "I'm clean. Or as the

doc said, no little dogs swimming through my blood. I'll run you over to the hospital. Hey, you, you little shit—"

"What?" I said.

"Not you," Leonard said. "Red on the head! You, kid! Get that goddamn gum off the doorknob. Now."

The kid sidled over to the knob, peeled off the gum, put it into his mouth, slid back into the chair beside his mother. If he had been a cobra, he'd have spat venom at us. Leonard and I went out.

As Leonard drove, I said, "You got to feel sorry for a kid like that. Raised with those kind of attitudes."

Leonard didn't say anything.

"I mean, he's off to a bad start. He doesn't know any better. You talkin' to him like that, that's a little much, don't you think?"

"I don't feel sorry for him," Leonard said. "I really was going to kick his nasty ass. I'm kinda hopin' his mama brought him there to be put to sleep, like a sick cat."

"That's not very nice," I said.

"No," Leonard said. "No, it isn't."

# 3

At the hospital they did some routine tests and put me in a cold room wearing what they referred to as hospital gown, which is pretty ludicrous. There you are sitting in the cold wearing a paper-thin sheet split up the back with your ass hanging out, and they call it a gown. You'd think they thought it ought to go with heels, maybe a nice hairdo and a brooch, a dinner invitation.

Leonard sat in the room with me. He said, "You have the ugliest goddamn ass I've ever seen."

"Well, you've seen a few."

"That's right, so my opinion is worth something."

"Not to me. And besides, it's so bad, why's the doctor always want to put his finger up it?"

"Probably lost his high school ring last time he poked around in there. I figure he pokes a little deeper, he might find an old boyfriend's rubber."

"That's your game," I said. "Dig in your ass, reckon they'll find dog hairs."

We joshed around with that kind of adolescent bullshit for a while, then Leonard started trying to tell me about him and Raul again. About that time, Doc Sylvan came in and Leonard went out.

"That insurance you got," Doc Sylvan said. "We're familiar with it. I made some calls to be sure. Sucks."

"Which policy sucks?"

"Both of them. The oil rig policy will pay more in the long run, but it's the short run that's a bitch. The other policy seriously sucks the dog turd. You see, this is what they call outpatient business. You know, give you a shot, then you go home. Come back for an examination, another shot. You go home. But, if you go home, the policy has a five-hundred-dollar deductible."

"It's going to cost that much?"

"Time I get through, it may cost more. It's not that it actually cost that much, but doing the shots here at the hospital makes it more expensive. And being a small city hospital, well, that gilds the lily."

"Then why didn't we do it at your office?"

"I told you why. Listen, what we're gonna do is we're gonna check you in for a few days here at the Medical Hilton."

"Won't that be more expensive?"

"Certainly. A lot more, but you do that, the offshore policy will pay eighty percent. The other policy will pay a bit."

"The one that sucks the dog turd?"

"Right."

"You mean to tell me the policy won't pay I go to the

house, but it will pay I stay in the hospital and it'll cost more?"

"Now you got it figured. Between the two policies you come out only owing a few hundred bucks' deductible. Policies might even overlap so you come out ahead, but I doubt it. You'll owe something. It's the way of the insurance and medical professions."

"I think I'm being snookered a bit so you can make some extra insurance money, that's what I think."

"Considering you owe me a few past-due bills for a number of things, maybe you can live with that."

"How long have I got to be in the hospital?"

"Way the policy works—"

"The offshore or the dog turd?"

"Both . . . I'd say seven or eight days."

"Ah, hell. You're kiddin'?"

"No, I'm not. You see, you take a shot now. Then you take one in seven days. That should be enough time to make sure the policy covers things. Those policies, way they're written, you almost have to be standing on your head and get hit by lightning while trying to pick your nose with a pop bottle up your ass for them to pay. You got to get a better kind of policy, Hap. You know, a real one."

"I get some real money, I'll do that."

"Anyway. One shot now. One in seven days, and one in twenty-one to twenty-eight days. You got a little option on the last shot. But not much. Thing about rabies, you miss those shots, you can kiss your ass good-bye."

"I go to the hospital, I got to wear this damn gown all the time?"

"You play the game, you suit out."

A hospital is dangerous to your health. All kinds of disease floats around in there. First day I came down with a cold. Worse than the cold was the boredom. Man, was it boring. And I had to lie there with this needle and glucose tube in my arm and there wasn't a damn reason for it, but they did it anyway, and the food they fed me explained why someone had written in blue ink above the commode lever in my room's toilet: FLUSH TWICE, IT'S A LONG WAY TO THE CAFETERIA.

So I spent my time lying there, a little mad actually, 'cause my best buddy in the whole goddamn world hadn't come by once. I hadn't seen him since he stepped out of the room that day Doc Sylvan came in. I phoned his house repeatedly, but no answer, and he didn't have an answering machine, so I couldn't leave a message. The only connection I had to the outside world was the TV set and Charlie Blank.

The TV bit the moose. There were only a few channels and they all seemed tuned to the same stuff, or at least the same sort of stuff. I'd seen enough talk shows involving stupid relationships to last me a lifetime. I could have told those people quick-like why they were having so much trouble with their lives and their relationships. They were dumb shits and proud of it.

I had known people just like them all my life, just because you couldn't avoid them. They were like shit, always turning up on your shoes. I wouldn't have given those happily-stupid-by-choice-assholes the time of day, much less want to hear what they had to say on television.

And if that wasn't enough, at night I had to put up with this political show starring a fat guy in a ritzy suit who spent an hour talking to an audience as mean-spirited and narrow-minded as he was. It was a great setup. He liked to show clips from political speeches, then criticize them out of context. And his audience, with the sum of their intellect added together, multiplied by three, it still left them—in defiance of mathematics—collectively half-wits.

I was getting desperate. I longed for something as awful as a Jerry Lewis movie to watch, or maybe an info-mercial on makeup.

First evening I was in the hospital, Charlie Blank came in to see me. He had been promoted to lieutenant. Wasn't that the chief liked Charlie so much he wanted to move him up, but the old corrupt bastard was happy he was rid of Lt. Marvin Hanson, and someone had to get the job, and Charlie, who was also a good honest cop, was next in line, and probably in the chief's mind a better trade, if for no other reasons than he was an unknown quantity, and was, more important, white.

Hanson and his car had met a tree at high speed on a wet highway and he was now in a coma over at his ex-wife's house, doing an impression of a rutabaga. Just lying there, being fed by tubes and getting his ass wiped by his ex, shrinking up slowly, flickering an eyelid now and then, moving just enough to give the ex-wife and Charlie encouragement he was going to come out of it and ask for a ham sandwich and an update on pork belly futures.

I figured Hanson came out of it, you might as well plant him in the dirt and hope he grew. Chances were, he awoke, it would be as if he had never been. The world would be new to him. Amazing and beyond his comprehension. If he learned to play a passable game of checkers against himself without cheating and knew better than to shit in the kitchen sink it would be a feat of Olympian proportions.

Charlie was wearing his brown Mike Hammer hat, as I called it. Porkpie, I guess it's really called, and he had on a blue silk Hawaiian shirt decorated with brightly colored palm trees, parrots, and hula girls. He wore his usual cheap brown suit coat, black plastic Kmart shoes, and his deadpan look. I tell you, there's nothing better to view from a hospital bed than a Hawaiian shirt flashing out at you from between the lapels of a cheap suit coat, a porkpie resting on top of it all like a rusty bird feeder. He was also carrying a white grease-stained paper bag and another one, brown, minus the grease.

"I hear you had some squirrel trouble," Charlie said.

"Some," I said.

"Looks like he gave you hell."

"Yeah. You oughta see *him*."

"We're checkin' now to see the squirrel had an accomplice. You know, a spotter from the woods. We hope to make an arrest before the week's out. A few other squirrels or blue jays talk, a possum comes in with a word, we might have the bastard's partner by nightfall."

"Hey, make fun. But this mad-squirrel business, it isn't a light thing. Let me show you where he bit me. Look at that. There's four stitches there."

"I've had worse."

"From a squirrel?"

"No. You got me there. . . . You sound funny."

"I have a cold."

Charlie opened one of the bags and pushed it toward me. It contained a hamburger, french fries, and a malt. "I've spent a day or two in the hospital," Charlie said, "so

18

I thought you might want this—unless they've suddenly started hiring French chefs."

"Oh, God," I said, pulling out my sliding table and placing the food on it. "I never thought I'd look forward to a McDonald's meal."

"Stay in here a bit," Charlie said, "you get so the idea of eatin' out of trash cans is kind of appealing. By the way, I kept the Spider Man toy comes with it."

"You're welcome to it."

"You say that now, but you see it, you'll want it."

"Then don't let me see it."

Charlie put the other sack on the bed and took off his hat and hung it on the back of the guest chair.

"What's in the other bag?" I asked.

"Books. A magazine."

"Whatcha got?"

He took out a magazine titled *Boobs and Butts*, tossed it at me.

"Oh, great," I said.

"What's the matter? Read that one?"

"Yeah. Right."

"Well, at least you ain't sharin' the room. You can whack off without anyone seein' you."

"You can take this back," I said. "I got enough on my mind without thinking about what I'm not gettin' and haven't been gettin' for a long time."

"Hey, I'm married and I'm not gettin' it. Wife still wants me to quit smokin' before she'll give me the business, so to speak. I'm tryin' to quit, but I haven't beat it yet. I smoke three or four cigs a day now, but she knows. She's got like this second sense. She smells smoke, her pussy closes up. So when she ain't lookin', I read the magazines. Stay in the bathroom a lot. Run the shower. Wife thinks I am one clean sonofabitch, but I'm in there whacking off."

"Perhaps you should try and develop something more than just a sexual relationship, Charlie. You could meld with her mind, her emotions. Really attempt to understand what makes the both of you human beings. Appreciate her more as a woman, less as a sex object."

"Yeah, well, that's all right, but I still want to fuck her."

"I hear that."

"You know, I don't get it. My wife, she's into like saying the right thing. You know. I'm not supposed to say *pussy* 'cause it's degrading. I call her a pussy, I can see that's degrading. There's some women I think are cunts, you know. Some guys that are dicks. I mean, you can have a cunt and not be a cunt, and you can have a cunt and be one. But I don't get Amy's reasoning. I say I want some pussy, I'm sayin' I want some lovin', I'm not calling her a pussy, I'm callin' her pussy a pussy. And like, you know, that's as good a slang for what's down there as dick or cock is for what we got in our drawers. Someone called me a dick, I might get mad, but Amy told me she wanted a little dick, the reading is different, don't you think?"

"When it comes to women, I don't know which way to go. So you're askin' the wrong boy. I haven't got anything against women or men in general. I just think some of them are assholes."

"There you go. You just said *assholes*. Can you say that, or does that like go on your cosmic record?"

"Reckon it depends on who's keepin' score."

"Yeah, that's another trip, ain't it. All this religious business. Christians think you got to do good 'cause you want to go to heaven, but if you do good 'cause you want to do good and don't believe in that shit, then they figure it's the slow oven for you anyway. They like a god that's a bully, makes you want to do good 'cause he's gonna rough you up. Life is just one big mess after another, ain't it?"

"It's funny how sex can make one philosophical, isn't it, Charlie."

"I'll say, and while we're being philosophical, that magazine you got there, let me tell you, there's a redhead in there would make you write a hot check and rob a filling station pretty damn quick."

"Skip the details." I put the magazine on the bed table. "What are the books?"

Charlie took out a Harlequin romance and put it on top of the magazine.

"You're kiddin'?"

"Hey, my wife tossed it out. She reads 'em by the hand-fuls. I don't have a lot of money, you know. I made do with what I could get my hands on. Millions of readers can't be wrong. I did nab you this one, however."

He handed me a paperback western.

"We'll, one out of three isn't bad," I said.

"Got it at a garage sale. There's a few pages torn out, but it reads pretty good."

"You see Leonard?"

"Nope. Not in a while. I thought he'd be up here nesting in a chair."

"Hasn't even come by. He's been having boyfriend problems. I figure that has something to do with it."

"Raul?"

"Yeah."

"Leonard doesn't have patience with that boy. Raul is all right."

21

"I don't like him. I get this feeling there isn't much to him, and what there is to him isn't much."

"It's a friend thing, you know. Hard to understand the girls or boys a friend picks. They all seem wrong. I was the same way with Hanson. Though I got to say, this ex-wife of his, Rachel, he shouldn't have lost her. She's all right, way she's takin' care of him. And she's a looker too."

"I don't get it, Charlie. They been divorced for years. He throws his head through a windshield, bounces it off a tree, and suddenly she's puttin' a pee tube in his shank and feeding him processed green beans."

"She ain't feedin' him shit. He gets his food through a tube. And maybe that ain't such a bad marriage. She don't have to put up with his bullshit, nor he with hers. He may be luckier than everybody. He don't put up with no bull-shit at all. And he gets his dick handled more than I do, and I'm awake. But I was talkin' about you and Leonard. Close as you guys are, I think you're kinda jealous of the time Raul steals from you and him. It's almost like a marriage thing without the fuckin'. Well, actually, my marriage seems to be pretty much without the fuckin'. Still, you need a woman, Hap. Even like, you know, the local poke."

"Oh, that's an elevated view. Very modern, Charlie."

"I'm just sayin', a little goomba, it goes a long ways. Kinda gets the fluid out from behind the eyes, straightens the back. Maybe clears the complexion."

"My complexion is just fine."

"Hey, give it time. It'll go. Way things been goin' at my house, I'm noticin' not only some bumps, but I got a wart or two on my hand."

"It's the whackin' off."

22

"Damn. You might be right."

"How's the eyesight?"

"A little squinty, now that you mention it."

"Can I ask you a favor?"

"You can ask anything you want. I don't know I'll do it, but you can ask."

"Will you check on Leonard for me? See he's okay?"

"Hey, he's all right. You said yourself, boyfriend problems. I bet him and Raul are back together. They do this stuff all the time. They probably been stretchin' each other's assholes, or whatever it is they do, and that's why he hasn't been by."

"Anyone ever tell you that your ability to understand human relationships is unsurpassed?"

"Hear it all the time."

"Thing with Leonard is, I still don't think everything is all right. This isn't just some spat. It's more than just hurt feelings. Leonard took this breakup hard. And Raul's got himself a boyfriend."

"Uh-oh."

"Motorcycle guy, wears a beard and leathers. I don't know a lot about it. Leonard was trying to tell me when the squirrel got after us. Then, having to stay in here because of the insurance, and him not coming by, we haven't talked. He really wanted to talk. I mean, he's seriously frustrated. Other day in the doctor's office he threatened to kick this little brat kid's nasty ass."

"From what I've seen in the cop business, there's some kids' nasty asses I'd like to kick."

"This wasn't a juvenile. This was a kid-style kid."

"Advantage there is you don't have to lift your foot so high."

23

"He called the kid a little shit."

"My dad called me that a few times. And he was right."

"Seriously, Charlie. Will you check?"

"Yeah. Yeah. All right."

# 4

Second day I was there I didn't hear from Leonard or Charlie. I lay there and read the Harlequin romance and found it better than I thought. Then I read the western and found it worse than I had hoped, though I liked to pretend those missing four pages would have made it magic.

Between bouts with the paperbacks and poking at the bad meals, I spent a lot of time lying on my side looking out the window and sniffling with my cold. The window had become more interesting than the television. I learned to identify certain pigeons that roosted on the windowsill, and I named all of them. Original stuff like Tom, Dick, and Harry. Fred and George, Sally Ann, Mildred and Bruce. I called the little piles of shit they left on the ledge Leonard.

Beyond my window ledge and the pigeons, I could see

a lower blacktop roof and a puddle of water that had collected there, probably from a week ago. I liked the way the sun hit it and made a rainbow in the puddle.

As night fell and the pigeons went away, I could see only the black roof and the moon reflected in the puddle, like an anemic prowler's face looking up at me from the darkness. And as time passed the moon gave way to a veil of clouds and turned the sky black, and a spring rain began to splatter on the glass.

About midnight, I closed my eyes and listened to the rain, hoping it would lull me to sleep, but it didn't. I opened my eyes as someone entered the room. I turned to see in the darkness a young slim woman in white. A nurse. She came over quietly and turned on the light beside the bed.

"Still awake, huh?"

"Yeah," I said.

I saw now that she was not so young, just slim and pretty, her hair a little too red, her face strong with experience, her lips soft with what we Harlequin romance readers like to call promise. She had legs that would have made the pope abuse himself in the Vatican toilet and maybe not feel too bad about it.

"I need to take your temp," she said.

"I haven't seen you before."

"I come on at ten-thirty. I work the late shift. I been off a few days. My name is Brett. Open your mouth."

As she leaned forward to put the thermometer in my mouth, I could smell the sweetness of her perfume, see the swell of her breasts against her uniform. I guess it had been too long, because just the smell and sight of her gave me an erection. I lay there embarrassed, glad I was covered by a sheet and blanket. I felt kind of sleazy and satisfied at the same time. It's a boy thing.

After a few moments she reached for the thermometer and gave my nostrils another treat. She examined the thermometer, shook it, and smiled.

"Well, that looks okay. No fever. According to your chart, you're due another shot in the morning. Says you were bitten by a rabid animal."

"A squirrel."

She smiled. She had a beautiful smile. It was almost a night light. "No shit?"

"Well," I said, "it was a big squirrel."

She laughed.

I said, "Do you think you could take this glucose business, or whatever this is, out of my arm? I don't need it. I'm just here for shots, and the insurance won't cover it I do it as an outpatient."

"Honey," she said, "I've been there myself, but I can't take anything out of your arm, not even a knife. Not without permission. But, you know, it could come loose."

She reached down and pulled loose the tape that held the needle in my arm. She pulled the needle out and smiled at me again.

"Oops, little sucker slipped out," she said.

"Good to see someone that likes their job," I said.

"Oh, I hate this crap," she said, and sounded like it.

"Really?"

"No, I'm lyin'. Sweetie, there ain't nothin' I like better than pourin' shit out of bedpans. Unless it's givin' an enema or puttin' a catheter in some ole boy's dick."

That made me blush, but she certainly didn't seem embarrassed. Cussing seemed to be her life.

"You seem happy enough," I said.

"It's smile or die, darlin'."

"Then why do you do this?"

"'Cause I'm divorced and the landlord won't fuck me for the rent."

I laughed and she laughed.

She said, "You didn't tell me your name."

"Hap. Hap Collins."

"I'll see you, Hap Collins."

"I certainly hope so, Brett."

"I might even get to give you your shot."

"Oh boy."

"In the ass, if you're lucky."

"Double oh-boy."

She turned off the light, and I watched her crisp white uniform move through the darkness. Then she was gone and I was left again with the rain, the scent of her perfume, my thoughts and the absence of her smile.

As for thoughts, my ass was my major concern. So far the shots, one deadener and one rabies, had been given to me in my arm, but what if she did give it to me in the ass? Leonard had made fun of my ass. Suppose he was right? What if I had the ugliest ass in the world? What if it and my bald spot were both shiny and white beneath the glare of the hospital light? I mean, I rolled over and she got a look at my ass and the bald spot on top of my head, would she bolt? Or would she think they were sort of coordinated, like the correct pants with the correct hat?

I went to the bathroom and combed my hair, but I still had a bald spot. I wasn't silly enough to try and comb hair over it from the side. I mean, boy, does that look natural. It was sort of like wearing a sign that screamed I'M NOT ONLY BALD, BUT LOOK HOW STUPID I AM. Besides, my hair was cut too short to do much with it anyway. I wondered if my insurance covered hair transplants.

I went back to bed and did a few buttock-tightening exercises, but just a few. Hell, I had five days before Brett might give me my second rabies shot. I didn't want to overdo it.

I listened to the rain for a time, then rolled over, turned on the light, and tried the phone. Leonard's number rang and rang, but he didn't answer.

I lay on my back and thought about Leonard for a while, wondered where in hell he might be. When I wore out that line of mental inquiry, I started thinking about Brett. I wondered where she lived and how she lived and if she needed a middle-aged man in her life, about my size and disposition, with an ugly ass and a bald spot.

Probably not.

I even thought about the *Boobs and Butts* magazine in the drawer, but I had such a strong constitution I didn't turn on the light and take it out for a look. . . .

Well, just a brief one.

I finally drifted off, but the sound of hospital business jarred me awake all night. In spite of what one might think, the hospital is not a place to rest. Someone is always coming in to look in on you, or take your temperature, or someone is laughing or crying in the hall, or banging stuff around. I awoke feeling as if I had climbed Mt. Everest and fallen off, only to be discovered by an abominable snowman and taken home to his cave to be his love puppy.

I had my breakfast, which was a little better than having to chase it down myself on all fours and eat it raw. After breakfast I saw Brett again, briefly, long enough for her to take my temperature. I was going to try and talk her out of her phone number, but she seemed considerably more businesslike this morning, harried. Maybe it was the bald spot. I just smiled and spoke politely. She finished and went away, left me with her perfume again. I asked an orderly her last name, but he didn't know it.

I waited for Brett to come back, but she didn't show. A nurse with a face like a callused fist that had been punched through glass came in instead and insisted I have the glucose put back in my arm. I insisted it not go.

She went away in a huff and threatened to tell my doctor. I half expected Sylvan to show up, ready to paddle me.

Couple hours later another nurse came in. She was about Brett's size, and even reminded me of her a little—without the charm, the foul mouth, and the red hair. She looked like a younger, calmer brunette sister.

I said, "You're going to try and make me put that thing in my arm, it isn't going to work."

She laughed at me. "I came in to tell you Brett likes you."

"Wow," I said. "I feel like I'm in high school again. Next thing you know, we'll be using you to pass notes."

"She didn't tell me to tell you, I just wanted you to know. She's a friend of mine. She told me she was interested in you. She could use someone in her life. Someone that isn't a crud. You aren't a crud, are you, Mr. Collins?"

"Gee, I don't think so. What's your name?"

"Ella Maine."

"Thanks, Ella."

"You're welcome."

"Did she tell you what she likes about me?"

"Your sense of humor."

"Not my eyes? My noble chin? My dazzling smile? My throbbing pectorals?"

"Your sense of humor."

"That beats nothing," I said.

"Mr. Collins?"

"Yep."

"Treat her right."

"She gives me half the chance, I will."

"Don't tell her I spoke to you. It might embarrass her."

"I don't think she embarrasses that easy."

Ella laughed. "Now that you mention it, neither do I."

A few minutes after Ella departed, Charlie Blank came in. He had an expression on his face like a man who had just been told he was going to have to swallow and pass a bowling ball, then bowl a strike with it. He didn't ask to look at my ass.

"Leonard?" I asked. "He okay?"

"I don't know."

"What do you mean, you don't know?"

"I mean I don't know. I went by his place this morning. Knocked. He didn't answer. Seein' how you been callin', not gettin' him, I got a little nervous. I picked the lock and went in, but he wasn't there. I looked to see anyone had stuffed him in the closets or tried to cut him up in the bathtub. No Leonard. Not even a cut-up one. The bed hadn't been slept in, though he really ought to wash those sheets. Nothing looked out of place, but where the fuck is he? Tight as you guys are, it's not like Leonard to go off without at least tellin' you."

"You think it's foul play? That what you're sayin'?"

"I ain't sayin' it's nothin'. But . . ."

"But what?"

"I'm not finished here. Give me some room. That biker. One with Raul. You got a better description than you gave me?"

"I've never seen him. I gave you the description Leonard gave me."

"That description included him being alive and having a head, didn't it?"

"Say what?"

"Last night, out on Old Pine Road. Couple of motorists, alias two kids parked by the side of the road doin' the hole-punch boogie, found a biker. His Harley had slammed into a tree, but that wasn't what did him in. What set him back was a shotgun blast to the head. They're gonna be pickin' up teeth and head fragments for a few days to come. They might even find a jawbone over in Louisiana."

"Damn."

"Leonard owns a shotgun."

"Now wait just a goddamn minute, Charlie. You know Leonard."

"Yeah. That's why I'm worried. Listen here, Hap. Leonard, he's a little hot-tempered. You can't deny that."

"He's not that hot-tempered."

"Yeah, he is. Especially lately. What about this stuff with Raul and Raul's boyfriend, who, I might note, is a biker? Am I right?"

"Yeah. But . . ."

"And you know why Leonard lost his job at the Hot Cat Club?"

"He pissed on a guy's head."

"That's excessive even for Leonard."

"He was making a point."

"Uh-huh. What you said about Leonard sayin' he was going to kick that kid's ass. Remember that?"

"I don't think he really meant it. Not really."

"That shows some temper, don't it? And you haven't heard a word from him. Any of that seem right to you, partner? And this biker, it was a twelve-gauge made him the headless horseman. And like I said, Leonard owns a twelve-gauge pump."

"So does every other Texan. Leonard also owns rifles, handguns, a collection of silverware, and a TV set. Hell, so do I. So do you."

"I haven't pissed on anyone's head, nor have I threatened to kick a kid's ass."

"Ah-hah! But you sympathized."

"I was kidding."

"So was Leonard."

"You weren't so sure."

"You don't even know it's the same biker."

"True. But after I went by Leonard's, didn't find him, heard about this biker, I went back and looked in Leonard's closet. Twelve-gauge wasn't there. You and I both know that twelve-gauge isn't one he takes out much. Got it from his uncle, who got it from his father, or some such thing. Uncle gave it to Leonard when he was a kid. You've heard him talk about it. It's an heirloom. It goes so far back it isn't registered. Guy's going to do something like kill a lover or a lover's boyfriend, he might want to do it with a weapon that's special to him."

"I thought you were Leonard's friend."

"I am, Hap. That's why I'm worried."

"I can't believe you came to me with this bullshit. Leonard didn't kill anybody. Not like that, anyway. Hell, you know that."

"There's more. Last night, biker bar on the outside of town. The Blazing Wheel. Heard of it? Only biker bar we got. Well, some black dude with a bad attitude went in there and whupped the shit out of a biker with a broom handle. It was one serious ass whuppin'. And when the other bikers started to light down on this black dude, he knocked a couple knots on their heads and pulled a pistol. Then, when they followed him out to the car, he jerked a twelve-gauge off his car seat and pointed it at them. Shot the neon out of the Blazing Wheel sign and shot up some bikes. It looked like a fuckin' demolition derby out there. This biker, one got the dog shit beat out of him—guess what?"

"It's the dead guy?"

"Guess what else?"

"What?"

"This black guy did the damage, he was driving a Rambler. How many guys you know got the acorns to go in a biker bar like that and start trouble, carry a gun? How many black guys you know drive an old Rambler? How many whites you know drive a Rambler? Who the fuck do you know wants to drive a Rambler? That alone takes balls."

"I don't think Leonard likes the Rambler," I said. "He got it cheap."

"Yeah. Well, add this shotgun stuff in with the other stuff. The boyfriend business, Leonard not being home. It kinda adds up big-time nasty, don't it?"

"What about Raul? Any word there?"

"Zip. Which don't look good neither."

"Any charges filed against Leonard?"

"Not yet. I'm the only one that's put any of this together. Incorrectly, I hope."

I got out of bed and started for the closet.

"What are you doin'?" Charlie said.

"Keep what you think might be to yourself, will you, Charlie?"

"I'm an officer of the law, Hap. I can't— You're not goin' anywhere. It'll fuck up your insurance if you leave."

"I got to find Leonard. I got a better chance than anyone else. All you got to do is not tie things together just yet. Give me a little time. This way Leonard isn't forced into hiding if he didn't do this business."

"Didn't do it, he won't need to hide."

"State he's in, he might think he needs to. But I can tell you now, he didn't do this. Well, he probably did beat the hell out of that guy and shoot up the bar. And he probably drove that Rambler with a sense of pride. That's his style. But ambushin' some guy. Blowin' off his head like that. That's not his style."

"There's one other thing."

"What?"

"A Rambler, formerly white, before it was gutted by fire, was found in a pasture off Highway Fifty-nine."

"Was it Bill Duffin's pasture?"

"It was. And if I remember right, wasn't that the pasture where the squirrel jumped you? We're gettin' lots of coincidences here. Black guy knockin' knots on a biker guy's head, shootin' a twelve-gauge, drivin' a Rambler."

"Then I've really got no choice," I said. "I have to leave."

I slipped on my pants without underwear, pulled the gown over my head and tossed it on the bed. I put on my T-shirt.

"All I'm asking, Charlie, is you give me some space here. Okay?"

35

"Hap, I've done you guys a lot of favors. But—"

"Do us one more."

"You see how it looks. He went in there, lost his temper, knotted up a biker's melon, ran off in the Rambler, bikers chased him down. He shot the guy off the bike from the car. Then the others overtook him, burned the car to slow down identification . . . then . . . well, I don't think they took Leonard out to dinner."

I pulled my socks and shoes from the closet. I said, "They didn't find a body, so I'm going to figure on Leonard being alive. He isn't indestructible, but he isn't any pushover either. Did they find a shotgun and a revolver in the car?"

"No, but so what? Bikers could have taken that before they burned it. Why not? Good shotgun and a revolver. They'd want it."

"Maybe. But I'm thinking he got away, and he's out there somewhere, needing help."

"Hap, man, say he is alive . . . I'm crazy about the guy. Leonard, me and him are tight. But we're talkin' murder here. I don't never get that tight with nobody. Hear what I'm sayin'?"

"Sounds like self-defense to me."

"What? He goes in and beats a guy up and the guy goes after him and Leonard kills him. Biker wasn't armed, Hap."

"You say the Rambler was found in Duffin's pasture. That isn't near where the biker was killed, is it?"

"So they chased him. He tried to dart into the pasture and hide. They caught him. It stands to reason."

"He certainly ran them a merry chase from Old Pine Road all the way out to Duffin's pasture."

"Yeah. All right. That's a point. But it could have happened way I said."

"Bikers say they saw Leonard shoot this guy? Anyone say that?"

"No. They just say they chased him. But a lot of questions haven't been asked yet. They caught up and killed him, they ain't gonna admit it right away. For all we know, they're tannin' his hide somewhere, gonna make him into a rug."

"He's already tanned. I don't want much time, Charlie. Leonard did this, you can have him. It's not like he's going to go on a murder spree. And if he is dead, what's the rush, huh?"

It was Charlie's turn to consider. "All right. Twenty-four hours, then I got to let my cat out of the bag. And in the meantime, I got to start seein' there's more in the bag than just one cat. Investigation might bring something forward I can't hold back. Things can develop. A cat can have kittens. Understand?"

"Yeah," I said. "Fully. And Charlie. Thanks."

I sat down in the guest chair and put on my socks and shoes. I checked my wallet. Yep. Still had my two dollars and a couple of large uncashed checks from offshore work.

The nurse who had threatened to tell my doctor I was a bad boy came in just as I was starting out.

"Mr. Collins, what do you think you're doing?" she said.

"Don't worry, I'm not checking out. I'm going for a morning constitutional. I'll be back in time for my next shot."

"You can't do that," she said. "That's five days from now."

"Hide in the bushes and watch," I said, and went out.

A moment later I came back in. Charlie was listening to the nurse fuss about my departure. He was nodding and saying nothing. They both turned to look at me.

"Charlie," I said, "I know this messes up my exit, but you think you could give me a ride? To the house. I forgot I don't have my truck here."

# 5

Charlie drove me home and let me out. He didn't have much to say on the way over, but as I started walking toward the house he called out through his open window, "Just a little bit, Hap, then I got to bring Leonard in for questioning."

"Yeah. I know. What time is it?"

He told me.

I said, "Twenty-four hours. From right now. Okay?"

"Okay," he said. "But I mean twenty-four hours. Not twenty-five. And if something new comes up, deal's off."

I nodded at him, and he drove away. I got my key and walked up on the porch feeling ill. Partly it was the cold I had, along with a bit of fear about leaving the hospital like that, knowing I still had shots to take, and thinking about the doc's story about the boy who died tied to a bed, biting at the air.

I tried not to worry too much. I had five days before the next shot, and nearly two weeks after that before the last. But I had to wonder what I had been so all fired excited about.

Now I was out of the hospital and at the house, I didn't have a clue what I was supposed to do next. I felt as if I had tried to play a scene from *Hamlet* during a grade-school production of *Red Riding Hood*. It had been a dramatic moment, but it was inappropriate. It sure didn't add up to anything that could help Leonard.

As I went into the house the smell of mildew and dust hit me like a blow. I had been gone for months, and since I had returned to East Texas, I hadn't even been home. I had gone off with Leonard to shoot cans and talk. Things had gone downhill from there.

I felt a combination of pleasure and dread as I entered. Dread, because my place is essentially a shit hole. Much in need of repair. There's also the fact that the contents of my house spoke of, if not a miserable existence, certainly a lame one. I still had aluminum-foil-covered rabbit ears for my TV. Not even a roof antenna or a satellite dish.

The happy feeling that wrestled with the dread was due to the fact that I was home, free of the offshore drilling job where I had for months served as a heavy oiler, which is a glorified title for an idiot who pours oil onto machinery. I hated the work and vowed never to do it again. I also vowed, for the umpteenth time, to change my life. To find something better, to finally prepare for the future. Which, considering half my life was over, might not be a bad idea. Perhaps, if I had real plans, I could begin to think of my glass as half full, instead of half empty. Or half empty with a bug in the bottom.

I left the front door open, threw up the windows and let some fresh air into the living room. The air was rich with spring and I could smell the scents from the woods.

I went to the kitchen, opened the refrigerator, knowing full well there was nothing there, but it was something to do. I closed the fridge, found the cookie jar and looked inside.

There were a few cookies—the vanilla ones I stocked for Leonard—but the ants liked them too and they had been there first.

I used a long spoon to break up the cookies, poured the crumbs and ants into the sink, turned the water on them and watched them swirl down the drain.

Fuckers couldn't swim for shit.

I found a can of coffee, opened it, got a pot going, then discovered a tin of sardines. I used the key on the can to peel back the lid, got a fork, sat at the table and ate the fish, wishing I had crackers.

I poured a cup of coffee and sipped it while I walked around the living room thinking. That was when I noticed there were footprints in the dust in front of my bedroom door. I turned and looked about. The footprints led from one of the windows I had opened, and they were overlapped with my footprints, but they definitely were not mine. I realized that when I had opened this particular window, the one with the footprints below it, it had not been locked.

That hadn't struck me as odd then, as I'm not always wise about remembering to lock my windows, but when I examined the window more closely I saw the lock had been busted. Someone had forced something under the frame and prized it up.

I felt strange suddenly, realized there was a bad smell

coming from under the bedroom door. I had sniffed it earlier and had attributed it to dust and mildew, but now that I was closer I could really smell it, and it was not dust or mildew. Closer I got to the bedroom door, stronger it became.

I walked quietly back to the kitchen, set my coffee cup on the drain board, got a butcher knife out of the utensil drawer, and crept toward the bedroom. I inhaled a deep, sour breath and turned the knob slowly, expecting to be jumped at any moment.

I slid into the bedroom. It was hot in there. Dust swirled in circles. The midday light flowed through the curtains like a rush of yellow toxin. The window glass that peeked out between the curtain slits was filmed with cataracts of dust and fly guts. The window screens were layered with pollen.

Dead roaches and other desiccated insects lay on the windowsills with their legs poking at the air. The carpet was still brown, though it had originally started out a kind of bright rust color. Sunlight and lack of proper shoe cleaning had brought it to its present dried-shit hue.

My dresser was in its spot. The old-fashioned poster bed was still the same—except for the fact that there was someone lying on it, under a sheet, their head covered. This someone had stained through the sheet and turned it black. Their feet were sticking out at the bottom and were housed in black Roper boots, and the soles of the Ropers were gummy with some sort of black mess that might have been dried cow shit; it was evident the stench was coming from the boots and the body.

I took a deep breath, didn't like the taste of it, eased around to the head of the bed, took hold of the sheet and lifted it.

Leonard, the twelve-gauge beside him, a revolver in his waistband, his face sweaty, scratched, dirty, and unshaven, cracked one eye, said in sticky voice, "Howdy."

"You piece of shit," I said.

He opened both eyes, though not wide, said, "No. Actually pieces of shit are all over me, but I'm still just me. What you got that knife for?"

"What the hell are you, nuts? You've got cow shit all over my bed."

"Actually, it's pig shit, and it's a cold manure. Did you know that? It doesn't work as well for fertilizer because it doesn't heat up the same. Don't try and compost it. Just doesn't do right. Just a tidbit of information I thought you might like. I'm full of stuff like that."

"You're full of what's all over you. Get out of my bed."

"Do I have to? I'm really tired. I've been, to say the least, a little busy."

"I thought you might be dead."

"Disappointed?"

"A little. I can't believe you didn't take off your fuckin' shoes and clothes before you got in my bed. I do that to you, get shit on your bed?"

"I don't even remember having on shoes and clothes, Hap. You didn't bring home anything to eat, did you? I couldn't find nothing but ants and sardines, and I don't eat either ants or sardines, though I think I'd prefer the ants to the sardines. Goddamn ants ate my cookies."

"Those were *my* cookies."

"Yeah, but I know you keep them for me." Leonard swiveled to a sitting position on the bed. "Is that coffee I smell?"

"All I smell is shit," I said.

"That's because you're not used to it yet."

43

"What in hell has been goin' on?"

"I'm just too pooped to pop right now. I need some food, some coffee, and a blood transfusion."

"You're injured?"

"I've got a cut or two, but nothing serious."

I had plenty of questions but decided for the moment it was hopeless. Leonard was too goony, hungry, and stinky to be around. I said, "Get off your ass and take a shower. I'll run to town and get some food. You and I have some serious talking to do. And throw those clothes away. Wear some of my stuff."

"I think not. None of your underwear's got designs or colors, or, for that matter, room enough for my equipment."

"I sure hate you aren't going to have colored underwear. You got a date?"

"Not anymore."

"Raul?"

"It's a nightmare."

"Leonard, you are in some serious shit."

"Serious pig shit."

"Look. Take a shower. I'll be back shortly. But I do have one question." I nodded at the twelve-gauge. "You haven't shot anyone lately, have you?"

"No, but I've certainly wanted to."

"Never mind right now. Listen up. Don't answer the phone. Don't answer the door. Don't go anywhere and don't shoot anybody. And don't piss on anyone either."

"I'll do my best."

# 6

When Leonard went into the bathroom, I took the sheets off the bed, folded them together, toted them to the trash can out back, and stuffed them inside. I got my keys and climbed in my truck.

The truck I loved had been lost in a flood in Grovetown, Texas, and my latest ride was a blue, '79 Datsun pickup with a rust hole in the side. I didn't love the Datsun, but at least I didn't have to push it up hills. While I was offshore Leonard had made a point to come out and start it and drive it a bit to keep it running, and it hummed like a sewing machine.

I hummed it into LaBorde, cashed my checks, put some money in the bank, pocketed the rest, bought some groceries and cold medicine, got some food at Taco Bell, and drove back to the house.

When I got home the place had aired considerably,

and Leonard, wearing my blue jean shirt with the sleeves rolled up and a pair of my black jeans, was seated at the kitchen table with his legs crossed, wiggling one bare foot. He was drinking a cup of coffee. He looked a hell of a lot better than when I left him.

"You look like a black man again, instead of a gray man."

"Well, I feel like an asshole. Hope you brought plenty to eat. I'm starved. Say, aren't you supposed to be in the hospital? I mean, now that I notice, you don't look so good yourself."

"I got a cold."

"You got out of the hospital for me, didn't you, Hap?"

I told him what Charlie had told me. I told him about leaving the hospital. I told him Charlie was giving me a bit of time to sort things out.

"Goddamn," Leonard said. "This has turned into one serious fiasco."

"Thing is, it hasn't gotten out of hand yet. Charlie's keeping the connection between you and this biker's murder to himself. But that won't last. He'll have to say something eventually, and who's to say someone else won't put it together? Once the connection is established, you better have a damn good idea what's clickin', and it better be plain as day."

"I don't know exactly what is clickin'."

"Did you kill the biker?"

"I told you I didn't shoot anybody. I didn't even know the sonofabitch was dead until just now. You think I'd kill someone and not tell you?"

"I had to ask."

"All right. You've asked."

Leonard looked pouty for a moment or two. I said,

"Start by tellin' me what happened. You didn't just decide to roll in pig shit, did you?"

"No. That was sort of a natural by-product of my adventure. And believe me, without you it just wasn't the same. We're like the Hardy Boys, you know."

"No. I'm a Hardy Boy, and you're Nancy Drew."

"I'll let that slide. Hap, when we were at the hospital, and I went out of the waiting room, I didn't really plan to go anywhere. But the Doc was taking his time, and I thought, well, I'll step out, get something to eat for us and come back. But it didn't work that way. I drove off and couldn't get Raul off my mind. The boy drives me crazy."

"Aren't we a little old for this kind of infatuation? All this huffin'-and-puffin' shit?"

"I guess, but I got to thinking about him and drove out to the house. I thought he might be there. Had his fling with the biker, and maybe it was over and he'd come back. Wild thoughts, but that's what I was thinking. Thing was, I didn't know how I'd feel about him coming back if he did, but I wanted to see him again. It's that simple. Little bastard had my nose open."

"Want to open your nose, you should try pig shit. I have a cold, and that opened my nose right up. That mess on the carpet, you're cleaning that."

Leonard nodded. "What say we eat first, then go out on the back porch and talk?"

We finished the Taco Bell food, and I opened a can of tuna and a jar of mayonnaise, whipped a tablespoon of mayonnaise with the tuna and put it on bread. Leonard ate the sandwich and then another. When he finished, I made another pot of coffee and we went outside with cups of it.

The back porch wasn't much. It was close to giving up the ghost. The boards were gray and fiercely weathered, but the view out there wasn't bad. There was the dark East Texas woods, topped by the sky, which was a peculiar blue this day, made all the more beautiful by the golden brightness of the sun; the clouds flowed across it like lilies cast upon a great and tranquil ocean. Off to the right was a creek. You could hear the water gurgling, like a happy woman humming. There was a slight breeze. Outside you couldn't smell the mildew, dust, and pig shit. Leonard talked.

"Stuff I was gonna tell you about me and Raul, it don't seem like much now. Not after what's happened. All I can say is things were falling apart. I guess I knew they would in time. We were just too different. He was a little too young for me, from another world really. Wanted someone didn't like guns and boxing and martial arts. Someone more refined."

"I hear the word *refined*, Leonard, I think of you."

"You bet. But we weren't doing so good, and he got so he wasn't coming home like he should, and here I was staying up nights watching Dave Letterman and John Wayne movies, and he'd come in tired and cranky and short on explanation. Hell, I guess I knew he was fuckin' around. But I love the guy, you know, so it blinds you. I thought maybe I was just being stupid jealous. Thought the trouble we were having was a stage we were goin' through. I believed his shit about he was working—"

"Working?"

"Yeah. He finished hairdressin' school. Kind of elite business. He was gettin' into this deal they got now where the rich folks have the hairdresser come around to their place to do the work. Big money in that. Kind of like hiring a bartender for the night. Or maid service."

"I didn't know Raul knew a comb from a scissor."

"It was a short course. Three months. He took it while you were out helping exploit the earth of its natural resources."

"Go on. You were sayin' . . ."

"Well, things were tense, and the next-door neighbors were still pissed I'd burned their crack house down, and from time to time some of that bunch would come by late at night, throw things at the house, even took a shot at it once. They fucked with our mail. I finally had to have the address temporarily changed. Had my mail sent out to my old place. It was just one thing after another. But after I found out where those shits are now living, I went over and explained to a couple of people that any more crap happened around my house, even if I didn't know it was them that was responsible, even if I thought it might be them, I'd frown on it tremendously. Well, they knew I meant business—I mean, hell, I done burned their crack house down three times now. So things started cooling. But it was just one more aggravation to make things more tense with Raul. Maybe it was gettin' to him too, making him act crazy. Anyway, he wasn't home much. He was hangin' out in LaBorde Park, which is where lots of gays meet, and I didn't like that much 'cause that sounded suspicious, him roamin' around out there. It's not just a pickup spot, it's where those guys got beat up. You know, four or five just last year."

"One this year," I said. "That's the place the preacher carries the sign, isn't it?"

" 'Gay Equals AIDS Equals Death.' "

"That's the one."

"Yeah. That's the place. So I thought him being there all hours wasn't such a good idea. 'Specially him having all the fighting skills of a dirty sock. And worse yet, all these friends of his, they're classic queers. All that swishin' shit. Obvious targets."

"Do I detect a little prejudice toward other homosexuals, my friend? Those without weight-lifter arms and the ability to sight down a rifle?"

"I'm just sayin' Raul's with them, and since they're like flashin' neon, and they're in a bad place, it's just not smart. It shouldn't matter, but it does. So don't give me that liberal bullshit, Hap. I'm not up for it.

"So I'm worried, and I tell Raul I am, but he ignores me, and by the time I find out he's not only hanging out at the park, but he's screwin' Harley Greaseballs, it's too late. He's done run off with him. Can you reckon on that? I'm too macho for him, so he runs off with a guy looks like he wiped a couple old transmissions with his hair. I asked around at the park, found out where the biker guy hung out, found out his name was Horse McNee and that he was a closet fag."

"Horse?"

"It was a nickname. As in hung like a horse."

"Who told you this?"

"Another faggot. I kinda know him through Raul. Fusses like an old woman. But you know, you want some dirt, this guy seems to have it. He's been around for years. An old queen. Fact is, they call him Queen Mary. He's got a younger friend everyone calls Princess Mary. Princess likes to hang around bus stations hoping for a lube job. I can't stand him. But that's beside the point. This Queen Mary, he's always hitting' on me, and everyone else. I wouldn't fuck him if we were both wearing bags over our heads and I was using your dick. Hell, I wouldn't fuck him if we were double baggin' and using your dick with a rubber on. But I admit I played up to him a little—"

"You prick-teased?"

"Just a little. Anywho, I got the info, decided to drive out to the biker bar."

"With a shotgun, a revolver, and a broom handle?"

"You heard about that?"

"Yeah. And it doesn't sound like you. Not that I haven't seen you go off, but this seems radical even for your charming self."

"I know. Romance. Lust. Whatever, it fucks you up. I'm thinkin' I can go out there and Raul will be with Horse Dick, and I can talk him into coming back. And, to be blunt, I wanted to whip the guy's ass stole my boyfriend."

"It's not the guy's fault Raul's playin' around."

"Yeah. But I don't care. I'm wantin' to whip him anyway. Maybe I'm thinkin' I thrash Horse Ass—"

"Horse Dick."

"Whatever. I think if I thrash him, Raul won't think he's so hot. I mean, he doesn't want a macho queer, so he runs off with a greasy macho queer? You got to think Raul protests too much. So, I got my companions, the twelve-gauge shotgun and the thirty-eight snub-nose revolver, and went out there. As for the broom handle, well, I keep that under my car seat as a kind of attitude adjuster. I figured I had to be seriously prepared. As you recall, you and me learned us a little lesson last year."

"Yep. No matter how tough you are, you can't whip a bunch of guys at one time if they want to whip you bad enough. And if they whip you damn good and dead solid, it hurts like a sonofabitch."

"That's the lesson. Not only is the Blazing Wheel a biker bar, it's a seriously Caucasian bar. Dixie flag. The whole works. You're not even gonna find James Brown on the jukebox in this joint. Charlie Pride wouldn't be welcome. And here I am, a nigger with an attitude and a stick. A very solid stick, I might add. And I see this guy I've seen with Raul, and I walk over to him, holding this damn honkie knocker by my side—"

"Honkie knocker?"

"Sorry. Slipped out. No offense intended . . . And I say, "I'm Leonard Pine, and you've been fuckin' with my boyfriend.""

"That's original."

"Wish I'd thought the line over better, but that's what came out. Horse Dick threw a right cross at my head, and I drilled his arm on the inside with my stick, went to knockin' apples on his head. That first noggin shot I hit him so hard I bet his fuckin' dog back home shit a turd in the shape of a praying Jesus. All this happened quick-like, and these guys decided they were gonna skin me for knockin' their buddy, so I pull my pistol, shoot a hole in the floor and scare them back. I go out to the car and they follow."

"And you pull the twelve-gauge and shoot out the neon sign and blow up some bikes."

"You heard about that?"

"Same place I got the news about the shotgun, the broom handle, and the revolver. Charlie."

"That goddamn Charlie is one knowledgeable sonofabitch, ain't he?"

"That he is."

"So I went away from there, and a few of these guys followed, but I lost them. Or thought I did. I decided

Duffin's pasture was a good place to hide. I pulled in, killed the lights, parked, and sat. I think, all right, I've lost them. I start to relax. I have a bag of cookies in the car there, and I'm eatin' them, and I glance in the rearview mirror, and what do I see?"

"An old gentleman and eight tiny reindeer."

"The biker fucks. I wasn't slick as I thought. They'd seen me turn in, left their bikes down the road somewhere, and were sneakin' up on my highly attractive shiny black ass."

"But you were sneakier."

"I slid to the other side of the car, opened the door and slipped into the grass, draggin' my twelve-gauge with me. I crawled along for a bit, then got up and ran. Them sonofabitches seen me. They let out a whoop, and the race was on. I went into the woods. I looped wide and doubled back and got down in the creek and saw them crossin' down a ways, goin' up on the bank. I went down the creek about a mile and came up in the woods, and goddamned if some of them hadn't wandered up right where I come out. Asswipes had me surrounded."

"So they scalped you and ate you."

"I crawled right between those fuckers, and they didn't hear nor see me, so I kept on crawlin'."

"Isn't this story attributed to Daniel Boone?"

"You know Webb's hog farm?"

"Yeah. And I see this comin'."

"I crawled up to the edge of the farm, through the slats of one of the hog pens. They say hogs shit in one corner of the pen, but someone forgot to tell these fuckin' hogs that, or Webb needs to get his ass out there with a shovel more, 'cause I can seriously testify that this entire pen had the intense aroma of pig shit gone bad and then made worse.

"I was in this swill, lookin' out, and I seen the bikers trottin' along the side of the farm there. I knew they hadn't seen me, but they were close enough I could have smelled them, if I hadn't had my nose full of pig shit. You know what I did, Hap?"

"Is this question rhetorical?"

"No."

"You eased into the pig shit and hid."

"You ought to be on fuckin' *Jeopardy!*, Hap. That's exactly what I did. I slid myself into that muck so there wasn't nothing but my head and arms and that twelve-gauge stickin' out. I made up my mind they came for me I was gonna' start blowin' kneecaps off. But when they got downwind of that pig shit, they began to cuss and head back into the woods."

"It takes a real man to lay down in pig shit and not complain," I said.

"I fought off a couple of amorous pigs, climbed through the fence, made the road, but stayed more in the woods. After a while, I heard their bikes and hunched down in the underbrush and watched them drive by. I waited a few minutes, thought about going back for my car, decided they'd expect that and might have a guard there. I crossed the road, went across Murdoch's old pasture, crossed into the woods behind your house, jimmied a window with a tire iron out of your truck, and climbed inside. I was plumb tuckered out. I lay in your bed there all the mornin' and the day until you showed up and woke me."

"Just like Goldilocks and the three bears."

"Well, yeah."

"What about my tire iron?"

"It's under the porch. Damn, Hap, you're supposed to show me some sympathy. Fuck your tire iron."

"You brought this on yourself, man. And you fucked up my sheets. And you damn well better not have lost my tire iron."

"If it makes you feel better, I've got hog shit in my twelve-gauge."

"I'm tryin' to figure on this thing, Leonard, and it isn't adding up so good. Horse Dick lost his head out by Old Pine Road. That isn't anywhere near the Duffin pasture. But all these bikers were chasin' you and he wasn't. Seems to me, I was Horse Dick, and it was my noggin with the bumps on it, I'd have been leading the pack. But he went off in another direction and got himself shot."

"Maybe he got confused. Those were some serious adjustments I made on his punkin. I hit him so hard I may have even changed his past, but I didn't kill him."

"Oh, by the way," I said, "you know your Rambler? They burned that mother to the ground."

"Crap! You enjoyed telling me that, didn't you? You've always hated that car, and this from a man with a Datsun pickup."

"I think you ought to turn yourself in, Leonard. Not just because you drove a Rambler, but because Charlie will make sure the right thing is done."

"I'm not sure there's much Charlie can do."

"Once we start shooting holes in what at first seems obvious, we can clear you. You don't turn yourself in, they can say you're runnin' and hidin' because you're guilty."

Leonard shook his head. "I don't know what the hell to do. I'm damned if I do, and damned if I don't."

I heard the phone ringing in the house. I said, "I'll answer that while you clean the hog shit off my floor and carpet."

"Do I have to?"

"Damn straight. And don't just wipe the surface. You use some cleanser and de-stinker. It's all under the kitchen sink."

"De-stinker?" Leonard said.

It was Doc Sylvan on the phone.

"Are you out of your mind?" he asked.

"I'm not sure one way or the other."

"I can believe that. You have to have those shots, Hap, or you will die."

"Come on, Doc, I got five days before the next one."

"What about the insurance problem? You forgot about that?"

"Can't you fudge a little? I had to leave the hospital. It wasn't by choice, but I had to."

"Why?"

"I haven't done laundry in days."

"You went home to do laundry!"

"I had some bills to pay."

"Why don't you just say you needed to wash your hair?"

"Well, it does need it."

"Hap, listen here. You come back to the hospital tonight and stay, and I'll work something out. But you got to be there tonight. I can rig something for you being out of the room a while. Say I had you over at the office for tests, but that's as far as I go. Doing something like that, getting caught, I could lose my license, and I don't think you make enough to support us both."

"Not in the style to which you are accustomed. Fact is, I don't make enough to support *me*. In any kind of style."

"You be in the hospital tonight, and I promise I will have you out of there within two days, and still make the insurance work. It'll take some finagling, but I'll do it. Just to get you out of my hair."

"Got you."

"I will be by the hospital at eight-thirty tonight, Hap. Be there. In bed."

"In one of those little gowns?"

"You bet."

"Shall I wear a little perfume?"

"Please do."

"I think you just want to see me naked, Doc."

"It's all I think about."


Leonard came in with a scrub brush full of hog shit, a pail of stinky water, and a couple of towels.

"These towels weren't the good stuff, were they?" he asked.

"Not anymore."

"They have holes in them."

"Yeah, and the bad towels have more holes in them. You clean the mess up?"

"Yeah."

We went out back and Leonard dumped the water on the ground and used the water hose to clean the brush and towels. He hung the towels on my clothesline. He said, "I've been hesitating to ask. But what about Raul? Charlie know anything about him?"

I shook my head.

Leonard said, "That worries me. I hope he's all right."

Leonard's voice would have sounded calm to anyone

who didn't know him, but I caught the tremolo there. He was not only worried, he was scared. Maybe not for himself, but certainly for Raul.

"He's probably all right," I said.

"Maybe you could check around. Just to see. It's not like I can go out and look for him."

"I wouldn't know where to start, Leonard. He may have run off back to Houston. He's done that before, right?"

Leonard nodded.

"I figure him and Horse Dick had a fight," I said, "and he went away, then you stepped into the picture a day late and a dollar short and got your ass in a crack with all this business. Right now, way I see it, and you better believe me on this, Raul is the least of your worries."

"I guess you're right," Leonard said. "Just forget it."

# 7

But that wasn't the end of Leonard's wheedling about Raul. He worked on me for an hour, and since nothing else was shaking and our time was ticking away, I decided if I could locate Raul I could find out better what this was all about. Raul might have some idea who would want to kill his new boyfriend, and if he did, that could lead to placing Leonard in the clear.

I also decided that if I was going to start looking, I had best do it before the net was put out for Leonard. For all I knew, some cop other than Charlie had already put two and two together and they were seining for my buddy at this very moment. Even Charlie, if put in the wrong position, might have to break his promise to me and cast the net himself.

I left Leonard with a glass of milk, a bag of vanilla cookies, and a sad expression, drove into town and over to his place. I thought if I was Raul, I might go to Leonard's place to hide. It wouldn't be smart, since the cops were bound to look there, but if I was Raul and had all the street savvy of a broken knickknack, that might be what I'd do.

On the way, I tried to figure Raul for the part of Horse Dick's murderer, but that didn't play. Raul didn't have the temperament to step on a slug, let alone aim a shotgun at someone and blow off their head. Not even in self-defense could I imagine Raul doing such a thing.

But where the hell was he?

When I got to Leonard's house the day had turned off a little warm, but not uncomfortable. A light breeze was blowing and the blue sky was as clear as the Virgin Mary's conscience. All the lily-white clouds had blown away, or sunk into the sky, and it seemed like a day when you shouldn't have a care in the world.

I got out my key to the house and went inside. Raul was nowhere in sight. But the house didn't look like Charlie had described it to me. It had been turned inside out.

The living room couch had been pulled out into a bed, and the thin mattress had been tossed on the floor. The stereo was turned over and the back was ripped off the television set. In the bedroom the dresser mirror was broken, and the mattress had been cut apart and the cotton stuffing strewn about like the guts of a cloud. The closet door was thrown wide. Leonard's shotguns and rifles lay on the floor, and everything in the closet from clothes to coats to ammunition to income tax records were heaped to one side.

In all the rooms the drawers had been dumped, books pulled onto the floors, and in the kitchen the flour, sugar, baking soda, stuff like that, were strewn about or were in the sink. In the bathroom the ceramic lid to the back of the toilet had been dropped and broken on the floor and someone had been pawing about in the plumbing.

I checked the back door. It had been jimmied, the lock snapped free by a crowbar, or some similar instrument. I pushed it open, stepped onto the screened-in porch Leonard had rebuilt, examined the aluminum-framed screen door that led outside. I was surprised to discover it was locked.

I went down the steps and looked around. The rain from the other night had left the ground soft and there were footprints in the mud. Big goddamn shoe prints. Bastard must have worn a size fourteen. The tracks were leading away from the house, not to it. I followed them into the woods, and from there I lost them. I was a fair tracker, but I wasn't the Deerslayer.

Still, I took a flyer and went on through the woods a piece, over to where the foliage gave way to a muddy country road, and started up again on the other side. I walked out to the edge of the road just as an old pollen-coated brown pickup with two young men in it clattered by. They waved at me and I waved back.

I walked onto the road and looked around. It was a dirt road, so there were plenty of tracks, of course. Nothing odd about that. I walked along a piece and found a tire-smashed armadillo and a flattened copper-head, and finally took note of what I determined were the marks of motorcycle tires. Normally, that wouldn't mean much, but they ran off the side of the road, and I discovered where they trailed red mud across the grass and into the woods. The bike had been pushed, because there were shoe tracks alongside the tire marks. The same big shoe tracks.

It didn't take an Einstein to figure someone had driven off the road, pushed their bike into concealment, made their way on foot through the woods and into Leonard's house. The tracks got lost in the thick leaves, so I went on through the woods and back to Leonard's house and looked out back carefully until I found where the footprints exited the woods and came up on the south side of the back porch. I hadn't seen these tracks earlier.

Whoever had entered the house had entered here, probably that way instead of through the screen door to stay down and out of view.

They had cut the screen loose at the bottom of the porch with wire cutters, pushed the screen up, slid under and inside. Then they'd jimmied the back door, and gone in. I assumed they had been quick and silent and purposeful about their task, entered at night, and taken their time ransacking the joint. Gone out the way they'd come in.

I decided I was thirsty, went inside the house and opened the refrigerator. The ice trays had been emptied on the floor and they had melted and water had run into some of the flour. There was a big footprint there, mixed with mud. I managed not to step in anything.

Some of the stuff inside the fridge had been thrown about. There were a few beers and Cokes in the fridge. I got one of the Cokes and popped the top and went out on the back porch and sat down on the steps and tried to think while I sipped it.

It might have been a common burglary, but I couldn't figure what they had burgled. It didn't look like vandalism either, least not completely. Someone had been looking for something. And whoever had done the looking had owned a motorcycle. Horse Dick had owned a bike. The bikers who chased Leonard owned motorcycles. The kid that delivered newspapers on this street owned one too. But he didn't wear a size-fourteen shoe. Who the hell did?

I finished the Coke and looked at the tracks again, those leading into the woods, and those coming up on the side of the porch. I studied them carefully. They were pressed in pretty deep. Whoever had made those tracks was one big sonofabitch, and not just his shoe size. Guy could have been anywhere from two-fifty to three hundred pounds, or more. Maybe it was Bigfoot. Or Smokey the Bear. The thought of someone that huge made me a little queasy.

I went back through the house one more time, looking for clues, but nothing important jumped out at me. Which didn't surprise me. I wasn't much of a detective. I had enough problems just keeping up with socks that matched.

I closed the back door as best it would close, went through the house, locked the front door, stood on the front porch, finished my Coke and looked around.

The spot where the crack house used to be next door was nothing now but a patch of scorched earth and lumber. Someone's chickens were loose and pecking around in the ruins. I wondered what would happen if the chickens found some old drugs in there. A little crack, some cocaine. They would certainly lay interesting eggs.

Across the street where MeMaw used to live a new owner had moved in. The new owner had painted the house hot Pepto-Bismol pink with chocolate trim, and they liked dark blue curtains and had yard butts on the brutally mowed lawn.

Yard butts are what Leonard and I call those stupid, painted, plywood cutouts that are supposed to look like an old man or an old grandma bending over in the yard, the grandpa showing you his overall-covered ass, the grandma's dress hiked up, showing you her white-lace panties.

Leonard once told me he wanted to buy one of those plastic vaginas and butt holes you could get in sex shops and glue it on the seat of one of those grandmas. He figured if you were supposed to be looking up her dress, you might as well see something. It certainly would have been funny to see the owners of those yard butts come out the next morning to discover grandma giving the neighborhood a show.

I guess those dumb yard butts were better than those wooden Holstein cow sprinklers with a hose for a tail that swirled around and around tossing water. But not much.

I looked down the street, both ways, for no particular reason. Still looking for clues, I guess. All I noted was the street seemed to have changed a lot in the last few months. Some of the big trees along the pocked asphalt road had been cut down, and where there used to be shade there was sunlight. This neighborhood wasn't the best in the world, with its poverty and drug problems, but I had liked coming here.

Now, Leonard's house no longer seemed like Leonard's house, like my home away from home. Things had changed. On the street. In the neighborhood. In the house. In our lives.

Perhaps I missed Leonard having a new crack house to

burn down next door. He had burned two of them. Well, three of them, if you count the time I helped him do one.

Who knew? Maybe they'd move a new one in any day now. Hope springs eternal.

I took a moment to think about the sex life I didn't have. Damn. I was getting as bad as Charlie. This kept up, me and him would be fucking.

I thought about Lt. Marvin Hanson, lying in bed in a deep coma. I assumed if I thought about how bad he had it, I could feel a hell of a lot better about being me.

It didn't work. I still felt like shit.

I watched a couple of blue jays fighting in Leonard's oak tree. Listened for a while to a small dog bark savagely at something somewhere off to the south. The dog didn't want to stop barking. A car drove by, an old black man at the wheel, one arm out the window. He was wearing a blue baseball cap with the brim pushed up. He looked hot and tired and satisfied. I looked at my watch. Three-forty-five. Guy was probably just off work from the early shift at one of the plants around town. Must be nice to have a shift. A regular check. Probably had a wife to go home to. A dog. Some kids. A TV with cable instead of foil-covered rabbit ears. I used to have an antenna, but the wind blew it away. I wondered where my antenna was. I wondered where my youth was. I wondered if that fucker who drove by got the American Movie Classics channel.

The wind died down and I began to feel uncomfortably warm. I unbuttoned my top shirt button.

I watched the blue jays fight some more. The dog had stopped barking. I still felt warm. I checked out the pink house with chocolate trim again. The colors hadn't changed and the lawn butts were still in place.

I looked at my watch once more.

Three-forty-six. Time was certainly shooting by.

I scratched my balls, got in my truck, and drove away from there.

# 8

I stopped at a pay phone and called Charlie. Before I could tell him the state of Leonard's house, he said, "I hope you got something good."

"It's not that good. It's about Leonard's house. I just went by there. It's been ransacked."

"Maybe Leonard did it himself. Came back, grabbed some stuff he needed, made a mess."

"I didn't say it was messy. I said it was ransacked."

I described the place to him. He was silent. If he had an opinion he didn't voice it. Just before I started collecting Social Security, he said, "You need to come up with Leonard."

"I'm working on it. Am I to think you no longer think he got nailed by bikers?"

"I think all kinds of ways. It keeps me from getting

bored. And if you know where Leonard is, you ought to tell me."

"So far, nothing."

"You wouldn't lie to me, would you, Hap?"

"Gracious, no."

"I'm not fuckin' around here. This is some serious business."

"I know that."

"You put him up, hide him out, that's a crime. You know that. Right?"

"Of course."

"Are you talkin' through a cardboard tube?"

"It's my cold. It's getting worse."

"My cousin, he had a cold like that, neglected it. Fucker died. You takin' medicine?"

"I've bought some, but no, I haven't taken it yet. And I don't believe you had a cousin who died of a cold."

"Maybe it was my mother's cousin."

"You really aren't that concerned about my cold, are you?"

"Hey, you're sick, I'm sick."

"You think you'll soften me up, then I'll confide something to you, don't you?"

"You said it, I didn't."

"Let me ask you something. Raul. Is he a suspect in this case?"

"Everybody is a suspect. I'm thinking of running my wife in."

"Come on, Charlie. You got Raul in custody? Know where he is?"

"No, and if you know where he is, you'd best tell me."

"I just called 'cause I thought you should know about the house. You might want to go over there, bring some of your people, see if you can find a real clue. You could even bring your little Dick Tracy fingerprint kit."

"You probably fucked up anything might have been there to find."

"I don't think so. I know I'm not a real policeman like you—"

"You're not even a stuffed animal in a police hat."

"Very true. But unlike you, I don't have to step in shit to know a pile when I see it. And there is some shit goin' on here that's got nothing to do with Leonard. Not directly. At least I don't think so."

"You don't sound all that certain to me. Maybe you got to step in shit after all."

"Could be. But I did find a couple clues. You might take note of some footprints out back. They look to belong to Andre the Giant."

I told him about my trek through the woods to the road, what I found there. I told him what I had touched. I said, "By the way, as you well know, it won't be any surprise to find my fingerprints all over that house. And here's an idea, and this is just an idea, mind you, and I don't want you to take offense since it's from a layman and you're a real policeman with a badge and gun and everything, but you take fingerprints, what I'd do is see you have any other than Leonard's, Raul's, or mine."

"My," Charlie said, "you're a regular Boston Blackie. This stuff about fingerprints. And that footprint business. Shit like that'll bust the case wide open. All we got to do is make a cast of those footprints, make a shoe from that. Then we can go door to door and have people try it on. Shoe fits, we run the fucker in. . . . All right, Hap, get this. Time is running out, and I better not find you're fuckin' around on me."

"I wouldn't do that, Charlie."

"The hell you wouldn't."

"Charlie, you really got to either smoke more so you'll be less irritable, or you got to quit smoking so you can get some poontang and be less irritable."

"What I'd like is to fuck like a snake, then afterwards smoke like a chimney. Hap, you listen here. We're buddies, but when it comes to murder, that don't buy much. Hear me talkin'?"

"I hear you. I keep hearin' you. What the hell is with you? I still think you're pissed about Kmart closing down."

"It's not an easy thing to get over. But don't change the subject. I'll make sure Leonard gets as fair a shake as he can get. If it's self-defense, I'll do all I can to get him off. But I'll tell you now. I'm comin' after him, and if I discover you've had anything to do with hiding him, then I'm coming after you too."

"You said I had twenty-four hours. My understanding of that was I found him during that time, could straighten out things, you wouldn't bother me. Even if I did know where he was. Isn't that right? I had twenty-four hours, didn't I?"

"*Had*. You got a lot less now. But I also said no promises if things changed around here."

"Has something changed?"

Charlie let me hear the electricity in the phone for a while.

"Well, has it?" I asked.

"Just find Leonard," Charlie said, "and listen close. I'm coming after you," and he hung up.

I thought about that a moment, then understood what Charlie was trying to tell me. I called Leonard. I let it ring a couple times, hung up. Let it ring a couple times, hung up. Then repeated it. I hoped he'd realize it was some kind of code.

The third set of rings someone picked up the phone. I said, "This is me. If that's you, might I suggest a stroll in the forest?"

The phone went dead. I took a moment to wonder if my phone was tapped, decided things had happened too quickly for that. I was okay. I was just feeling a streak of secret agent.

I pushed out of the phone booth and walked over to my truck. Down the road a piece I saw a yellow '66 Pontiac parked next to the curb. There was a man sitting in it wearing a cowboy hat. He didn't look like any of the cops I knew. He didn't look like a cop. He didn't look like anybody I knew, period. He didn't seem to be watching me.

The phone booth was next to a 7-Eleven store. I went inside and bought a Diet Coke in a plastic bottle and a bag of peanuts. I drank the Diet Coke down a bit, poured peanuts into it, and went outside. I climbed into my truck and looked in my mirror. The Pontiac was gone.

Probably just some guy waiting for someone in one of the houses along the street. Or maybe he'd stopped to check a map. Pull his dick. Anything. I had to lighten up. I was starting to be one paranoid sonofabitch.

I drove away, an eye on the mirror, watching for yellow Pontiacs or low-flying stealth aircraft with radar.

# 9

I didn't go directly home. I was sort of afraid to. I figured Charlie would be searching my place, and if Leonard had heeded my warning, he wouldn't be there. It might also be better if I didn't come up on Charlie and his folks going through my underwear drawer. I wouldn't want to embarrass them.

I drove downtown and went to the all-day dollar movie and had popcorn. The popcorn was okay, but the movie wasn't very good. I walked out about halfway through and stopped off at the yogurt joint and had a cone.

When I finished my cone, I cruised over to the bookshop and looked around the magazine rack. I didn't see any *Boobs and Butts* there. Where did Charlie find that stuff? I hung around long enough the clerks began to watch me suspiciously. I bought a couple comic books, a *Batman* and a *Spider-Man*, and left.

When I got home, Leonard wasn't there. I gave the house the once-over, went out on the back porch, and saw him strolling toward me from the woods. He had the twelve-gauge in one hand, a shovel over his shoulder, and I could see his revolver in the waistband of his pants.

Leonard smiled. "Thanks for the phone tip. I watched from the woods. Charlie and a blue suit showed up with the sheriff. They worked your lock and went inside and looked around."

"That means they have a search warrant."

"Probably. They were inside about twenty minutes."

"They did good. I can't tell they've been here. They even locked the door on the way out."

"They looked around outside too. Found the sheets covered in pig shit."

"They take the sheets with them?"

"No. At this point they probably haven't put the pig shit and my daring escape together. I was smart enough to bury my clothes in the woods. I was going to do the sheets next. Actually, I don't think putting me and the pig shit together is going to mean anything anyway."

"You're probably right about that. Something new has happened. Now you're connected to all this officially, and Charlie had to come check my place as a likely hiding spot."

We sat down on the back porch and I told Leonard what I had found at his house. Told him about my conversation with Charlie.

"Any ideas?" I asked.

"Was the stuff really wrecked? Were my books ruined?"

"They're messed up. Some of them."

"The TV's screwed?"

"Looks that way. And the stereo."

"Shit."

"Your J. C. Penney's suit was tossed on the floor too."

"Now that fucker is dealing with dynamite."

I nodded. "I knew that would get you."

"Seems to me someone thinks I have something I don't. If I do, I don't know what it is, and I don't know how I came by it or why I'd want it. And even if I did, that's no excuse to fuck with a man's J. C. Penney's suit."

"Or maybe they think Raul has something."

"I hadn't thought of that," Leonard said.

"Or maybe they thought Horse Dick had something, and now they think Raul has it, and they thought he was hiding it at your house."

"Or someone thinks what Horse Dick had and Raul had, I now have."

"Or maybe it's a disgruntled hair patron of Raul's," I said. "A little too much off the ears and he's ready to flatten the kid's head."

"Come to think of it, he cut my hair once or twice, and I sort of avoided him after that. He tended to poke you with the scissors."

"I'll tell you this," I said. "If I had something that the guy owning that shoe printed wanted, I might be inclined to give it to him. Help him carry it out to the car, give him a blow job, wipe his ass, give his car a push uphill."

"That big, huh?"

"No. I just made all this shit up for your amusement."

Leonard sighed. "Sorry. I'm beginning to think I was born under a bad sign. . . . Do you think Raul's dead?"

"I don't know. Maybe that's the news the cops got. Maybe to them it's looking like you did him in too. I'm not saying he's dead, I'm just saying if he is, it'll compound things."

"Jesus, I hope he's all right. And not just for my sake."

"We're jumping a lot of ditches here for no reason, Leonard. We don't know anything. Not really. Charlie gave me the impression something was up, though, but I think now it was just the fact they were going to search here and he figured you might be here. He's trying to help. Guess it was good I called him when I did."

"Long as we're speculating, though, I just thought of something. What if the bikers didn't know Horse Dick was gay?"

"Who says they care?" I said.

"I'll stand by it for the moment. Considering most people aren't that liberal about homosexuality, and these guys are about as open-minded as a scorpion. It's a fuckin' Dixie No Nigger Bar, for Christ sakes. You think it's No Niggers But Queers Okay?"

"You never know."

"Yeah, well, let's place bets. So if the bikers first heard about Horse Dick being gay from me when I knocked knots on his head and uttered my classic line about his fuckin' around with my boyfriend, could be they got rid of him themselves. They figured I'd get the blame, and that way they could kill two birds—or two fags, if you will—with one shotgun blast."

"That's a possibility, I guess, but that doesn't explain your house being tossed. My guess is the incidents may not have anything to do with one another. They just unfortunately came together at the same time."

"Maybe," Leonard said. "Now what?"

"I think you ought to continue hiding out in the woods. I've got a pup tent, some camping gear, and I suggest we put it together and you use it. I'll find you at the Robin Hood tree when I get some word, or I need you."

The Robin Hood tree was a massive oak. It reminded Leonard and me of the great oak in the Robin Hood tales, therefore its nickname. It was near my place, on property of Leonard's, and it was out back of the house he still owned, but had boarded up until he finished repairing and selling the house he had inherited from his uncle. A chore that had turned into one of the labors of Hercules.

"I'm going to be at the hospital tonight and tomorrow night," I said. "I don't know I can slip out during the day or not. I do, I'm going to wind up owing so much money I'll spend the rest of my life trying to pay, and still won't be able to."

We put the gear together, along with the two comic books I'd bought, and Leonard took the stuff and melted into the woods. I'd have to get him a suit of Lincoln green. For that matter, I had a green suit I had bought at J. C. Penney's. I could loan it to him. Make him one of those little Robin Hood hats out of green construction paper, rob a tail feather from a chicken, stick it in the hat. I could call him Little Leonard.

When I had a few things packed, I took some cold medicine and drove into town on my way to the hospital. The sky was a gigantic charcoal smear backgrounded by a dying burst of red sunlight, bright and jagged as if God's heart had exploded. Bats filtered about, radaring for bugs.

I drove over to a burger joint and had a burger, thought about everything that had been going on, then thought about nothing. By the time I arrived at the hospital God's heart had bled out, and all that was left was a dark stain, like blood drying on a brick.

I was uncertain what I was supposed to do at the hospital, so I parked and went right up to my room. My name was still written on the paper in the slot outside the door.

I peeked inside. It was dark in there. The bed next to where I had slept was still empty. My bed, where I had had such joyous moments watching pigeons, was also empty.

I turned on the light, pulled back the closet door, and looked in there. My gown was dangling from a hanger. At least I assumed it was my gown. Same style. Same color. Plenty of room for my ass to hang out. I knew for a fact I'd had one just like it.

I looked at my watch. I was a half hour early. I sat in the visitor's chair beside the bed and wished I'd gone home first to get something to read. I looked out the window. It was dark, but I could make out the pigeon poop on the sill, the stuff I'd named Leonard.

I turned on the TV and watched a news program.

About eight-twenty Doc Sylvan came in. "Thanks for showing up. It's nice of you. You know, I didn't think you would. If you hadn't, I'd have made sure the insurance didn't cover shit."

I clicked the TV off. "I'm sorry, Doc. I wasn't trying to give anyone a hard time. I really did have an emergency. I just can't talk about it."

Doc Sylvan eyed me. "Yeah . . . Well, all right. Gown's in the closet. Suit up."

He went out and shut the door. I put on the gown and stuffed my clothes in the closet. Sylvan came back after a while. I had crawled into bed and had the covers around my neck.

"You stay here tonight and tomorrow night," Sylvan said, "and we'll be through with this insurance foolishness. You do that, I can make the insurance work. I think. You come to my office for the remaining shots."

"We could have done that in the first place."

"Insurance, Hap. Keep that in mind. Just keep telling yourself. Insurance. I'm tired of having to sound like a broken record."

"Yes, Yoda."

"You look like shit."

"I got a cold. I picked it up here."

"I don't doubt that. I hate coming to the goddamn hospital to examine patients. They always give me something."

"You could let them die."

"Believe me, there's some I wish would."

"My God, Doc, isn't that against that Hippocratic oath?"

"Hippocrates never had to deal with some of the assholes I deal with. He did, he'd have shoved that oath up their ass."

"Are you indicating any patient in particular?"

"Could be," Sylvan said. "Could be."

Sylvan got his stethoscope and checked me over. He used a tongue depressor on me. He clucked and clicked. "Upper respiratory. Bit of a sore throat. I'll have them check you out. Give you something for the symptoms."

"Thanks," I said.

"Hey, what else can I do for my favorite patient?"

"Let me see . . ."

"Hap, get out of this bed before day after tomorrow, I'll kill you."

"Any news on the squirrel's head?"

"Other than the fact there are tire marks on it, not much. It'll be a while before we hear. They got boxes of heads at the lab in Austin. We've had several rabid dogs and raccoons since you came into the office. Goddamn woods are full of them this year. It's epidemic. I'm leavin'."

"Will you tuck me in before you go?"

Sylvan grunted and left. I closed my eyes, was surprised to discover that so early into the night I was sleepy. I suppose it was the cold, or the medicine I had taken before I left the house. Don't take cold medicine and drive. I wasn't driving. I couldn't quite figure out what it was I was doing. I drifted off.

I came awake and checked my watch about eleven P.M. I was surprised. I felt as if I had been asleep for only moments. I used the bed-lift button, raised my back, turned the TV on again.

The entire television industry hadn't revamped itself during my nap. Everything that was on the standard channels sucked the big ole donkey dick. I tried for some of the specialty channels. No luck. Didn't have any. You'd think if you had to eat the food in the hospital, least they could do was get cable.

I turned off the television and sat in the dark. About fifteen minutes later Brett showed up pushing a metal table on wheels. She turned on the light beside my bed. She lifted a brown paper bag off the metal table. She smiled at me. God, I liked that smile.

"Well," she said. "I heard you ran off."

"Sssssshhhhhh," I said. "Doc Sylvan and I like to think of it as a bit of a sabbatical."

"Since you're back, I figured you'd be needing this."

She opened the brown paper bag, took out the copy of *Boobs and Butts* Charlie had given me, laid it on the nightstand beside my bed.

"One thing I like to see in a man," she said, "is attention to culture."

"That's not really mine."

"It was in the nightstand drawer here."

"Yes, but Charlie, a friend of mine, gave it to me."

"I see. Well, just so you'll stay occupied, I brought you a little something."

She reached back into the bag. She brought out a *Playboy* magazine and a *Penthouse*. "I thought you might as well move up to the classics. Though I'm afraid both of these have words in them."

"Actually, *Boobs and Butts* is very precise. Very modern. They have words. It's just minimalist. They choose what they have to say wisely and place the words under the photographs."

"Yes. I read a few of those words. Did you know they misspelled *pussy?* They used one *s.*"

"No. I'll have to drop them a line."

"Let's check the vital signs."

She did the general routine, pronounced me a bit feverish.

"Doctor's notes say you have a bit of a cold," she said.

"I think I have more than a bit. In fact, when you're in the room I think I gain a couple of degrees on the thermometer."

"Is that a compliment, Hap Collins?"

"I hope so."

She took a water pitcher from the table, poured me a plastic cup of water, gave me a couple of pills. I swallowed them. She said. "Those have plenty of saltpeter in them."

"That's a good idea," I said. "In fact, maybe you could arrange for me to have an ongoing prescription."

"I might be back later," Brett said. "You're not asleep, perhaps I can sit by the bed and read you the captions from the *Boobs and Butts*."

"I wouldn't sit too close."

"Sleep tight, Hap Collins."

"I doubt it," I said. "Wait. What's your last name? I never caught it."

"I never gave it. It's Sawyer. Brett Sawyer. I'm in the phone book. I don't have an answering machine. I don't fuck on the first date, and some men find me forward."

"I can't imagine that."

"That I don't fuck on the first date?"

"That some men find you forward. Hey, I'm gonna be busy some when I get out of here, but you think after that I could give you a call?"

"I've done everything but stick my butt in your face," she said, "so I'll leave some of the work to you. I'm in the phone book."

She gave me that dazzling smile and went away. I lay for a while hoping the cold medicine she had given me would put me to sleep quickly and that it really did have saltpeter in it.

It didn't. I turned off the light and lay there in the dark and looked at my dick making a pup tent of the blanket. I experienced all sorts of unclean thoughts. I certainly hoped Jesus wasn't in the room with me right then. In fact, I might even have shocked the devil.

After a while the pup tent folded, and I fell asleep. If Brett came back, I never knew it. For the first time in a long time, the hospital let me sleep through the night.

# 10

After lunch the next day, Charlie came by. He was wearing a poorly cut brown suit with a light brown shirt and a dark brown tie. He had on tennis shoes, white socks, and his porkpie hat.

"When do you get out of this pit?" he asked.

"Tomorrow morning."

"Then maybe I ought not get you too excited before then."

"My God, are you fixing to strip?"

"Be the best thing you've ever seen, but no. You got to tell Leonard to come in."

"We been over that," I said.

"No. You got to have him come in. Way it looks now, he's in the clear."

"How's that?"

"Bikers at the bar. They all called Leonard a mean nigger and numerous names so foul that if I was to air them politically correct liberals would start to fall out the sky clutchin' their hearts, and the fuckin' super-conservatives would like it too much."

"Get on with the meat."

"They all agree he was too busy running from them, tryin' to hide, to have killed McNee, who they call Horse."

"Yeah, I know that."

"That they call him Horse?"

"That he's called Horse and that his real name is McNee. But what about Leonard?"

"Leonard wouldn't have had time to whack anybody. It's not like they're tryin' to give him an alibi, it's just their stories give him one anyway."

"You wouldn't pull me, would you? This isn't some kind of trick?"

"You tell Leonard to come in. He'll end up owin' a fine for shootin' up the place, assault charges, maybe. Might have to buy the Blazing Wheel a new sign. He'll have to answer a lot of questions, but in the end he won't have to hide out. We can say he was hiding from the bikers for fear of his life. Say he's been in the woods all the time . . . Has he?"

I didn't say anything.

"All right, have it your way," Charlie said. "But, way it looks, his head is off the chopping block."

"I'll be goddamn."

"Yeah, me too. You have him at the station no later than tomorrow morning after you get out of here."

"It'll be more like after lunch. Hospital has to process me out."

"So you knew where he was all along?"

83

"Let's just say I think I can get in touch with him."

"Yeah. Right. After lunch tomorrow. No later. Hear?"

It went pretty smooth, all things considered. Leonard didn't get off scot-free. A court date was set, and it was certain he'd be paying a fine, and he wasn't entirely out of the woods on being a suspect in the death of Horse Dick, but no one was really trying to push him hard in that direction. Not with the bikers actually giving him an alibi. He got processed and out of the cop shop almost quicker than I got out of the hospital, and he didn't have to ride in a wheelchair out to the curb like I did.

I've never really figured that. You go to the hospital, they check you out, no matter if you're skipping rope and climbing the walls, they got to take you out in a wheelchair. It's one of life's little mysteries, like UFOs and the Loch Ness monster.

The morning after Leonard was set free it was hot and bright, but there was a cool wind with it. We met at his house to clean up the mess there, but finally said to hell with it.

I drove out to my house and he followed in the rented Chevy he was driving. We got cane poles and some fishing goods, walked through the woods to where the creek widened, sat there fishing for perch.

"I just couldn't face that mess today," Leonard said. "Besides, it makes me think about Raul."

"The mess?"

"No. The house, stupid."

"Any idea about the mess?" I asked.

"I figure it was the bikers. They found out where I lived, went looking for me, didn't find me, trashed the place. That fits in with you finding the motorcycle tire prints."

"Yeah, but I don't know," I said. "The bikers have been pretty candid about stuff. They didn't admit to that."

"They've only been candid when they could say what an asshole I was. And you know what, they're right."

"I never doubted that. Thing is, that mess bothers me. I think you ought to seriously watch your ass for a while. Those footprints out there don't belong to the tooth fairy."

"Yeah, all right," Leonard said, but he didn't sound too sincere. "You think Raul's alive?"

"I don't know. Haven't a clue. I got to say this. Seems to me he'd have shown up by now. I'm sure you're aware with you in the clear he's considered the prime suspect in the murder of Horse."

"I figured as much. They're just replacing me with him. You know I can't let that stand. Raul couldn't murder anyone. . . . Shit, Hap. I love that kid. He's a dip, but I love him."

We caught a couple of perch, put them in a can of water, sat and talked. Leonard told me about Raul, and how things had gone sour, and how the kid was wilder than he'd realized. It was a pretty standard story. I'd heard it before, but it had been men talking about their women. Love was love, however, and the problems didn't seem to change much, even if the lover was of the same sex, except there was a lot more fucking. Gay or not, men are men, and men seriously love to fuck, and you can write that down in your little black book, tear out the page, crumple it up, and smoke it.

When Leonard finished telling me his woes, I told him

about Brett. Then we talked about Hanson, and how we had to go see him and watch him do his coma.

Next Leonard told me how he had gotten a tick on his balls while staying in the woods. He said he still had it. He couldn't get it off.

"It's in a hard-for-me-to-reach place," he said. "Maybe you could pull it off for me."

"Not on your life. I'm a pretty good shot, though. I could shoot it off."

"I'm serious here. This is a problem."

"Use a match. You light it, blow it out, then stick the hot end against the tick's butt, and he'll back out."

"You've done this?"

"No, but I've heard about it."

"You've had ticks on your nuts?"

"Yep."

"But you didn't try this method?"

"Nope."

"Why didn't you?

"Afraid I'd burn my balls."

"Some help you are. I think you just don't want to be handlin' no queer's balls."

"I don't want to be handling anybody's balls but my own."

"Yeah, well, you'll be sorry, I get that tick disease. You'll wish you'd pinched that tick off."

"I don't think so."

"Way this sonofabitch is swellin' up, I'm gonna have to put a camp chair beside the bed so my balls and the tick got a place to sleep."

"Hey, you want, I'll get your balls and the tick a blanket and a fluffy pillow, but I'm not pulling nothing off your balls."

As usual, the conversation degenerated from there, finally drifted, and we just sat there silently and fished. The wind stopped and turned hard and hot and the air was difficult to breathe, but still we sat, and finally the heat began to fade, and it was cool again, without the wind, and the air was fresh and the brightness of the day fell down amongst the trees, and the sky turned purple, then black, and the stars came out, big and bright and splendid.

We walked home through the dark with our gear, a can of perch and a flashlight, arrived at my house in time to clean the fish by porch light, fry them up, and have a good supper.

After supper we watched a little TV. Then Leonard left early. I promised to come over the next morning and help him clean. He drove off and I watched something on TV I wasn't really paying attention to for about an hour, then cut it off, went to bed, and read a science fiction novel for a while.

Next morning, early, I got up and drove to town and bought some sausage and biscuits at the drive-through of a fast-food joint, went over to Leonard's place.

When he let me in, the house smelled of coffee, and most of the living room had been picked up, and the kitchen porcelain was shiny and the kitchen floor in front of the refrigerator was bright and damp from a recent mopping.

"You've been busy," I said.

"Yeah," Leonard said. "Couldn't sleep last night. Stayed up cleaning. Come in the kitchen, just step careful. Floor's still damp."

I did that. Put the sack on the table, pulled up a chair.

I said, "You pour us some coffee, and I'll give you a sausage and biscuit."

"That's a good-enough deal," Leonard said. "You know what's odd? I discovered something missing."

"Oh?"

"Videotapes. The blank ones, and the ones with movies on them. They're all gone."

"You mean someone broke into the house and stole movies?"

"Looks that way," Leonard said. "I got to figuring, and thought, well, the *Gilligan* tapes are gone, so it could have been Raul. Maybe he's the one wrecked the house. You know, pissed at me. Maybe thinks I did Horse Dick in. So he comes here, throws stuff around, and takes his *Gilligan* tapes. But the thing is, why would he take *The Treasure of the Sierra Madre*, *The Outlaw Josey Wales*, and a bunch of others?"

"They're good movies?"

"He didn't think so. Anything that had gunfire in it he was against. I'm not sayin' my tastes run to *Battleship Potemkin*, but all of Raul's taste was in his mouth, and besides for my dick, which spent a goodly amount of time in his mouth, I don't think he knew good taste."

"Maybe he stole them because you liked them? A kind of revenge."

"I thought of that," Leonard said. "But why did he steal the blank videotapes?"

"So he could tape stuff on them."

"All right. All that works, but why just the videotapes? There's music CDs here he liked, and he didn't take those. He didn't take anything else I think would have interested him. And this mess doesn't strike me as vandalism. There's a lot of things could have been broken for fun, but weren't. Most of the stuff is just tossed around. What's broken seems to have been the result of a search. It wasn't a vandal. I think someone was looking for something, and that doesn't fit in with Raul. He knew where everything was, so why would he throw stuff around?"

"He was mad at you."

"Could be. But, I don't think he took the videos at all."

"Someone else took the *Gilligan* tapes?"

"That's my guess."

"Man, a crime like that, it shows you what the world is coming to. Fucking crooks are like bottom feeders now. Who the fuck in their right mind would want a tape of *Gilligan's Island*, let alone the whole series?"

"Bob Denver?"

"Shit. Don't you know he gets tired of wearing that stupid sailor hat and trying to look perky?"

"You think the series waddled in shit, you got to see the reunion movie," Leonard said. "Raul made me watch it. And man, that one is really deadly. It sort of numbs you, you know, like a kind of nerve gas. I was weak for two days."

"You just hit on the secret," I said. "It was stolen by the State Department to use as a means of covert warfare."

"Way I figure it," Leonard said, "them folks already got a complete set of *Gilligan*. It goes with their *Three's Company* collection. It's what they watch when they're supposed to be solving the nation's problems."

We worked on the house until early afternoon, had some sandwiches, decided we ought to drive into town and buy a few cleaning supplies. We went in my truck. On the way back to Leonard's house, he said, "This Old

Pine Road, where Horse Dick got it. Could we drive over there?"

"Why?"

"I don't know. Guess I'd like to see the spot where this guy they thought I killed bought it."

"I don't know that's such a good idea," I said.

"Come on, Hap."

I didn't much care for it, but we drove out to Old Pine Road, which isn't much of a road, really. It's narrow and winds through a heavily wooded area and links up with a highway that leads to Lufkin. It's shady because of the trees, and not too heavily traveled.

We drove along, finally saw some tire tracks burned into the road, heading through the underbrush and into a large oak tree. Beyond the oak the ground was covered in a deep carpet of kudzu vines and wildflowers, and the hill rolled down steep and turned level as it met the woods.

We pulled to the side of the road, got out and looked around. It was a bright, hot day, and everything I looked at seemed to be viewed through a piece of transparent, lemon-colored rock candy. The air was full of pollen. Every time I took a breath it was like sniffing flour. Within minutes my throat was scratchy and my nose was plugged. It didn't help my cold much.

We looked at the oak, could see where the bike struck it. It was a damn good strike. A chunk had been taken out of the tree as if with an axe.

"If the shotgun hadn't killed him," Leonard said, "you can bet this tree wouldn't have done him any good."

"Without the shotgun, he wouldn't have hit the tree," I said. "Now you've seen it. Make you feel any better?"

"No. I don't really know why I wanted to see it."

We stood under the oak out of the sunlight while Leonard dealt with his thoughts, stood there hugging the shade. Not that it helped. It was still hot and the pollen was thick.

"You know," Leonard said, "I bet I could put a weenie on a stick, poke it out from under this shade, and the sun would cook it. . . . What's that?"

Leonard was turned away from the road, looking down the hill, toward the woods. I looked and saw a scattering of mosquitoes buzzing at the edge of the woods where shadow gave way to light. The insects rolled and rose and dropped like a tiny black cloud amongst the trees. I could imagine them looking up at us, thinking, *Come on down and we'll strip your bones, for we are the piranha of the air.*

It was the mosquitoes I thought Leonard was talking about, but then I followed his pointing finger and saw what he saw. It lay partially buried in the vines near the woods. It was silver, and the sunlight bounced off of it as if it were a mirror. The reflected light was painful to view and caused me to squint my eyes.

"I don't know what it is," I said.

"Could be a piece off the motorcycle," Leonard said.

"Cops looked the place over," I said.

"Don't forget, it's the LaBorde cops we're talking about. Charlie, excluded, of course. I bet they didn't even go down the hill. At least not all the way. Especially the fat ones. They went down too far, they wouldn't have been able to get back up."

"What if it is part of the motorcycle?" I said. "So what?"

"It could lead to the solving of the case."

"What, a fender? The handlebars?"

"You need to read some Agatha Christie, man."

"Why? Am I being punished?"

"You read her, you'll find nothing is too small. Let's go down and see what it is."

"It's a steep hill."

"I bet that's exactly what the fat cops said."

"They were right."

"We're manly men. We can do it."

"Will you carry me?"

"Nope."

We went down the hill, our ankles clutched by kudzu and all manner of undergrowth, and when we were within twenty feet of it I thought it was a huge wad of aluminum foil. Then I saw that what I thought were the natural crumples of a wad of foil were not crumples, but dents, and it wasn't foil, it was a motorcycle helmet. I could see part of the visor, and it was cracked, and I could see something behind the visor, and Leonard, who was slightly ahead of me, could see it too because he stopped walking, made a kind of startled move and let his breath out slowly.

"Shit," he said. "Goddamn shit."

I went on past where he was standing, got closer. There was a head in the helmet, and there was a body attached to the head, and the body was twisted down into the vines. I couldn't see the body from atop the hill, just a piece of the helmet, but I could see all of it easily from this angle, and the legs and arms looked as if they were nothing more than the limbs of a scarecrow, stuffed with straw, twisted into the kudzu.

I squatted down and looked at the face inside the helmet. The head was turned in there too far and was covered in what looked like molasses but wasn't. There were ants and maggots on the part of the face I could see. The wind had changed and the smell of death rode on it and blew into my nostrils and defeated the plugs of pollen. It was all I could do not to get sick.

I got up and turned Leonard by grabbing him by the elbow and started us up the hill.

"It was Raul, wasn't it?" Leonard said.

"Yep."

# 11

We made an anonymous call to the police department and they came and got the body, and next day they made a big deal out of it in the papers, about how the cops had done this great detective work.

There was stuff about the murder of Horse Dick, though he wasn't called that. There was no mention of the fact Raul was found just down the hill from where Horse bought it. But it was pretty clear, if you read between the lines, that Raul had been on the back of the bike.

It wasn't clear how Horse, between collecting knots from Leonard, ended up with Raul and the two of them had gone riding. But it appeared when Horse got his head blown off, the bike had gone into a tree, and so had Raul, and Raul had hit the tree so hard it had knocked him willy-nilly down the hill and into the vines.

That was pretty much the sum of all that was known.

Two days later Raul's parents came from Houston and had him buried in a little graveyard out in the country. It was a quiet shady place with Civil War veterans, black folks, and paupers, and for some reason they decided not to haul him home but to have him planted there.

Leonard wasn't invited to the funeral or the burying, but he went to the burial anyway. The graveyard was on one side of a blacktop road, and there was a cluster of oaks on the other side. We parked beneath them, sat on the hood of the rented Chevy, and watched the service.

We didn't have on black. We didn't have on ties. The coffin was bronze. The family was weeping.

The whole thing was over in short time, then the cars filed out. One of the people attending the funeral stood by the fence for a while, started across the road toward us. He was dressed in black, all neat. At first he was hard to recognize without his Hawaiian shirt, cheap suit, and porkpie hat.

"Thought you might be here," he said to Leonard.

"Yeah," Leonard said.

"I'm sorry," Charlie said. "You should have been invited."

"Family don't like queers," Leonard said. "Far as they were concerned, Raul wasn't queer. He was just a little confused. Any day now he'd quit suckin' dicks and start dive-bombing pussy."

"Easy, Leonard," I said.

"Yeah," Leonard said. "Easy."

Charlie climbed onto the Chevy's hood, sat by Leonard. "I wasn't invited either. Came anyway. Thought whoever did it might show up. You know, like in the movies. Returning to the scene of the crime."

"You don't mean me, do you?" Leonard said.

"No," Charlie said.

"Well, you sure don't mean me," I said.

"No," he said. "Actually, I came 'cause I thought I might see you two. Raul's body was on Old Pine Road, just down the hill from where Horse Dick bought it. Down there all the time."

"So we heard," Leonard said.

"Shits went out there to investigate the site didn't do much of a job," Charlie said.

"Boy, that surprises me," Leonard said. "A dead queer, I thought everybody would be in a hurry."

"It ain't one dead queer," Charlie said. "It's two."

"All right," Leonard said. "Two dead queers."

"Could it be one of you boys called in about the body?" Charlie asked.

"Could be," I said.

"Thought so. You boys are too nosey to let something lay."

"Hey, we did better than you guys," I said.

"That's what gets my goat," Charlie said. "Want a little tidbit, boys?"

"Sure," I said.

"The two dead queers," Charlie said. "One of them was a cop."

We both stared at Charlie. I said, "Well, since it wasn't Raul, that leaves Horse."

"See," Charlie said, "your powers of deduction. Phenomenal."

"Don't fuck around here," Leonard said. "I'm not in the mood. Horse Dick was a cop?"

"Yep," Charlie said. He reached inside his suit coat, brought out a flattened pack of cigarettes. He put one in his mouth, got out a lighter, and lit it. He said, "He was working undercover."

"Under Raul's covers," Leonard said.

"He was on special assignment," Charlie said. "Didn't know it till the other day. It wasn't part of my business. This was something the chief set up."

"The chief set up stuff with a gay cop?" I said.

"Didn't know he was gay," Charlie said. "Chief knew, guy wouldn't have been a cop, let alone on assignment. I'd seen the guy around, but he wasn't part of my action. I didn't connect the death of the biker with the cop's death, not until it got to be more common knowledge. It was slow to leak around the department. Chief thought it made him look like an idiot, so he wasn't blowin' any trumpets."

"I'll be a sonofabitch," I said.

"Guys are running a lot of drugs through the Blazing Wheel," Charlie said. "So Chief got Horse . . . McNee . . . and that's another alias. His real name is Bill Jenkins. Anyway, Chief got him to go undercover. Horse got involved with Raul, then he and Raul got dead."

"You think it had something to do with Horse being a cop, or being gay?" I said.

"Don't know," Charlie said, shaking his head as he blew out smoke. "Maybe both. Maybe neither. Whatever, I wanted y'all to know, 'cause truth of the matter is this one may not get the attention it deserves. Cop gets killed in the line of duty, we're all over it. But, like you said, Leonard, couple of fags, Chief being like he is, seeing this as some reflection on the department and himself . . . It could fall between the cracks. Might already be there. I maybe can't do what ought to be done. Get what I'm sayin'?"

"Yeah," Leonard said. "We get what you're sayin'."

"I didn't really know Raul that much," Charlie said. "I hate he's dead, though. I mean, you liked him."

"Good enough," Leonard said.

Charlie finished his smoke, climbed off the hood. "See you boys later."

Charlie went down to his car and drove away.

We sat there for a while watching the grave digger with his backhoe. He threw the dirt in fast and got things tidy, drove the backhoe through a large gate on the other side of the graveyard, wheeled it onto a trailer hooked to a truck. He fastened the backhoe down. He locked the gate up. He drove the trailer and the backhoe away.

Two men took down the striped funeral tent and placed the flowers and wreaths the bereaved had ordered onto and around the grave. They loaded up and got out of there.

We walked down to the graveyard, went through the gate. Walked past gravestones. I read some of them. Civil War dates. One worn stone bore the faded words BELOVED SLAVE AND SERVANT chiseled on it, which I thought was kind of ironic.

One said JAKE REMINGTON, adding, NO RELATION TO THE ARTIST OR THE GUN MANUFACTOR OF THE SAME LAST NAME. There was a Jane Skipforth, who died in the early 1900s, FROM COMPLICATIONS WITH MEN. A Bill Smith, who died in World War I. HIS PLANE WENT DOWN, BUT HIS SPIRIT SOARS. A Frank Jerbovavitch, who got old and died. A Willie, no dates, just Willie. A Fred Russel, just dates. No mention of his relationship to the famous western artist of the same last name.

And so it went. But it really didn't matter what was said

or wasn't. Now they were all brothers and sisters under the dirt.

Leonard stood at Raul's grave, said, "Somehow, it don't mean nothin', a grave. Just like when my uncle got buried. He's dead, and that's all there is to it."

Leonard kicked some dirt onto the grave and we left.

# 12

When we got back to Leonard's house we drank some coffee and chatted a bit, but it wasn't a lively sort of chat.

After a while, I took a hint, told Leonard I was going home, and I'd call him the next day. He almost helped me to the door. He stood on the porch as I was getting in my pickup.

"Hap," he said, "ain't no one I'd rather have around than you. But sometimes I don't want no one around."

"I understand."

"This is one of those times."

"No problem."

I drove home, wheeled by Leonard's old house, the one down the road from me, gave it a longing once-over. It was boarded up and graying, and the old television antenna shooting up the side of the house, spreading out on top of the roof, had been ravaged by wind. It looked like some kind of giant alien hand gone to rot, leaving only bones. Paint flaked like psoriasis off the porch and the front door. The grass was tall and nodding in the wind.

I wished Leonard would move away from his uncle's house and come home. The place wasn't much, but I liked him down the road from me. We had had some good times out here, and maybe we'd never have them again. Life was starting to get in the way.

I was pretty wired when I got home, so I tried a shower, but that didn't help. I sat around for a while, trying to read, trying to watch television, trying to listen to music. None of this did me any good.

The day wore on. I got to thinking about Brett. I looked at my watch. It was late afternoon, but she wouldn't have to go to work until late. I dialed her number. She answered on the third ring.

"Honey, I was beginning to think I was going to have to part my hair on the other side," she said.

"Come again?"

"I thought I was losing my touch."

"Do you practice it much?"

"Actually, I don't. And I'm not normally such a floozy, but I haven't met anyone that's interested me in ages."

"That's flattering. What interested you in me?"

"I just love that little bald spot."

"I don't think you mean that."

"You know, you're right. I don't." Brett laughed. The laugh was as nice as her smile. "I don't know. Not really. There's just something about you. You remind me of a big puppy dog. I think that's it."

"Woof, woof," I said.

"How about taking me to dinner? I haven't eaten yet, and I've got to go to work before long. I've had one of those days where all I've had to eat is coffee."

"Well, I've had one of those days too. Maybe we can cheer each other up."

"Forty-five minutes," she said.

We went to an expensive place called the West Coast. The place looks better than the food tastes, though the food isn't bad. The West Coast is on a hill and has a large advertising sign out front that lists the specials of the week, most of the specials being some kind of seafood or steak.

The restaurant itself is made of great slabs of lumber and vast expanses of glass. It has well-manicured bushes and lots of parking places. For some reason, people dress up when they go there.

I dressed up a little myself. Dark slacks, dark blue sport jacket with a light blue shirt. I wiped off my shoes with a wash rag until they almost looked as if they had been polished. I had a tie in my coat pocket that I decided not to wear. It was a nice tie. Maybe later I could get it out and show it to Brett, just to give her some idea of what I might have looked like had I worn it.

When I picked up Brett, I wished I had on the tie. She looked nice. She had on a white blouse with a blue design on it, a blue skirt, dark blue shoes, and dark hose. Her makeup was spare and her hair was as lustrous as a goddess's. The blouse revealed the tops of her breasts and she smelled so good I thought I might have to pull over to the side of the road and cry for a while.

"I hope I look all right," she said. "I started to just shit in the face of all feminists tonight and wear an all-purpose deluxe tight-as-sin polyester screw-me-to-death outfit and no panties. I wear that, when I walk it looks like my thangamajig is shellin' a walnut."

All I could respond with was, "I'm sure that would have been very nice too."

"Well, this will have to do. I didn't want you to spring a leak on our first date."

"It's fine," I said. "Looks great."

"I hope so," she said. "Actually, it's kind of painful. I got on one of those bras hikes your titties up. They aren't as form-fitting as the goddamn box says they are. I feel like I got a truck jack under each one of 'em."

We made romantic small talk like that on the way over, and once inside and seated at our table, a guy dressed in a white dinner jacket stood up at an organ and played and sang in a manner so awful I thought for a moment he was a comedian. When I realized he wasn't, I said, "I'm sorry. I could have taken you to Burger King and we could have listened to Fats Domino on the jukebox. This clown wasn't here last time I came."

"That must have been Christmas Eve 1984, because I been here a lot and he's been here since I've been coming, and he's never been able to carry a note in a sealed Tupperware container. He can do a damn good 'Pop Goes the Weasel,' though, and come Christmas he has a medley that ends with 'Rudolph the Red-Nosed Reindeer' that'll break your goddamn heart."

I smiled at her. "You are definitely different, Brett."

"Not really," she said. "I just put up a bold front. I'm really a chicken shit. This dating business is confusing to me. I don't know if I want a real relationship anymore or a quick fuck. What about you?"

"I'd really hate to choose."

"I'll tell you a secret too. I don't come on to every man like I did you."

"You keep telling me that."

"Do I?"

"Yep."

"Well, I really do like you. If you had money I'd like you even more."

"I like you too, but I don't have money."

"I didn't think you did. You don't look like you got more than a couple dimes to rub together."

"Don't worry. I can pay for the meal."

She smiled again. Damn, I liked that smile.

"I don't mind you don't have money," she said, and she reached out and placed her hand on top of mine. "I just said it would be convenient you had it. As for you liking me too, that's good, but men like women right off if they look a certain way. And there's some men, they go long enough and it's late enough and they're drunk enough, and some of them don't even need the drink. . . . Well, they'd fuck a three-hundred-pound cross-eyed sow in a John Deere cap."

"You got to be proud of those old boys," I said. "To think appearance doesn't matter. That's very modern, don't you think?"

"What I think is I may not be a *Playboy* model, but I been around enough to know I look better than a tie rack. Figure that won't last much longer at my age, so I better use it while I got it."

"I may let my biology bark now and then," I said, "but I make my final judgments with my heart, not my eyes. And just for the record, on the visual part, you're a long way off from having ties hung on you. But that's not the long and the short of it for me. How you look, I mean. I

104

grew up in the sixties. I'm for equal rights and I'm for women. I even think of myself as a supporter of feminism as long as it doesn't come across as stupid and strident as extreme machoism. . . . Is that a word?"

"Who cares? I get your drift."

"All right. Whatever, strident on either side wears me out. Like I said, my biology barks now and then, but when it comes down to it, I like to think I'm not the sort of guy can be pulled around by the ying-yang. I like to believe I'm made of sterner stuff than that."

"I grew up in the sixties too," Brett said, "but I hope there's at least a drop of male chauvinist pig in you, or I've spent too much time brushin' my hair. They still use that term, don't they? 'Male chauvinist pig'?"

"I'm not sure," I said.

"Men and women, biology and the goddamn federal budget," Brett said. "All a mess, isn't it?"

I agreed it was.

Brett said, "If you're a woman and you like sex, you're a whore. If you don't like it, then you're frigid. If you use what charms you have to get sex, then the feminists hate you, and if you don't want to marry every goddamn hard dick gives you a poke, then the men think you're a ball breaker, or you're back to number one again. You're a whore."

"It is confusing," I said.

"And you know what?" Brett said. "I think you could be pulled around by your dick a little bit, I wanted to pull it."

"You're right," I said. "I take all that bullshit back. Start pulling."

A well-dressed waiter came by then. A good-looking college kid about nineteen. He was very polite and acted

105

as if he couldn't wait to give us menus, take our order, and be our food slave for the next hour or so. I caught him peeking at Brett's titties, but I thought it might be ruder to ask him to stop than to ignore him. Besides, I couldn't actually blame him. It's easy to talk a line of shit about how looks don't matter, and they shouldn't, and as you mature they don't matter as much, but the eyeball is connected to the crotch in men, and that is the sad way of the world, and no matter how many volumes are written on political correctness, the one-eyed snake that lives between the legs of men will not read and strives only for satisfaction.

The waiter took our drink order and went away. While I studied the menu, I found myself feeling guilty. I was having fun, about to eat a good meal, sitting there with a good-looking date, and Leonard was sitting at home with a can of tuna fish, a handful of bad TV stations, and no vanilla cookies.

Well, he could always go down to Burger King.

When the waiter came back with our drinks we ordered a dozen oysters, steaks, and salads. The oysters came and Brett ate hers with lots of lemon and sauce, and I ate mine with just the lemon. The salad came and it was a good salad, or as good as salads get in Texas. A Texan's idea of a salad is a few bananas and strawberries inside a mold of lime Jell-O.

The baked potatoes had all the fixings. Cheese, sour cream, butter, bacon bits. The steaks weren't bad either, both of them cooked medium rare. I drank a nonalcoholic beer, and Brett had another mixed drink. And if I could remember the roster of all the songs that talentless sonofabitch in the dinner jacket sang, I'd go to my grave a happy man.

As we ate we blocked out the singer's frantic organ playing and tired voice and talked about ourselves. My side of the story was pretty easy to tell. It was mostly about bad jobs, growing up, this and that, but I left out the part about being an ex-con because I was a draft resister; that would come later when we knew each other better.

Brett told me she had been raised in Gilmer, Texas, had been a cheerleader and later a majorette, and that she'd once had a fantasy she might like to fuck the football team. But the fantasy wore off before she got the opportunity, and in the long run, after knowing a few of them, she decided the knob on the end of her baton was about as stimulating. Real lady talk.

"When I was eighteen," she said, "even without the football team, I was a walkin' sperm bank. A psychologist will tell you it's because there was something wrong with me, and who am I to argue. They'll tell you my parents beat me or fucked me or doodled with my asshole while I slept, or a next-door neighbor liked to pay me nickels and ice cream to have me strip naked and sit on his coffee table while he beat off to violent Bugs Bunny cartoons. And I'm sure it happens, but I had a good home life and was well loved and was popular in school, went to church, got baptized, and even attended charm school."

"I take it you didn't get a diploma from charm school."

The great smile again. "Actually, I did, smart ass. But as I was sayin', ain't none of that bullshit applies to me. I do have a sneakin' suspicion what my problem was and is, however."

"What?" I asked.

"I got on the pill when I was sixteen because I think I

just simply and dearly loved to fuck. I still do. Though I've got morals now."

"You don't do it on the first date."

"That's it. That's the moral. And I make the man wear a rubber. But I suppose that's nothing to do with morals. You could call that disease control. Has to be, because I hate those goddamn rubbers."

"So do men. Go on, tell me more."

Brett told me she had a twenty-seven-year old son named Jimmy who lived in Austin and was into Taoist philosophy and the martial art of aikido. Jimmy believed the source of his energy came up from the center of the earth and moved through his colon and all around inside of him. He had lots of internal energy. What the Japanese call ki power. Three people couldn't lift Jimmy off the ground because of his ki. He could hold his arm out and you could swing on it. For all this internal energy, however, he lacked common sense and didn't have a bank account. He wrote to Brett at least twice a month for money, and last time she heard he was in love with a former cocaine addict turned Christian Scientist who was healing an unexplained open wound on her leg—more of a running sore, actually—with prayer. Jimmy said he was certain in time his girlfriend could cure it right up. For the time being, however, she had also consented to the use of gauze, peroxide, and adhesive tape, though this was not common knowledge she shared with her church.

Brett had a young daughter named Tillie, who lived in Denver. She said the last letter she got from Till, as Brett called her, was encouraging. Till said her pimp didn't beat her as much these days and most of her old injuries had gone away, though she did sport a small white scar over her right eye, and on cold days she walked with a limp. She had bought a new spitz puppy she named Milo, but her pimp didn't like it and shot it and she was kind of happy about that now because she didn't really need a dog in a small apartment where she had to entertain men.

The apartment, Brett told me, was a room over an all-night garage, and most of her customers were brought there by taxi after reading her name off a Fina station's shit-house wall. The pimp lived uptown in a condo. Brett finished by saying, "Guess I can't be too hard on Tillie, she's just doin' for money what I used to do for free, though admittedly I didn't advertise in the Fina station toilet."

"I always felt bad about not having kids," I said. "But I'm feeling better now."

"I must admit, I've come to understand why certain animals eat their young," Brett said. "But I wouldn't have missed them growin' up. I love them. The problem was their father was an asshole and I was too young to raise babies. It's our fault they both turned out to be worthless pieces of shit. I had the first one when I was sixteen. The second one when I was eighteen. I did the best I could but I was a kid myself. Earl didn't do a goddamn thing except suck the end of a bottle and hump truck-stop waitresses. After we were married for a while, Earl decided he liked to toss me over the TV set on Friday nights, bounce me around the bedroom, punch me, then butt-fuck me as a little treat when his arms got tired. This went on longer than I like to admit. I kept thinking I could change him."

"I'm sorry to hear it."

"That's all right," Brett said. "Nineteen eighty-five I finally got tired of it. I hit him in the head with a shovel while he was digging for fishing worms in the backyard. I seen him out in the yard digging, and just the night before he'd given me one of them beatings I was tellin' you about, and he put a beer bottle up my ass and poured the beer into me, and I was not in a cheery mood about it. Anyway, I seen him out there, so I made my plans. I hit him in the head with that shovel and I'd brought some lighter fluid and kitchen matches with me, and after I hit him I set him on fire. You might call it premeditated. You may have seen something about it back then. It made all the papers and TV. I burned the back of my hand a little when I was doing it, but Earl got the worst of it. He's in some kind of home now in Houston, a ward of the state, and he can't do things for himself and has trouble with simple math problems. Stuff like, if you have two apples and you eat one, how many are left?"

"Jesus, Brett. Did you do some time?"

"Judge let me off. There was plenty of evidence Earl had it coming. I dressed nice that day, best hot pants I had—you remember hot pants, don't you? Well, I wore pink hot pants and a tight top, and as the judge was a known lecher, he let me off on a kind of self-defense thing. Earl's relatives tried to sue me, came back on me for every kind of thing there was for about six months, but after a while they got to feelin' good about Earl being gone too. He was always borrowin' money from 'em and he was known to conk the sisters now and then, and I figure he'd been fuckin' the youngest one, 'cause she had a kinda twitch to her eye and didn't like men much. Earl's mama thought Earl was a lot like her husband, Earl's daddy, who used to beat her. Her husband, Earl Senior, died of a heart attack one morning in a moment of fury

110

over runny breakfast eggs. So, his family kinda got to respect me a little, 'cause down deep they didn't like that sonofabitch Earl Junior neither. I'm not sayin' they exactly thanked me for settin' Earl's head on fire and bangin' his brain around, but they began to feel fortunate he didn't have anything upstairs left to use for devious means. Instead, he was tryin' not to mess himself too often and learn not to lick his fingers when he got single square breakthrough. That's kind of his lifetime career now. Keepin' shit off his fingers."

"Always an important point," I said.

"His family sent me a Christmas card for a few years after I moved away," Brett said. "All this happened over in Gilmer, and I can't say I've missed the place much or looked back, though I do miss the Yamboree now and then. You know, the big sweet tater celebration they have over there every year?"

"I've been to it."

"What kills me is the main float they make. It's always this big yam, or sweet tater, but it looks like this big brown turd. I rode on it back when I was in high school. I was the Yamboree Queen one year. I remember I drank some Boone's Farm apple wine and rode on that turd down Main Street waving at people, got so goddamn tickled I nearly fell off. People thought I was just hysterically happy that I was that year's turd queen. That's back when I first was datin' Earl. He wasn't so bad then, and I've got some good memories, but the best one is the last one, when Earl was running across the yard with his head on fire, just before the neighbor tripped him and put out the blaze with a water hose."

"Did he beat the flames out with the hose, or did he have the water on?"

111

Brett laughed. "He had the water on. When I think about that day I get a kind of warm feelin' inside. Not as warm as Earl's head got. But warm."

"I don't suppose any of your other relationships have ended in tragedy?"

"Don't worry. Earl's the only one I ever set on fire, and I haven't taken up a shovel since, unless it was to plant flowers. It was just one of them things. Enough was enough. I burned up his car too. I was so goddamn angry after he got his head fire put out, I pulled his car into the drive, poured gasoline on it, and set it ablaze. I did that 'cause he treated that car better than me."

"You certainly had a big day that day."

"You betcha," Brett said. "And you know what? I got a friend goin' through that shit right now. You met Ella, didn't you?"

"She's a nurse too?"

"That's the one," she said. "She told me she talked to you. Her husband beats her regular, and she won't leave. I've tried to get her to leave, but she won't, and she ain't for settin' his head on fire."

"Actually, that's for the best, Brett."

"I reckon, but she ought to do somethin'."

"I wish her luck," I said.

"Luck ain't gonna have a goddamn thing to do with it," Brett said.

After dinner I drove Brett back to her place and she made coffee, then dressed for work. While she dressed I sat on the sofa and drank my coffee and looked around the living room. It was neat and simple. She had a row of books, mostly nursing text books and a few best-sellers. A few knickknacks. No shovels or lighter fluid.

There were photographs of her two kids. They were probably in their teens in the photos. Handsome kids. The girl looked as if she were going to grow up to resemble her mother. Probably did by now. Except for the scar and the limp. The boy was nice-looking. Probably wowed a lot of women in the aikido class during his discussions of Taoism. I wondered what he could do with a left jab to the nose, a swift kick to the gonads.

Brett came out wearing her nurse duds. "I'm sorry I had to deflate my titties," she said, "but duty calls."

"That's all right. Would you like me to run you to work?"

"No. I got to come home sometime, and I don't want to be dependent on you. I had a good time, really. I hope you did, even if you didn't get any nookie."

"Listen, Brett. You don't need to keep that up. I like sex. Really. But I like you too. I want to know you better. I'd prefer not to spend a lot of time with you around shovels and lighter fluid, but I do want to know you better. You don't have to come on so strong."

"I guess you're right. But I got to tell you, sweetie, when you been fending for yourself long as I have, you use ever' tool you got in your toolbox. I guess I bring out the monkey wrench sometimes when a pair of pliers would do."

"It's all right," I said. "I'll see you again if you'll let me."

"You bet. And soon."

"One thing," I said. "You got any photos of you riding that turd in the Yamboree?"

"Somewhere. Next time we get together I'll let you see 'em. I even got one of me when I was a baby on a fake bearskin rug I'll show you."

"Great. Good night, then."

"Wait," she said. "Come here."

I went to her and she started to kiss me. I said, "I'm on the tail end of a cold."

"I've had colds before," she said. We kissed. It was very nice. I kissed her again.

"I got to go," she said.

We went out and she locked the house and we kissed again and I walked her out to her car. She drove away in her Ford and I got in my truck and left her place tasting the lingering sweetness of her on my lips and tongue.

# 13

When I got home Leonard's rented Chevy was in the front yard and I could see the glow of the TV through the windows. Inside, he was sitting in my recliner watching a true-crime show. His face was drawn and his skin looked gray. There was a Jiffy bag package by the chair.

I said, "I thought you wanted to be alone?"

"I did," Leonard said. "But when I got alone, I decided I didn't want to be alone. Where you been?"

I told him.

"Glad to hear it. I thought you'd given up dating."

"So did I," I said.

"How'd it go?"

"Good. I think."

Leonard grew silent. I could tell something was wrong, that he was trying to maintain a front of control, so I didn't throw off his game plan. I let him lead.

Eventually, he said, "I have something I'd like to tell you, something I'd like to show you."

I sat down on the couch and waited. Leonard had his pipe with him, the one he smokes now and then. He packed it carefully because his hands were shaking. He lit it and puffed. He used the remote to turn off the television.

He said, "So I'm sittin' home alone, thinking, always a dangerous thing for me, and I ask myself, this videotape business, it's obvious someone is looking for something, and it's on video. What could it be?"

"And the answer is?"

"I didn't come up with anything. I asked myself another question. Why would they come to my place to look for the video? That one seemed obvious."

"Raul," I said. "We've determined that possibility already."

"That's right. Raul got a video belongs to someone else, and whoever it belongs to, they go looking for it."

"So why didn't they check Horse Dick's place instead of yours?"

"I thought of that. I called Charlie and said, 'You know my place was trashed because someone was looking for something. What about Horse Dick's joint?' Charlie tells me, yeah, it was wrecked. I tell him about my videos missin', and we get to talkin', and he says he was the one inspected Horse's place and didn't remember seeing any videotapes there. Didn't think about it at the time. Wasn't looking for any. But he recalled a VCR, and now that he thought about it, that didn't make sense. Could be that way, you know, like Horse Dick only rents videos, but usually where there's a VCR there's a videotape or two. You know what else Charlie told me?"

"No."

Leonard took a deep breath on this one. "This is hard, man. Raul, he didn't die from hitting that tree. Wasn't shot either. Charlie, he got back to headquarters after the funeral, and he's bawlin' his men out, ones looked over the hill, and they showed him pictures and video, Hap. Pictures of the tree, the hill, and Horse Dick's body, and all along the woods, and guess what?"

"I wouldn't know where to start."

"Raul wasn't there."

"They overlooked him."

"No. They didn't miss him. Charlie pushes for the autopsy report, looks it over. Coroner, he'd been told to just take it like it looks: someone, assailants unknown, killed Horse Dick, and Raul died in the motorcycle crash. Chief, he don't want to deal with any other possibilities because of fearin' it might connect with a gay killin', then it would come out Horse Dick was a butt-hole bandit and a cop. Thing is, Raul was thrown off the bike, but that didn't kill him. Whoever *they* is, ones shot Horse Dick, somebody . . . They took Raul with them."

"Oh, shit," I said.

"Yeah," Leonard said. "They took him, kept him a while, hooked some kind of battery to his balls and gave him a jump-start. Several times. Coroner thinks they wetted him up to get the kind of contact they wanted with the cables. They broke his foot. Probably stomped it. They used some kind of bat or board on his knees and shins. They pushed all his fingers back till they broke. They broke his arms and twisted them behind his back and cranked them around some more, making those nerves jump. They finally twisted his neck with some kind of garotte, stove in his head with something heavy, stuck his noggin back in the helmet, took him out there and dumped him where they got him."

"Christ, Leonard. You're sure?"

"Charlie's sure. The coroner's sure. Raul was lyin' out there rotting these last few days, but he hasn't been there the whole time."

I sat amazed, a little sick to my stomach. "I'm surprised Charlie would tell you all this."

"You heard what Charlie said earlier. Chief's tied his hands. Won't let Charlie do what needs to be done. Ain't no one gonna do much about this shit. Couple queers aced is almost good business far as the chief's concerned. As for Charlie, he sounds dispirited. Like he's losin' his will to be a cop. So, it's you and me, bubba."

I thought about that a moment. I said, "I don't know it's our place to deal with something like this, Leonard. It's police business. I think what Charlie's implying is we find something good, something helpful, we report it. But he's not suggesting we take the law into our own hands."

"You're not listening, Hap. It's police business when they want to make it their business. They don't make it their business, then I got to make it *my* business."

"I don't like the sound of that."

"Maybe I'll put it to music and you'll like it better. You want to hear the rest of what I think?"

"Yeah."

"I think they—whoever they is—tortured Raul for the whereabouts of the tape or tapes. Raul wasn't a tough guy, but he must have felt strong about this one, Hap, 'cause he didn't give it up. He lied. Told them what they wanted was where it wasn't. They tried him out. They checked Horse Dick's place. No dice. So they talk to him some more in that special way they have. So now he puts them on my place, thinkin' he's gainin' some time to maybe get away. Or maybe he is a tough guy. Tougher than I knew. Whatever, he puts them on me 'cause maybe he thought I could handle them. Figured he sent them there and I was there, I'd handle them. Or maybe he didn't give a shit about me. But the thing is, they tossed my place and didn't find anything. They decide to give Raul a little more business, or maybe they just got tired of his bullshit and finished him. Or maybe he died sooner than they expected. Thing is, he goes out without giving them what they want to know."

Leonard paused to relight his pipe. I said, "Question immediately comes to mind is, how do you know they didn't find the video? Maybe it was at your place and you didn't know it. Raul had a house key, could have hid it there. Or maybe they went to your place first, hit Horse Dick's second. Maybe he had it."

"I thought of that," Leonard said. "But I also thought Raul might have hid it somewhere else. So my next question was, where would he hide it? Remember what I told you about all the crap going on at my place, my mail being screwed around with—"

"The other address," I said.

"That's why you're my friend," Leonard said. "You can keep up with me. Almost. Mailbox out here isn't checked often. I come out maybe once every month or so. It doesn't get any mail to speak of anymore since I switched back to the town address. Mostly just junk mail. It's a huge mailbox, so it's a pretty safe place to leave something. I drove over tonight, got out my trusty flashlight, looked in the mailbox, and what do you think I found?"

"That Jiffy bag by your chair," I said.

"Bingo, my man. That and some junk mail. And you won't believe what's in the Jiffy."

Leonard grabbed the Jiffy bag, took a little notebook out of it and tossed it at me. I grabbed it and looked at it. It was a standard promotional-style notebook for King Arthur Chili, a local business.

"I couldn't make heads or tails out of that," Leonard said. "Wait before you look. There's a couple of video-tapes inside as well. I've seen one of them. I got it loaded in the VCR. I want you to see it."

Leonard plucked the remote out of his lap, turned on the set and the VCR. I moved over and stood behind him to watch.

There was static and darkness, then gray shapes. The gray shapes became clearer, but never too clear. One of the shapes was a tanker-style truck. It was parked and a hose was being fed from it into a hole in cement, a hole like a cistern, and you could hear the sound of a pump sucking up the contents of the cistern, running it into the truck. The other gray shapes were two men with the truck. One of them was scrawny, with longish hair and a dark cap of some kind. He had on jeans and a jean jacket with the sleeves cut out. No shirt. Classic TV and movie-biker garb. The other guy wore jeans and a dark T-shirt and jackboots. He had long hair tied back in a ponytail. He looked about fifty-five or so and was about the size of the Green Giant who sells peas on the commercials.

"Bigfoot!" I said.

"Bingo again," Leonard said. "He's also Big Man Mountain."

"Say what?"

"Professional wrestler. One of LaBorde's claims to fame. He was a villain on the circuit. Retired a year or

120

two ago. Read about it in the paper. Word is they retired him 'cause of some shit he had goin' down, but I don't remember what it was. But there was a scandal."

"I seldom read the papers," I said.

"Well," Leonard said, "you should. But that's him."

"How can you tell? I can't see his face worth shit."

"True, but how many long-haired guys have you heard of weigh about three-fifty and stand well over six foot?"

"I don't know of any."

"Well, I know of one. Big Man Mountain. Bigfoot, as you call him. He dressed that same way when he wrestled, as a biker. And it appears that's his normal attire."

There was more of this, two guys standing around while the hose sucked the contents of the cistern. Then the two guys got in the truck and the video jumped around in blackness and static. When it started up again, there were more clips of this activity with the tanker, and in some cases I recognized where they were, the back of restaurants in town. A Mexican restaurant where Leonard and I often ate because the food was cheap and good, another restaurant where the food was good, but not cheap, and we didn't eat there. We wanted to, though.

Besides the work with the tanker truck, there were also some clips of this big truck with sideboards and the same guys and two other guys dressed in similar garb. They were parked behind a building, loading barrels onto the back of the truck. As with all the video, the guys looked nervous and furtive.

"The rest of the tape is just more of this," Leonard said.

"I don't get it. Why would Raul mail himself a tape of some bikers sucking crap out of cisterns and putting barrels on trucks?"

Leonard cut off the VCR and the set. "Do you remember that article I read to you a few months back? Out of the paper?"

"No. I hardly remember where I was yesterday."

"Man, you got to pay more attention to the newspapers," Leonard said. "Grease nappers."

"Grease nappers? What grease . . . Wait a minute . . . The folks stealing grease from restaurants, selling it to the recycling folks. It was kind of a humorous article. Something about 'Police Set Grease Trap for Suspects.'"

"That's it. Except the police didn't catch anyone. And if you remember, there's lots of money in grease napping."

I went back to my spot on the couch. I said, "You tryin' to tell me Raul was filming grease nappers, and they caught him, tortured and killed him over it?"

"There's lots of money in grease," Leonard said. "Silly as it sounds, with just limited facilities, you can make up to a couple thou a day. Better-organized than that, hittin' LaBorde, Lufkin, Tyler, you could make a hell of a lot more. Maybe ten thousand a day. People have been murdered for a lot less than that. And if they thought the whistle was going to be blown, they could have murdered Raul, and it wouldn't be for grease. It would be for money."

"All right," I said. "Say the grease nappers were filmed by Raul. You got to ask yourself, why? I mean, since when is Raul an investigative reporter?"

"I don't know he was. I think these tapes belong to Horse Dick, the cop. He's undercover, acting like one of the guys. That's why it jumps around. Sometimes he's helpin' them do the work. Then, when he's standin' over to the side, smokin' a cigarette, pissin' or somethin', he filmed them with a hidden camera. Later he had the stuff put on video, for easy viewing. While he's doing this investigation, he falls in with Raul and they start swappin' spit and sperm, and pretty soon it's pillow talk, and Raul knows everything Horse Dick knows. That could be what led to Raul's demise."

"What about the chief? Wouldn't he have this information? If so, why would Horse or Raul hide it in your mailbox?"

"Maybe Horse Dick didn't have time to get the stuff to the chief. Maybe he was waiting until he had a full investigation. Maybe the chief has a copy. I don't know. Thing is, I believe Raul got wrapped up in this business pretty tight, got to thinking he was some kind of hot-shit undercover guy himself. Horse Dick tells him things are getting tight, maybe they ought to get rid of the tapes for a while, so Raul mails them to my old address. That's his handwriting on the envelope. Then, when Raul gets caught by the bad guys, he doesn't tell them where they are. How's that sound?"

"Lots of things wrong with that scenario. Why would Raul and Horse Dick not turn the evidence over to the chief, they thought they were in trouble? Why wouldn't Raul tell these thugs where the videos are? Torture like that, you'd tell anyone anything they wanted to know. And if you don't mind me saying so, Raul wasn't that tough."

"I don't really have an answer for that, but things occurred to me. Back when I was burning those crack houses, rumor was the chief was getting a slice of the drug pie, which was why the houses kept being built up. Him and the owner of the houses were supposed to be in cahoots."

"Never been any proof of that," I said, "though I don't doubt it."

"Chief sent Horse Dick in to investigate drugs through the bikers. Maybe this is law enforcement, and maybe its the chief's way of getting enough evidence on the bikers to make sure he gets a cut. Horse Dick figures this out, so he doesn't hand in the videos. He hides them. That kind of explains why the chief isn't pursuing this business. It could be more than just the gay thing."

"Problem with that theory, Leonard, is the video is of grease nappers, not drug lords."

"Yeah, you're right," Leonard said, and relit his pipe. "But it could all connect."

"I guess. Sounds thin to me. But if drugs were happening along with the grease napping, wouldn't there be videos of drug activity?"

"Maybe this was the best Horse Dick could get on them," Leonard said. "Could be like the way you use income tax fraud to get gangsters for worse business. Nail them for grease, you put the drug business out of business."

"There's something in that," I said. "What about the other video?"

"I was going to give it a look-see, but then you came home. My guess is more of the same."

We loaded the video. It wasn't about grease napping. It was two guys walking, and it was easy to recognize the place. It was LaBorde Park. I recognized the bench the guys were walking past. I knew the camera view was being taken through the shrubbery across the way. The lighting was bad, just some of the pole lights in the park, and the camera jumped this way and that, but it was enough to see the two guys. They stopped walking, and one guy put his hands on the other guy's shoulders. Now that their faces were toward us, code bars appeared, disguising their features. The guy who was being held by the shoulders got down on his knees and unbuckled his partner's pants, probed for goober, found it, put it in his mouth.

Suddenly some fellas burst out of the bushes. They rushed the guy doing the suck work, and the guy having it done on him stepped back and watched. The guy who had planned to treat the other one got kicked, slapped, and rolled in the dirt. This went on so long it was almost too much to watch. After a while the guy who had offered his dick came over with his tool still hanging out and a knife in his hand. He put the knife to the assaulted man's throat, made him do what he had wanted to do in the first place. While the guy on his knees sucked, the guy with the knife used his free hand to pull a cigarette pack out of his pocket. He shook out a smoke and put it where the bar code was. His hand put away the pack and came up with a lighter, then the lighter flame went behind the code bar. The lighter came down and was put away. From the way the smoker acted, he could have been alone.

The guy on his knees was still at work; the smoker used the knife to tap him on the head, to keep a kind of rhythm, sang, "Mama's little baby love shortnin', shortnin', mama's little baby love shortnin' bread," over and over. And he wasn't even in tune.

The others stood around and jeered and watched and wore their code bars. When the job was finished on the smoker, the others got in line and took their turn.

When they were all finished, they shoved their victim down and went away. The camera went off and the video showed us some blackness, some gray, then it was over. It was one of the most humiliating things I'd ever seen.

"Not exactly Oscar material, is it?" I said.

"Jesus," Leonard said. "What was that all about?"

"I'm not sure," I said. "Was it staged?"

"I don't know," Leonard said. "But I tell you this, if it was, it sure blurs the line . . . Amateur films?"

"Maybe. But what's the deal? One film on grease napping, the other on gay bashing? Or is it supposed to be some kind of sex tape?"

"It didn't have anything to do with sex, Hap. It's about power, man. Gays, they're more of a target than women or blacks. Most folks think a gay gets a beating, they get what they deserve."

"Could have been a gang of gays doing it," I said.

"That's possible," Leonard said, "but straights like their dicks sucked bad as anyone, especially when it humiliates someone and empowers them."

"I'm going to have to keep you away from those pop-psychology books," I said.

"You know, you're right," Leonard said. "I'm startin' to sound like you. You won't tell anyone I used that word *empower*, will you?"

"I'll try and keep it under my hat. But, whatever, the same question still begs to be answered. What is it all about? What's the connection between grease and a fucked-up film like this?"

Leonard shook his head. "I don't know. Maybe there's something in the notebook. Me, I couldn't make diddle out of it."

I got it and opened it. There were rows of letters. Stuff like YCU—ART—QWEP. Beside that, another set. And another. All across the page and down. I looked the notebook over slowly. There were ten pages of this stuff.

"What the hell do you think that's all about?" Leonard said.

"This look like Raul's writing?"

"No."

I studied the notebook a few moments. I said, "Same number of letters in each group. Some of them have the same first three letters. Think about it."

"I have thought about it."

"It's easy. It's not like some super code. Probably someone's personal notebook. It's put together like this so most people picked it up wouldn't put it together quickly, but it's nothing takes a lot of work to figure out. In fact, it's kinda stupid, really."

"You're tryin' to make me feel stupid."

"I like to grab the chance now and then."

"Come on, Hap. I'm depressed enough here."

"Phone numbers. You coordinate the letters with the numbers, and you got phone numbers. The first three are area codes."

I went to the phone, studied the letters on the dial, compared them to the numbers beside them.

I said, "Lot of this is Houston area codes. Some of the others show up a lot are Dallas. I don't know the rest."

I picked up the phone, dialed one of the long-distance numbers. A woman's voice said, "East Side Video."

"Where exactly are you located?" I asked.

She told me. I wrote it down on a pad while she talked.

"Thanks," I said. "I wasn't quite sure."

I tried several other numbers. They were all video stores. I wrote them down. I gave the list of names and stores and their locations to Leonard and let him look it over.

"It sort of connects," Leonard said. "You know, like I almost got an answer, but not quite."

"I think these are stalk-and-rape tapes," I said. "There's stuff like this comin' out of Japan. I saw something about it on one of those news shows a while back. I may not read the newspaper enough, but I try not to miss my TV. Stuff they do in Japan, they don't actually show the rape. May be set-up stuff, but like you were saying about what we just saw, it blurs the line."

"What's the deal with the Japanese tapes?"

"Japanese started selling that shit here in the States. Video stores sold and rented it. It was damn popular till pressure was put on the stores to remove the tapes. Where do you think those tapes went?"

"Under the counter," Leonard said.

"In a lot of cases, I think so. And if the Japanese government is getting pressure from our government, or just from watchdog groups, it occurs to me the U.S. might start producing its own videos. We are, after all, capitalists. Entrepreneurs here in LaBorde rough up gays in the park, film it, sell the stuff to the shitheads who'll market it. The market will mostly be big cities."

"That works," Leonard said. "Makers of this smut would have it pretty good 'cause most of the park gays, they're underground. They don't want to go to the police, admit they're gay. And if they aren't closeted, still, the idea of admitting to what happened, the humiliation, holds them back. Very few talkers."

"Correcto. And my guess is some of those reports we've heard of beatings in the park, they were worse than we know about."

"And the chief kept it under wraps?"

"It's hard to know how corrupt the old bastard is. He

may not be that crooked. We may be puttin' shit on him he ought not have to wear."

"You always like to think that way, Hap. For someone's been through things you've been through, you can be naive as a baby duck. There's folks out there think if they make a dollar off this stuff, and they didn't do what's on the video, and no one was killed, and it's a bunch of queers anyway, it's okay to sell it. I think the chief may be one of them folks. I think he may be one of them only cares about the dollar, not even if someone's killed or if he did it."

"I don't think it goes quite that far. But the real question is, what can we do about it?"

"These guys, whoever they are, they probably killed Raul to protect this racket, the grease, the gay-stalk tapes. And I'll tell you, my friend, if the law won't do it, I am gonna find out who's who, and then ain't nobody but the devil gonna know their names."

"Then you'd be just like them."

"Pullllleeeezzze. There's few people think a roach exterminator is a murderer. I'm not talkin' about beatin' up and rapin' innocent people who are lookin' for love in all the wrong places. I'm talkin' about stampin' out a plague, man. Listen. I know how you are, and there ain't no use talkin'. You do what you want? I've heard you rave about the horrors of the child sex trade in Thailand, the poor, the plight of blacks and women and gays, and all the stuff you gripe about, but me, I'm gonna do somethin'."

"I didn't say I didn't care, Leonard. I said—"

"Save it."

"Don't be mad. I—"

"I said save it."

Leonard got up, gathered the tapes and the notebook, shoved them inside the Jiffy bag, and went outside. I didn't follow. I sat on the couch until I heard his car start up and go away.

# 14

That night I slept poorly. My mind wandered from that sick video to images of what had happened to Raul, and finally to Leonard. Leonard and I often fought. Leonard was quick to lose his temper, but something like this, I didn't really know what to think, what to expect. I wanted to help him, but bending the law was one thing, breaking and stomping the shit out of it was another.

I did what Leonard wanted, I'd have blood on my hands, and I wasn't sure where we would stop once we got started. I had killed before, and I didn't like it. I didn't lose lots of sleep over it, as it had been self-defense, and no other alternative was available, but I thought about it and didn't like it, and didn't feel heroic. I didn't want to put myself in a position where I had to kill.

I tossed and turned, finally got that business off my mind long enough to think about Brett. I thought about what she had done to her ex-husband. Was that self-defense or vengeance? Too bad Leonard was gay. He and Brett might go well together.

Jesus, I liked Brett, but did I really need to fall for an unrepentant firebug woman with asshole children?

Come to think of it, was I such a good catch myself?

That's the way the night passed, back and forth, an occasional snooze here and there, but mostly me tossing and turning and considering.

I got up early, put on coffee, thought about calling Leonard, but didn't. It was too early, and since he was already pissed, that wasn't going to mellow him out any. While I mulled all this over, it started to rain. Good. Great way to start the day.

I hung out till daylight, finished breakfast, and decided to call Brett. She ought to be getting home about now, and I figured before she dropped off to sleep, I might speak with her. I calculated the time it would take for her to drive home, and phoned. She didn't answer.

I waited a while, drank a cup of coffee, and called back. She answered this time. She sounded tired.

"Hey," I said. "It's me, Hap."

"I still remember you," she said.

"Well, hell, Brett. Now that I got you, I don't know why I'm calling. I know you're tired—"

"Are you?"

"What's that?"

"Tired?"

"Actually, yeah. I've had coffee, but it isn't helping."

"You came over, I know something might invigorate both of us. That is, unless you're so tired you don't think you can be invigorated."

"That's me pullin' up in your drive now."

* * *

Fast as I wanted to get there, I took time to go by Leonard's. I figured he was sleeping, so I didn't knock. I wrote him a note and stuck it in the screen door. I gave him Brett's phone number, told him to call me after noon. I wrote that I was sorry. That we should talk. I signed it "Mom."

When I got to Brett's place she opened the door and let me in before I could knock. I stood just inside the doorway trying to get my breath. She was wearing a pair of brief red panties, some brand-new flip-flops, and a small dark mole like a chocolate drop on her right breast near the nipple. A very nice nipple, I might add.

"If you don't mind," she said, "I thought we'd call this a second date."

"I'm easy," I said.

"So am I," she said. "And I got a whole box of rubbers on the nightstand to prove it."

"That's what I call hospitality."

"Well, I am excited to see you," she said, "but actually I had to rub ice on my nipples so they'd stand up like this."

She took me by the hand, led me to the bedroom. We embraced and kissed. She started removing my clothes, and I helped her. We lay down on the bed together.

She said, "If you have a shoe fetish, I'll leave the flip-flops on."

I laughed and she flicked them off. I helped her out of the red panties. I didn't want her to be uncomfortable. I used my tongue to taste the chocolate-drop mole. Much better than chocolate, actually. We made love for an hour, then fell asleep to the sound of the rain.

When I awoke, Brett was leaning over me.

"I really enjoyed that," she said. "I even came."

"I hope you don't mean in spite of me."

She laughed. "No. I don't mean in spite of you."

"Me too," I said.

"What?"

"I came too."

She laughed. "Men always come."

"Ejaculating is not the same as coming, in my book. It feels good, but when you really get off, you know the difference. It's not just a release of pressure. It's a special state of mind. You know, like when you switch channels on TV, and surprise, it's your favorite movie just starting."

"By God, Hap, you're a goddamn philosopher."

"I know it."

"What's your favorite movie, by the way?"

"You're not going to ask me my astrological sign next, are you?"

"I don't cotton to that shit. I'm interested in movies."

"*Casablanca*. And I like slow walks in the park and I'm going to be a brain surgeon and try and help all mankind."

She laughed. "I like *To Have and Have Not*. That's my favorite."

"That's my second favorite."

"My second favorite is *The Sound of Music*."

"I like *Casablanca* and *To Have and Have Not*."

"That part where they sing the do-re-me song, or whatever it is. I love that."

"I like *Casablanca* and *To Have and Have Not*."

She slapped at me. "You don't like *The Sound of Music?* It's the greatest musical ever made! I bet you think it's kind of sissy."

"Yeah."

"Hap Collins, I thought you were a sensitive man."

"I am," I said, and pointed my finger at my eye. "Press right here and it hurts. But *The Sound of Music*, I'd rather have my dick nailed to a burning building than have to sit through that shit again, and I don't care if the popcorn is free and you're giving me each bite with your vagina."

"Vagina?"

"That's a medical term for *pussy*, honey."

"God, Hap, you're almost a doctor. . . . So you don't like *The Sound of Music*?"

"No. Actually, I loathe it. But you like *To Have and Have Not*. That's good."

"I was always nuts about Bogart. I like Walter Brennan too. I like where he talks about being stung by a bee."

"Me too. I like Lauren Bacall too."

"You would."

"Shouldn't I? You kind of remind me of her, actually."

"In what way?"

"You're both women."

"Asshole . . . You know what?"

"What?"

"What I want us to do is go in to the doctor and get checkups. Make sure there's no AIDS stuff going on. I want to get past this rubber-on-the-dick stage real quick. I say we start our relationship with complete confidence."

"You won't take my word I haven't got AIDS?" I said.

"I'll take your word you don't think you have it, and probably don't, but you might not want to trust my word. I've been sexually active my whole life, Hap."

"And all that practice has really paid off."

"It's not that I actually think I've been unsafe, but I want us to start with a clean slate."

"All right," I said. "It's a deal. 'Course, as you know,

135

I've just had a lot of blood work, so I think we can safely say I'm okay."

"All right," Brett said.

"You'll look at my charts, won't you?" I said. "Talk to the doctor?"

"Most likely."

"All right," I said. "One thing, though."

"Shoot."

"I'm old-fashioned in one way. Well, maybe lots of ways. But if this is a relationship, and not just a good time, I want it to be a relationship."

"You mean I have to quit screwin' the entire medical staff and the patients at the hospital?"

"Yep. And I'm giving up farm animals for you, baby."

She snuggled in close. "Wow. Now that's dedication of purpose. You know, there's still several rubbers in the box."

"I hate leaving a partial box, don't you?"

"Absolutely," Brett said.

"It's so untidy."

"Absolutely. By the way, Hap. Did I tell you that I used to be a man?"

I hit her with a pillow and she laughed and we made love again.

I guess it must have been around five o'clock when the phone rang and Brett stirred and got up and walked nude into the kitchen. After a moment she came back. "It's for you, hon."

"Thanks. I hope you don't mind. I told a friend I'd be here."

"Not at all," she said. She was standing in the doorway, one leg cocked forward, showing me what I wanted to see. I got out of bed and went by her and she took hold of me and said, "I still got supplies in that box."

I kissed her and she held me where I wanted her to hold me. I put my hand on her and said, "Did you shave it just for me, or do you keep it like that?"

"I shaved it just for you," she said. "I thought it might be a little different. Besides, it keeps the lice out. You like it?"

"If you don't know by now," I said, "I don't know what to tell you."

After a moment I broke loose, went into the kitchen, practically having to walk around my dick. I picked up the phone.

"Yes?" I said.

"It's me," Leonard said, as if I were expecting someone else.

"I'm so glad," I said.

"That lady I was talkin' to? Is she the one?"

"She's the one."

"Good. I'm glad."

"Did you call to congratulate me?"

"No, I called because your note said to call."

"I was feeling very brotherly then. Right now I'm not so sure I want to waste my time with you. This woman, I think she could make me take a tire iron to Minnie Mouse."

"That's great . . . hey . . . really, Hap. Peace, man."

"Peace, Leonard."

"I was pissed. I'd had a few drinks. I'm fucked up over all this."

"Nothing more needs to be said."

"I love you, man."

"And I love you. Listen up. Let's find out what we can. I'm with you, but . . ."

"I have to behave myself."

"Exactly."

"I can only promise that up to so far."

"We look around," I said. "We find something. See how the police can be made to do something, we keep the blood off our hands. Got it?"

"What if we can't?"

"We cross that bridge when we come to it."

"When do we get started?"

"Tomorrow."

"Where?"

"The place where Raul got his hair-cutting experience. What's it called?"

"Antone's."

"I'll pick you up at your place at nine o'clock."

"See you then," Leonard said.

I went back to the bedroom. Brett was holding the box of prophylactics. She shook it.

"I say we tap the box out," she said.

We didn't quite manage that, but when we were finished, Brett pushed up tight against me and closed her eyes. "Spoons," she said.

I held her, and soon she was asleep. While she slept, I looked at her and thought about her ex-husband beating her, raping her. How could he?

I thought about those nice long fingers of hers coiling around a shovel, squirting lighter fluid, striking matches. I kissed her cheek and lay against her and felt her warmth, and soon I too was asleep.

# 15

We awoke in the late afternoon and had dinner out of Brett's fridge. Ham on white. While we sat naked, eating sandwiches and crunching potato chips, there was a knock on the door, and we had to rush to put on clothes.

Brett finished first by pulling on a long T-shirt. She went to the door while I continued dressing in the bedroom. I was having trouble finding my pants but finally located them under the bed in a wad. Found a sock behind a chair.

I finished dressing, went into the living room area. Ella was there. She grinned at me. She really did look like Brett's younger sister.

"Well, I see you two have hit it off," she said.

"We're not doing much hittin'," Brett said, "but we are gettin' off."

"Brett!" Ella said. But I could tell she wasn't all that offended.

I smiled at Ella. Close up, I could see her very pretty face wore a black eye, partially hidden by makeup.

"You just come by to annoy us?" Brett said.

"No. I came by to talk to you about switchin' shifts with me next week. Can it happen?"

"It might," Brett said. "I'll have to think on it, though. Sometimes Ole Head Nurse Meanie doesn't like changes, and honey, I don't know she'll like you."

"Yeah?" Ella said. "What's wrong with me?"

"Same thing's wrong with me and a couple of the other girls." Brett gave me a soulful look. "We're just too good-lookin' for her. She thinks everybody ought to be uglier than her."

"Is that possible?" Ella said.

"I don't think so," Brett said. " 'Course, you take a few more shots to the head like that one, you might be in the runnin'."

Ella looked embarrassed. She said, "Brett . . . I . . . ."

"Sorry," Brett said. "I didn't mean to embarrass you. Hap here, he understands."

"No, I don't," I said.

"Hap Collins!" Brett said. "You do too understand."

"I don't mean to embarrass you either, but now that Brett's said something, I don't understand why you'd take this shit."

"Brett, you shouldn't have said anything to anyone," Ella said. "That wasn't right."

"You can't keep hidin' it, girl," Brett said. "That's the worst thing to do. You hide it, you're helpin' him do it."

"She's right," I said. "Dump the bum."

"He's been going to counseling," Ella said.

"Bullshit on counseling," Brett said. "The guy's a turd. Flush him."

"I love him," Ella said.

"I loved that shit-ass husband of mine, too," Brett said. "But one day I didn't and I had to set his head on fire."

"I'm not like you," Ella said. "I got to go."

"Ella," Brett said. "I'm sorry. I shouldn't have . . ."

"No," Ella said. "You're right. Think about the shift, will you?"

"Sure," Brett said.

Ella left quickly.

When she was gone, Brett said, "Bless her."

We were about to finish eating when there was yet another knock on the door. Brett answered. It was Ella. She was in tears. "My car won't start. I'm going to be late. He hates it when I'm late. I thought maybe . . . he . . . I'm sorry. What's your name again?"

"Hap," I said.

"Hap, I thought you might help me with my car?"

"Honest truth is I can't fix a wheelbarrow."

"Kevin will be so mad," Ella said.

"We'll drive you home," Brett said. "Okay, Hap?"

"Sure."

We took my pickup. We drove out to the east side of town. It was a beautiful day and the rain of earlier had given it a kind of glow, like the world had been washed down and polished.

About a mile and a half outside the city limits we came to a spot where an old country store had stood. I had stopped there once and bought a barbecue sandwich. It had tasted like shit. Now the store was just a shell of a building. Windows knocked out. A door halfway down. That's what happens when you make lousy barbecue.

We turned down a dirt road along a row of mailboxes and lights on poles, drove past a dog kennel where a half dozen hot-looking Siberian huskies watched us pass.

Shortly thereafter, we drove onto as ugly a stretch of land as I've seen. You could tell right off that not too many years ago woods had stood here. Someone had clear-cut it, sold off the lumber, then made a mobile-home park out of it. In this case, they hadn't even bothered to scrape it down to the clay. Some of the stumps still remained, burned black but still standing. Between clumps of stumps and pools of rainwater, trailers stood.

We drove past a row of run-down trailers with broken toys in the yard, sad dogs on chains, and finally drove around to a fairly nice little white trailer with pink trim. The yard was clean, except for the standard redneck sign-post—any kind of black car on blocks. This one was a Ford Mustang. When I was in high school I had wanted one of those. Thought I'd die if I didn't get one. I didn't get one and I was still living.

We parked and let Ella out. She thanked us, and as she started toward the trailer the door opened and a man came out. He had on jeans and was shirtless and barefoot. He was a stocky guy with a slightly protruding but solid-looking belly. He was about my height. Good-looking fella with a crewcut.

"Where the hell you been, Ella?" he said. "I been sittin' here waitin' on my goddamn dinner."

"My car, honey," Ella said. "It wouldn't start."

"My car wouldn't start," Kevin said in a mocking tone. "It's always somethin', ain't it, bitch?"

Ella turned to us. "Thanks. I'm sorry."

"That's all right," I said. "You sure you want to stay?"

"Yes," Ella said.

"Hey," Kevin said, "who you talkin' to?"

"Ella . . ." I said.

"What do you mean, 'do you want to stay?'"

"I mean you sound a little drunk, and maybe she ought not to stay."

"You keep your nose out of my business, old man."

"Old man?"

"Yeah. Old man."

Ella took hold of Kevin's shoulder. "Don't, honey. They gave me a ride."

Kevin pushed Ella down on the wet ground. Brett rushed over to help her up. "You get back in the truck, cunt," Kevin said.

"That's it," I said. I had been standing outside the truck with the door open, leaning on it. I closed it and started toward Kevin.

Kevin said, "What you gonna do, fuckhead?"

"I can either sit you down and have a nice talk, or punch your lights out. Since I figure you'll be a boring conversationalist, I like the second idea."

"Punch my lights out?" Kevin said. "I'll have you know I was a goddamn good boxer. I almost went pro."

"Then I'm sure you've seen a left jab," I said, and jabbed him. I hit him solid on the right eye and his head snapped back. Then I kicked hard off my back leg and caught him in the balls. I half-leaped then, caught his head as he bent over, drove it down with an elbow and lifted my knee into his face. When he came back up, his face bloody, I skipped in and caught hold of his arm and his shoulder, brought my right leg behind his right leg, and reared backwards hard as I could.

He went down quick and smacked his head against the dirt. Spittle flew out of his mouth and gleamed like a string of diamonds in the sunlight.

Ella rushed over, draped herself over him, held one hand toward me. "Don't, Hap! Don't hit him anymore."

"Why not?" I said. "I'm just startin' to enjoy myself."

"He doesn't mean it," Ella said. "He can't help himself. It's not like him. He's not himself."

"Then who the hell is he?" I said. "Was he that other fella when he blacked your eye?"

"I pushed him into it," Ella said.

"Jesus," I said. "You better get straight, Ella. I can see a couple having a spat, even taking a slap at one another in a moment of anger. But this. Him punchin' you around . . ."

Kevin had gotten up on one elbow. "You better go, man."

"Why?" I said. "You going to whip my ass, big man?"

Brett came over and took my arm. She said, "Let's go, Hap. Your testosterone is showing. Ella. You want to go with us, you can. You want to call someone about this. The women's shelter. Whatever. We'll make sure you get to do it."

Ella shook her head. She started helping Kevin to his feet.

"You want to see the left jab again?" I said to him.

"You caught me by surprise," he said.

"Looked to me I caught you in the eye," I said.

"Then you kicked, like a sissy," he said.

"Tell everybody a sissy kicked your ass, then," I said.

Ella started helping Kevin toward the trailer. She paused and looked back over her shoulder. "Thank you, but it's not your business. Really. It's not your business."

Ella went up the steps with her arm around Kevin. They went inside the trailer and closed the door. We got in the pickup and drove away.

Once we were out on the highway, Brett slid over close to me.

"You were magnificent, Hap."

"I think I got a little John Wayne."

"You know what?"

"What?"

"I just loved his movies. Will you take me home and seduce me?"

"Because I beat Kevin up you're hot?"

"No. Because you got pissed when he called me a cunt. I am sometimes, but I thank you anyway."

"You're welcome."

"I like what you tried to do for Ella. But she doesn't change, Hap. She never does. I've tried to get her to leave him, but she keeps going back. Someday he'll kill her."

"I fear you're right," I said.

# 16

We drove back to Brett's place, went to bed and made love, then showered together. I dressed and got ready to leave so she could have time to herself before going off to work.

As she kissed me 'bye at the door, I said, "I'll be back."

"Hell, I know that," she said. "You done had a taste."

I drove home, read until late, slept fitfully. Next morning I picked up Leonard and we cruised over to Antone's.

The air was sweet-smelling after yesterday's rain, but you could tell already it was going to be hot. It was going to be that kind of April where spring, except for an hour or so in the morning, was mostly forgotten. Ozone-layer problems, perhaps. I liked to blame it on all those evangelists and their goddamn hair spray. Hadn't they heard of spritzers?

Antone's was what used to be called a barber college

and hairdressing salon. It did business, but it mostly trained people for business. It was located where Main crossed Universal Street. Below Universal was a poor section of town, but on the opposite side of the street things began to look up. Drive a short distance and you were on the town square, where things were clean and bright.

Go the other way, you were descending into a toilet that might flush at any moment. A place where Those in Power liked to keep the people they thought of as rejects.

We parked in the parking lot next to Antone's and a recreation center that used to be a 7-Eleven before it got robbed so often it was sort of like a free-money drop for the thugs of LaBorde. Through the glass you could see folks who ought to have jobs, or kids that ought to be in school, shooting pool. There were a number of motorcycle types in there as well. I hoped none of them recognized Leonard from his little escapade at the Broken Wheel.

Leonard glanced through the glass at the pool players. He didn't say anything, but the look on his face told me plenty. Leonard thought most of these folks were lazy shits and worthless, and I suppose he was right to some degree. Many of them were just that. Plain sorry. But I never found that life worked that way, black and white. Good and evil. Most of the time it was a mixture. That's what made it so hard. You couldn't generalize and be a thinker. There were assholes on both sides of the coin, but there were good people shouldering bad breaks as well. Miss two paychecks, have the car break down, and you could go from lower middle class to living in a cardboard box under the river bridge, eating out of Dumpsters and pushing a shopping cart.

Inside Antone's there was a lot of activity, people cut-

147

ting hair and doing perms on folks with a desire for cheap haircuts, coloring, and curls. Always a scary proposition to get a haircut at a beauty and barber college.

I used to get my hair cut that way before I decided three bucks was too much for what they did to me, and eight bucks downtown at a real barber shop was just right. When I got my cheap haircuts it wasn't at Antone's. It was the original barber college, and it was located in another poor part of LaBorde back when we called LaBorde a town, not a city. The place was cleverly named Bob's Barber College, and it smelled of hair oil, shaving cream, and men's sweat. That's all you saw there. Men. It didn't do beauty cuts and it didn't do anything fancy, so it didn't attract women. It was a place where men talked the kind of talk that used to be called man talk. Hunting and fishing, cars and dogs and women. Usually in that order.

Got your hair cut there, way it was done was limited. There was the Dust Bowl Oakie cut, which seemed mostly a kind of hand-on-top-of-head-and-cut-around-it style, shaving from about the middle of your head to below your ears. Then there was the cut called by many of us the Mental Health and Mental Retardation cut. Same style they gave the mentally handicapped at the state school. This translated as cut what you see, and all you want, long as there's some hair left on the top of the head like a topknot. Got through with you on that, you looked a little bit like a turnip. There was also the GI cut, which was a shaved head. This was mostly given to those suspected of insects. And finally, there were standard jobs, like Little Man Number One. This was almost passable unless you wanted it blocked in the back. That didn't exist. The head got cut pretty good, but when it came to the back of the neck, it got shaved slicker than a snot-covered doorknob. There was Little Man Number Two as well. This one you got a haircut and a shave, as well as a few deep cuts soaked in some alcohol-based stink-water that made flies light on your face. Lastly, there was Little Man Number Three, but it was so dreadful it's difficult to talk about. This was the specialty of Bob himself, guy who taught the others. He gave all his haircuts while drunk and with a palsied hand, and many of us suspected his tools of trade were the Weed Eater and the garden snips.

Nothing like old memories.

Me and Leonard spent a few minutes watching a young blond lady with scissors snip hair out of an elderly man's nose, but when the hairs being snipped began to yield little gooies on their stalks, I lost interest.

Finally a man came over to help us. He was short and pale-skinned and had his dark hair combed back tight and plastered with something so shiny you could almost see your reflection in it. He had one of those pencil-thin mustaches like forties movie stars wore, ones make you look like you had a drink of chocolate milk and forgot to wipe your mouth. He had his colorful shirt open almost to his navel, and let me tell you, that was no treat to view. He had a chest like a bird and a little potbelly and a thin straight line of hair that ran from chest to navel and looked as if it had been provided by the nose hairs the blonde had clipped. He was wearing a gold medallion on a chain around his neck. The medallion reminded me of those aluminum-foil coins you unwrap and find chocolate inside. He must have been on the bad side of forty. A face, a body like that, you're not born with it. It takes some real abuse and neglect to create.

"May I 'elp you, *messieurs*. I am Pierre."

His accent was right out of Peppie Le Pew, the Warner Brothers cartoon skunk, with maybe a bit of the Frito Bandito thrown in. Not quite Spanish, not quite French, all false.

"Pierre?" Leonard said. "You're really named Pierre?"

"That ees correct."

"Where's Antone?" Leonard asked.

"There is no Antone," Pierre said. "It's jest a name I liked."

"Then you're the owner?" I asked.

He nodded. "What ees the thing I can due fer yew?" Pierre said, and his accent was even less identifiable now. Some German seemed to have slipped into it.

Leonard gave Raul's name and said, "Seems he was killed. Murdered. It's been in the papers, so you probably knew that."

"Oh, my," Pierre said. "I do not read zee papers."

Leonard gave me a knowing look, one that put me in Pierre's camp.

"I knew eee was missing. The cops, zey 'ave been 'ere. But ded, dis I deed not know."

"What we want to know," I said, "is about this deal you have with your graduates cutting hair in people's homes."

"Eet ees all zee rage," Pierre said. "Ze wealthy customers, zey love it. Raul, he was, a, how yew zey . . . goode one. Unlike some."

Pierre glanced at a young man who was cutting furiously at a woman's long blond hair. The guy had a strained look on his face like he had never done this before, and knew even if he did it again he wouldn't be any better.

Pierre turned back to us. "Some, zey are quite . . . how you say . . . 'opeless."

"Did Raul do a lot of these jobs?" Leonard asked.

"Some. Eee may 'ave done others I dew not know of. But many customers called 'ere, for referrals. We gave Raul some of zeees referrals. Eet ees part of our zervice to graduates."

"Can you tell us who these people were?" I asked.

"Are you with ze po-leece?"

"No," Leonard said.

"Zen . . . I don't know."

"We're not askin' you to turn over the secrets to the atomic bomb," Leonard said.

"We're friends of Raul, and we'd like to talk to people who knew him," I said. "It's for his parents. We're kind of . . . you know . . . trying to piece together his life for them. Something they can cling to. You understand?"

Pierre nodded, and when he spoke this time, he almost sounded tongue-tied. "I suppose zere is nofhing rong weeth zat."

We followed him into his office. He sat down behind his desk while we stood. He rummaged in a drawer, came up with a leather-bound file book. He opened it, ran his finger along a page. He stopped, made a satisfied noise, found a pad and pen and wrote down a couple of names for us, gave them to Leonard.

"Just these two?" Leonard said.

"Eee cut zere 'air regularly," Pierre said. "Others eee set up on ees own, for zem, I can not 'elp yew."

"Wee-wee," Leonard said.

"It's *merci*," I said.

"No," Leonard said. "I have to wee-wee. You got a john here, Frenchy?"

\*     \*     \*

We sat out in the parking lot and looked at what Pierre had given us.

Leonard said, "Hope that guy ain't gay. He could give our whole sexual orientation a bad name."

"Let me tell you," I said. "He's heterosexual, he's not doing us any good either."

"What kind of fucking accent was that?" Leonard asked. "It changed from one word to the next."

"It was a bullshit accent is what it was. Closest Pierre's been to France, or anything French, is a croissant. Maybe he's been to Paris, Texas."

"I hear that," Leonard said. "Don't you know that fucker is worn out at the end of the day. Trying to remember what spin he's been putting on particular words. Hell, he made me tired just to listen to him. What are the names he wrote down?"

"Charles Arthur. Bill Cunningham."

"Whoa," Leonard said. "Charles Arthur. You know who that is, don't you?"

"No."

"King Arthur, the chili king. King Arthur Chili, like it said on the pad in the Jiffy bag."

"I know who King Arthur is," I said. "I just didn't know him as Charles Arthur."

"The pad in the Jiffy bag, then the name coming up at Antone's, that's certainly coincidental."

"There's lots of those pads," I said. "They give them out free all over town. Raul cut Arthur's hair, probably picked up a notebook while he was there. King Arthur could have given it to him."

"With coded numbers written on it?"

"You got a point there," I said. "But Raul could have brought the book home and Horse Dick could have writ-

ten down the coded numbers for some reason. It could
have been something he was working on. That makes
more sense to me, actually."

"Maybe," Leonard said. "And still, Raul could have
picked it up while cutting Arthur's hair. Sneaked it."

"I have to ask the same question. Why?"

"I don't know. Why don't we drive out to the plant, see
if we can find King Arthur?"

"Big shot like him," I said. "I bet he's never there."

"Yeah, but we got to start somewhere," Leonard said.
"Or how else we gonna get in our annoyance quota."

KING ARTHUR CHILI ENTERPRISES, as the sign over the huge
gate read, was way out in the country and set on about
twenty-five acres. It was a cluster of big buildings that
stank. One side of the acreage was a meat-processing
plant, the other side housed the place where the chili
peppers were ground and the chili was whipped up and
shoved into and sealed in cans. The whole place smelled
of hot pepper and drying blood.

There was a rendering plant out back of it all, and
twice a week at night the stink of it was absolutely awe-
some. It was where the tougher meat, the hides and
horns, and the occasional old horse were processed into
soap, fertilizer, and other odds and ends. Or at least I
think they still made soap out of old horses. Maybe not.

Joint used to pump out dead cow and horse stink in
the form of greasy black smoke all the time, until city or-
dinances got tight and King had to start letting loose with
his garbage smoke late at night, twice a week.

It was such a stout stink that sometimes, the wind was
blowing just right, it would travel out as far as where I
lived, slip in through the windows and gouge my nose

until I came awake. On the side of town where Leonard lived, twice a week it would damn near slay you.

The lot was loaded with cars, but we found an empty space with some big shot's name written on the curb. We parked in that slot like it was ours and we were proud to be there.

The secretary was thin, young, silver-blond, and so goddamn cheery I wanted to strangle her. We told her we would like to see King Arthur, and she told us he was out. We asked to see someone in charge, and after twenty minutes in the guest chairs, the skimming of several stimulating magazines on the chili business, a nice-looking man about fifty with shiny gray hair came out. He was dressed in a plum-purple leisure suit with a white belt and white shoes. The leisure suit looked brand-new, and this baffled me. They had quit making those horrors years ago. It pointed to the scary proposition that this guy liked those fuckers so much he had them special-made. In my eyes he was already guilty of something, if nothing more than being a public eyesore.

He came over, shook our hands, told us his name was G. H. Bissinggame, and we told him ours. He asked us what he could do for us. I told him about Raul, how he used to cut King Arthur's hair, told him about Raul's murder, said we were curious about his death.

Leonard said, "We're kind of poking around, nothing official. We wanted to know if King Arthur could tell us anything about Raul might help us figure out who killed him."

Bissinggame furrowed his brow. "Why would Mr. Arthur know such a thing? Isn't this a matter for the police?"

"We're not saying he knows anything directly," I said.

"We'd just like to talk to him. Something Raul might have said, anything might give us a lead."

"Why would he say anything to Mr. Arthur?" Bissinggame said. "Mr. Arthur was a customer, not the boy's therapist."

"Then you knew Raul?" Leonard asked.

"No."

"Then how did you know he was young?" Leonard said. "You called him a boy."

"Whoa, here," Bissinggame said. "You're being a little nasty. You're trying to tie me into something, way you talk. You're not the law. You don't have the right to do that, and I'm sure there's no need for Mr. Arthur to talk to you."

"I just asked if you knew him," Leonard said.

"No, you didn't," Bissinggame said.

"You're right," I said. "Leonard, here, he and Raul were very close. He's a little touchy."

"I apologize," Leonard said, but with his tone of voice he might as well have gone on and called Bissinggame an asshole.

"Could you do this?" I asked. "Could we write down our names, phone numbers, and could you ask Mr. Arthur to call? We're trying to help out the family, sort of piece things together for them. You know, last bits of information about their son."

"You said you were trying to find leads to the murder," Bissinggame said.

"That too," I said.

"I'll tell you now," Bissinggame said. "Mr. Arthur, he doesn't return calls. That's why he has a secretary, and this Raul, I recognize who he is because Mr. Arthur often conducted business while getting his hair cut here at the plant. But I didn't really know the boy. Mr. Arthur said very little to him, as I recall."

"Let me ask this," Leonard said. "What if Raul had a King Arthur Chili pad, and inside the pad there were some letters written down that coincided with phone numbers, and say these phone numbers connected with video stores, and say me and Hap had the pad and a couple videos, would that interest Mr. Arthur?"

Bissinggame looked at Leonard as if he had just swung in on a vine. "What?"

"Never mind," Leonard said.

"You need a lesson in manners," Bissinggame said to Leonard.

"You gonna give it to me?" Leonard said. "A man wearing a fuckin' purple leisure suit is the one needs manners. Don't you know shit like that offends everyone?"

"Come on, Leonard," I said.

"I'm going to call security, you don't leave right now," Bissinggame said. "Our security people, they aren't a bunch of fat cops. They don't mess around."

"Come on, Leonard," I said.

"Security?" Leonard said. "Now I'm scared. What kind of leisure suits they wear? Lime green? Peach? You had on one of them peach kind, I'd have to hit you."

"We're going," I said.

"Best do," Bissinggame said. "Helen," he yelled to the secretary. "Call security."

Helen picked up the phone. I took Leonard's elbow and led him out of there. As we went down the corridor toward the exit, I said, "Shit, Leonard. I can't take you anywhere. Next time, you stay your ass in the car."

"I bet that dick's got on spotted boxer shorts," Leonard

said. "Man, them leisure suits, they're a crime against humanity."

"Well, you're right about that."

"Guy like that, way he defends his boss, I bet he's got naked pictures of ole Chili King doing the ass end of a dead beef. Pins that to his mirror while he whacks off with his dick poking out of that leisure suit. Know what I'm sayin'?"

"I got you."

"Fucker would give a snake a blow job, it wore a leisure suit."

"Give it a rest, Leonard."

"Cocksucker," Leonard said. "Hope he gets a bowl of bad chili. Probably likes it that way, strained through his goddamn shit-stained underwear."

"Careful. You start talking bad about chili, Texas is sure to be next. And you know well as I do that's not good."

"You're right," Leonard said. "I stepped over the line."

We had just gone out the door when a white car with KING ARTHUR CHILI written on the side of it parked in the middle of the lot and two guys in green uniforms with badges and no guns came over and stood in front of us. One of them was about the size of a moose, and the other may well have been a moose without antlers.

"We got a call you two were causing trouble," said the real moose. He was chewing on an unlit cigar as casually as a cow chewing cud. The other guy, the one the size of a moose, had an expression about as illuminating as a potted plant, but lacking the warmth. He could have been thinking about mayhem and murder, lunch break and a cigarette, sex or a gerbil up his ass. That face gave nothing away.

"How you know it's us?" Leonard said.

Moose grinned. "They said a white guy and a black guy."

"Yeah," Leonard said. "How do you know you ain't got the wrong black and white guy?"

Not A Moose said, "Because they said the nigger had a smart mouth. You're a nigger. You got a smart mouth."

"Now you've done it," I said.

"What?" Moose said.

"I said now you've done it."

"What the fuck's that mean?" Moose said.

"It means," Leonard said, "I'm in the mood to snap your dick off and shove it in your ear. Who you think you're connin'? You ain't even real law. Guys like you, we wipe our asses on you."

"Daily," I said.

"Yeah," Leonard said. "Daily."

"Sometimes twice a day," I said.

"That too," Leonard said.

"Yeah," Moose said, and his hand went to his back pocket and came back wearing a pair of brass knuckles.

Leonard said "Asswipe!," stomped the guard's foot, grabbed the hand with the knucks on it, swung under the guy's arm, then with a palm on the fucker's elbow snapped him to the cement, bouncing his head off of it, smashing his cigar into his face.

Not A Moose rushed forward then, about to grab Leonard. I kicked him in the leg, just above the ankle, stuck my thumb in his eye. He let out a yell and sat down in the parking lot, both hands over his face.

"I'm blind! I'm blind!" he yelled.

"Are not," I said.

"I can't see!"

"Take your hands off your face, you ignorant mother-fucker," I said.

As Not A Moose experimented with his vision, I turned to watch Leonard. Leonard peeled the brass knucks off Moose's hand and tossed them on top of the chili building, said, "Fetch that, dick cheese."

Dick Cheese, also known as Moose, came up on one knee and stayed there. He wouldn't even look at us. He let the mashed cigar fall from his lips as if he were shedding a tooth.

Leonard said, "Y'all through?"

Dick Cheese nodded.

"Good," Leonard said. "You guys need you another line of work. You're not even mediocre at this one. My preference is neither of you get up till we're gone. Hear me? That's just a preference. You get to choose for yourself. That's what makes this country great. Free choice. But you get up, me and Hap, we're gonna shake out the jams. Know what I mean?"

We walked past Not A Moose, who was sitting on the ground nursing his watery eye. I said, "I'd put ice on it, I was you, otherwise it'll get puffy all around. I'm sorry."

"You skinned the shit out of my ankle too," Not A Moose said.

"Ice might be good for that too," I said.

We strolled over to the truck and drove off.

# 17

A few days went by and no answers fell out of the sky on us. Raul was still dead. I hadn't won the lottery. The two security guards didn't show up with new brass knucks. Bissinggame didn't send us a fashion catalogue containing custom-made leisure suits in ugly colors.

There were events, however. Leonard had finally gotten the tick off his balls. Used a match, as I had suggested. It worked. 'Course, as he feared, he managed to burn his nuts, so I was on his shit list for a couple days. The tick ended up in the commode, a burial at sea.

Somewhere during all this we put the notebook and the videos back in the Jiffy bag, placed them in a metal box, hid them out at Leonard's old house inside a torn-out section in the back of his living room couch.

I got my last rabies shot from my surly doctor, found out the squirrel head had come back positive from

Austin. That part made me feel kind of weird for a day or two.

Oh, yeah, and the guy in a yellow Pontiac wearing a cowboy hat was glanced by Leonard and myself on several occasions, following us when we were together a couple of times, following me once on my own, and following Leonard a few times. It was, of course, the yellow Pontiac I had seen outside of Leonard's house the day I went in and found it tossed. So much for paranoia. Sometimes they *are* out to get you. They'd do better sneaking up on you, though, if they didn't drive yellow Pontiacs. A Yorkshire hog in a three-piece suit and a derby with a red turkey feather in it would have been less conspicuous.

We didn't let on we knew he was following us. We wanted him to make a move, but he never did. Kept his distance, wasn't always there, but just when you thought he was gone for sure, he'd show up again, like a pee stain in your shorts.

The only really good thing about those few days was Brett. We spent a lot of time together, getting to know each other, solidifying our relationship, allowing our souls to meld into one, and, of course, fucking like two anacondas during mating season.

So, life wasn't all bad on my end, but Leonard, well, he was like a pot of water on the stove. You never knew when he'd boil. Little things like that lousy tick and a burn on his balls set him off. And all those videos that had gone missing, his John Wayne and Clint Eastwood movies were in the batch. He really took that hard. And the fact his J. C. Penney's suit had been mistreated and had a stain of some kind on it didn't set well with him either. Just grumpy, is what he was. It was getting so I wanted to find Raul's killer just so I wouldn't have to hear Leonard bitch.

One day, because we hadn't figured out our next move, which with us was common, Leonard and I went miniature-golfing. Spring had choked off pretty much for good, it seemed. It was late April and unseasonably hot, like two rats in caps and sweaters fucking in a wool sock under a sun lamp.

The sand at the little golf course was turning pure white from the heat, was as thin as bleached flour, and the gravel that was mixed with it crunched wearily under our hot, heavy feet. No trees. Kids screaming and shoving. And the windmill on the tenth hole didn't work; wouldn't turn, so you had to kind of boost your ball over the boards on the side, shoot from the foul area, knock it back in. Done that way, it was hard to figure your points. I wanted to just pass up the hole altogether, but Leonard wouldn't hear of it.

"A man starts, a man finishes, no matter what," he said.

"Yeah, right, boss."

We batted the ball around for a while, and by the time we finished I had won and Leonard was in an even more foul mood.

"I used to be good at this," Leonard said. "You know me and Raul played a lot?"

"No. I didn't."

"Yeah. I always beat him. I can't believe you beat me."

"Look, you want the truth, Leonard, I boosted the ball with my foot on the windmill hole. Okay. It gave me the one-point difference."

"What I figured . . . You're not just sayin' that?"

"Nope. I boosted it."

"Cross your heart and hope to—"

"Leonard. I said, I boosted it."

"I thought I saw you do that out of the corner of my eye."

"Let's don't get too carried away."

"Then you didn't really?"

"I did, but I was very clever about it. You didn't see me."

"Good," Leonard said, "loser buys lunch."

There was a little restaurant in front of the miniature-golf course, and we went in there to eat. It was supposed to be a health-food place, so most of the food tasted like yesterday's dog shit reheated and hammered, but they made a pretty good meat loaf. We had that. We sat near the window.

The yellow Pontiac, which had followed us from home, was sitting across the street in the Kroger parking lot. It was a good spot. The traffic on North Street was heavy, and it would be hard for us to get over there before he spotted us, cranked up, and left.

"You think he thinks we don't see him?" Leonard said.

"I don't know," I said.

Leonard ate a bite of his meat loaf, said, "Remember how this meat loaf used to just pass muster?"

"Yeah."

"It tastes like it was rolled in someone's dirty socks now."

"Oh, good. I can't wait . . . Who do you think the guy in the Pontiac is working for?"

"King Arthur," Leonard said.

"You didn't exactly take time to think about that answer."

"No. You asked me what I thought, and I told you."

"You got to remember, I saw Mr. Pontiac before we ever went out to the chili empire."

"That's because he had my house staked out. He was waiting to see who came in. You happened to be there."

"But he quit following me. He just showed up again recently."

"Right after we went out to the Chili King's place of business. Seems obvious to me."

"Why did he stop following me in between?"

"Maybe he lost you and didn't find you again. Until lately. Hell, you gave Bissinggame your address and mine."

I nodded. "That works pretty good. I like it. I doubt it's true, but we'll go with it. I hate unsolved stuff."

"Me too," Leonard said. "Want to go over and knock on his door?"

"We'd never make it. He'd be gone before we got halfway across the street."

"You think he's takin' notes, snappin' pictures?"

"I don't care if he's playing with himself over there, I'm tired of him following us around. It makes me nervous."

As if he had heard us, the car began to roll. It went out of the Kroger lot and onto the street and headed north.

"Shall we chase it?" Leonard said.

"What?" I said. "And miss this meat loaf? . . . What the fuck we eatin' here for?"

"It's cheap and all we can afford," Leonard said.

"Oh, yeah," I said. "Pass the hot sauce."

After lunch we came up with an idea. It may not have been the best in the world, but it was an idea, and when we had one, we liked to grab on to it and hold it tight, 'cause we might not have another.

We stopped at a gas station, filled up, and headed south for Houston. It was almost a three-hour drive, and then we got lost, so we spent five hours from LaBorde to the store I had written down on my list, East Side Video.

East Side Video was in an okay section of town and it had lots of videos. We looked around the store for a while, then went over to the fellow behind the counter. He was in his late twenties, with longish red hair done up in corn rows. He looked up at us. He had a pimple on his chin like a volcano. It had such a puss head on it you wanted to hit it with something.

"Help you?" he said.

"Yeah," I said. "We're looking for a special kind of movie."

"What kind?" he asked.

"Well, I don't see it on the shelves. It's . . . a little different."

"Yeah," he said. "You mean in-and-out stuff? We got that, but we don't put it out next to Mickey Mouse."

"It's under the counter, then?" Leonard said.

"Yeah. We got some stuff you can look at."

"What we're really looking for is a little different from that," I said.

"How different?"

"Real different," Leonard said. "We were told you had some tapes, some stuff like they make in Japan."

The guy pursed his lips. "Yeah? Who told you this?"

"Some guy," Leonard said.

The counter man nodded. "We got some tapes we sell that are a little different."

"One we're interested in . . . well . . . it's got queers getting the shit kicked out them," Leonard said.

The redhead grinned. "Yeah. Some people think

165

JOE R. LANSDALE

they're real. They look real 'cause they're so sloppy. Yeah, we got that. It's not common knowledge, but we got it. We sell 'em. Not good quality. I mean, it ain't gonna be *Ole Yeller*, know what I'm sayin'?"

"Sell a lot of them?"

"No," said the counter man, "but at a hundred dollars a pop, we don't have to sell a lot. Come to think of it, I guess we do a pretty good business with it."

"Against the law?" Leonard asked.

"Why you ask?"

"Just wondering," Leonard said. "And if it is, maybe we got to think twice about buying it."

"Technically it's covered by the First Amendment. 'Cause it ain't real. Just looks real. But there's folks don't like the idea, so we keep it under the counter."

"We seen the one our friend had," Leonard said. "It looked real."

"'Tween you and me," the counter man said, "it might be real. But the people make 'em claim they ain't. They get cornered, they say they bought them from a video enthusiast and they're just showin' what someone took a video of. Kind of like reporting the news. You know, like that fellow few years ago did the video of executions. We got that one here, you want it."

"No, thanks," I said.

"These queer kick videos, I figure what the hell, one more queer with a black eye ain't nothing to me. I'd kick one of the little faggots myself, make him suck my dick I wanted it sucked, though I ain't so sure I'd want a queer's lips on my tootie-toot, know what I'm sayin'? AIDS and all. Fucker might bite me."

I could sense Leonard's tension. This guy kept it up, he

166

was gonna wake up with a shelf full of videos shoved up his ass.

"All right," I said. "We'll take one. If it's one thing we like to see, it's a queer get his."

The kid reached under the counter and brought out a tape in a cheap box with a photocopied cover that read: KICKIN' FAIRIES.

"Nice title," I said.

"Yeah, they ain't real original," the kid said. "But I seen this one, and I tell you, if it's set up, it's set up good. It looks real as a car wreck."

I peeled a hundred dollars out of my wallet, just like I had it to spare. I put it on the counter.

The kid took the money and shoved the video at me and said, "No receipt on this stuff. No returns. We don't buy this shit back. We can run off another one cheaper than we can fuck with that."

"I.R.S. might not like you not keeping records on this stuff," Leonard said.

"I.R.S. might not know," the kid said.

We drove into the nightfall, cruised mostly silent back to LaBorde, the video on the seat between us.

# 18

I won't describe the video we bought in great detail. We watched it when we got back to Leonard's place. It gave me nightmares. Like the kid said, if it was set up, then it was a horribly beautiful setup.

In this one some thugs in the park, presumably the same cowardly thugs from the first video, still wearing their bar codes across their faces, took a brick and knocked a young man's teeth out and made him suck them, bloody mouth and all. Then they kicked his ass and left him lying in the dirt. If it was special effects, it was damn good special effects. But considering the way the rest of the video looked, I doubted there was anything artificial about it.

"Do we show this to Charlie?" I said.

"Not yet," Leonard said.

"Why not? I don't like the idea of this thing being in my house."

"We'll put it inside the couch at my old place, with the rest of the stuff."

"I don't like that either."

I took the video out of the machine and put it back in its box.

"I never thought I'd live to see such a thing as this," I said. "I can't believe it. What in the hell has happened to everyone? Every time I turn around, I'm amazed at how little I know about human nature. About anything, for that matter. But this . . ."

"Whatever it is," Leonard said, "I'm tired of it being given names and excuses. Guy sells drugs, it's because his grandma died. Poor kids sell drugs, it's because they're poor. Guy goes off his rocker, kills someone, it's because he eats Twinkies and the sugar gave him a rush. I reckon sometimes it is those things, but you know what? I don't give a shit. I think a person ought to be responsible for being an asshole. Used to, person had to be responsible, had to pay the price, there was less of this shit then."

"There're more people now, Leonard. More pressures."

"There are more assholes," Leonard said, "and it ain't got a damn thing to do with pressure. Or say it does. So what? You ain't been pressured, man?"

"Leonard, you yourself are talking about going out and eliminating some people. What's the difference?"

"Difference is, I'm responsible for my actions. I ain't gonna say I got a bad hotdog and it gave me a bellyache and that made me do it. I'm gonna do it 'cause I want to do it, and I got my eyes wide open going in, and if I can do it and get away with it I will. As for you, I only want you to go so far. I don't want to be responsible for your actions."

"It would be hard for me not to help you," I said.

"I know," Leonard said.

"What about Charlie?"

"Wait a bit."

"How long?"

"A bit. I want to see we can find some things on our own. We solve it, we got things laid out so the chief can't tuck it under his ass, then we show it to Charlie and maybe I don't have to empty my box of shotgun shells."

A day later I started looking for honest work. The dough I had made offshore had been damn good, but at the rate it was going, it wouldn't be long before I had nothing more than an empty palm and a flapping wallet.

I went first to the aluminum-chair factory, but just walking in the door made my stomach hurt. Factories and foundries, and I've worked in both, were my idea of hell on earth. I stood there a moment smelling machinery oil and listening to the thud of the machines at work, watching people shuffle about as if they were pushing great boulders up a hill, and I went out of there.

I went to a local feed company for a try. The foreman told me quite frankly, "We mostly just hire niggers and wetbacks 'cause they work cheap."

"I work cheap," I said.

"Yeah, but the way we work someone, we wouldn't do that to a white man."

"Well, that's certainly white of you," I said.

"Yeah, ain't it," he said.

I left that cocksucker to it, drove all over town, tried a lot of places, but there wasn't much available, and what was available wasn't worth having. I put in some applications. One that looked promising was a job at the chicken plant, being a security guard. It wasn't exactly what I wanted, but at my age exactly what I wanted I couldn't get and what I could get I didn't want.

I began to think of the rose fields again, where I always found work, but decided against it. That hot sun, that dust up the nose, I just didn't think I could go back to it. It was a young man's job on his way to somewhere, a foolish man's job on his way to nowhere, or the last job a man could get.

It was a pretty sad situation. Here I was in my mid-forties and no real job, no retirement fund, dog-turd insurance, and a squirrel bite on the arm.

After a day of unsuccessful job hunting, I drove over to Brett's and took her to dinner at a kind of home-cooking joint, then we went back to her place, went to bed and made love, which was a damn sight better than looking for a job or working in the aluminum-chair plant. Though, considering most anything is, that isn't giving Brett the sort of compliment she deserves.

As we lay in bed, we began to talk. We talked about all kinds of things, and gradually we got around to me and my life and I told her about my job search, and how I had never really settled into anything, jobwise, that mattered. I told her about Leonard, that he was black and gay and that he and I were as close as brothers. Probably closer.

"Wow!" she said. "I've never really known any black people, you know, close up. Friend-like. Way you say you guys are."

"Is that a problem?"

"You know, I was one of them kind always thought that line about 'some of my best friends are niggers' made

171

a certain sense. I didn't mean nothing by it, I was just ignorant as a fuckin' post. Later on, I was all for civil rights, and I went out of my way to treat the blacks in school like they were my friends. Condescending is what I was. In other words, I was actually a blue-collar redneck trying to come across like a middle-class stiff ass trying to show those poor niggers what a liberal I was. So I haven't really hung around that many blacks."

"You didn't mention the gay part."

"Yeah, there's that, too. I always kind of thought of gays as perverts growing up. I never hung around any. Maybe it's high time I gave it a try. This Leonard, he's your brother, I reckon he ought to be mine too."

"You couldn't have said anything better."

"Great," she said. "I get to be the first in my family to hang around with niggers and queers."

I laughed at her.

"'Course," she said, "my family background was the kind of folks thought you touched a black person's hand you could get cut, like sharkskin can cut you. I grew up thinking all blacks did was fuck, which seems like a fairly legitimate pursuit, actually."

"I like it."

"Yeah. It passes the time. My daddy, he was the kind of guy thought miniature golf ought to be Olympic sports, called blacks darkies when he wasn't calling them 'shines' or 'niggers.' My mother, who was a kind of liberal for where we lived, called them 'nigras' or 'coloreds' and thought they ought to have the right to vote but should have their own toilets and water fountains. Later on, after civil rights, she never did like the idea of going into a filling station and thinking a black ass had been on the crapper ahead of her. So, you see, I've had some hurdles to overcome."

"Well, your old man might have been a racist, but I'll tell you, when it comes to miniature golf as an Olympic sport, he might have been on to something. It's a hell of a lot more entertaining than skating."

Brett grinned. "Give us a kiss."

I did. And another.

"Now," she said, "make love to me and try to have it last longer this time."

"Thanks for considering my ego."

"Not at all," she said, shifting herself under the covers to accommodate me. "You know where the hole is, don't you?"

"I'm a little bit limp right now," I said.

"Hey, baby, it's not the meat, it's the motion. We'll make it happen if we have to poke it in there with a stick."

"Oh, that's stimulating."

We didn't have to resort to the stick.

And Brett was right.

It wasn't the meat. It was the motion.

# 19

Along nightfall, when Brett was off to work, I drove home happy and satisfied. Feeling that, in spite of things, life was coming together. I went inside, and as I reached for the light switch the ceiling fell on me and the floor jumped up and hit me in the face. Next thing I knew there was pain in my side and I was rolling into more pain, then hands had me and I was pulled up and a big shadow came out of the greater shadows of the house and kneed me in the groin, dropped me to the ground. Then the knee found my chin and gave me a little merry-go-round trip. Someone behind me put his forearm around my neck and squeezed and lifted. I was as good as hung.

"Howdy," said the big shadow.

All three shadows dragged me outside. They were not shadows in the pale moonlight, but men, and one of them was a very big man, the man in the video, the man who belonged to the feet that had made the tracks around Leonard's back door. Had to be. Guy like that, you could take his shoe and a boat paddle and shoot the Colorado rapids. He was the man Leonard called Big man Mountain, the professional wrestler.

The other two were economy-sized enough. They were not easy to see there in the moonlight, but one had a pale face that appeared to have exploded from the inside. The acne scars on his skin held the shadow, made the grooves in his flesh look like whiplashes.

The other was a stocky black man with close-cropped hair and a forehead that shone brightly in the light of the moon. He had breath as sweet as a bean fart.

Big Man Mountain pushed me down on my face, and the other two helped pull my arms behind me. They tied my wrists together with something that felt like wire, hauled me up and pulled me out back of my house.

There was a '64 Chevy Impala parked there, probably black, but it was hard to tell in the dark. It might have been blue or green or any dark color.

I felt like a goddamn idiot. I had walked right into it. I hadn't expected a thing. I had been too euphoric. They had driven over and parked their car behind my place, gone in through the back or broken out a window, and they had waited on either side of the door for me. The big guy, he had probably waited in the kitchen. I had walked straight into bad business, stupid as a duck flying over a blind.

The two smaller thugs put me in the backseat between them. The giant forced his frame behind the wheel, fired up the Chevy. A car passed us as we headed out of my driveway; its lights were bright and Big Man cussed them.

We drove on down my little road, on out to a full-fledged four-lane, and away we rolled. Down the dark highway, away from town, out into deeper darkness where the highway lost its lanes and narrowed, where the trees hung thick like tar-baby fingers over the road.

Way on out we drove, heading toward Louisiana, which lay sixty miles away. I sat there and thought about what I could do, but it didn't add up to much. My hands were behind my back and I was between two guys who looked as if the last sentimental thought they'd had was watching a puppy go under their car wheel and hoping the little motherfucker didn't pop their expensive tires.

We rode on, the windows down, the wind blowing in cool and wet with the smell of swampy water. It ruffled our hair, dampened our faces. Cars passed us. Cars came up behind us. I wanted to stick my head out the window and yell, but I figured I did that, I was a goner for sure. I tried to stay alert, looking for possibilities. I had a feeling possibilities were somewhere other than Texas that night.

We went halfway to Louisiana, veered to the right down a red-clay byway, cruised into deeper darkness where the land turned swampy and the shadows grew great, and the head beams were the only light you could see.

Way out we drove. Way out.

"I don't guess this is a surprise party?" I said.

"Oh," said the black man on my left, "don't know. Might call it that."

"You surprised so far, ain't you?" said the man with the pocks. He put a cigarette in his mouth and lit it and tossed the match out the window.

"We kinda good at surprises," said the black guy. "Fact

is, I thought you 'bout as surprised as anybody I ever surprised. And I surprised me a few."

"Shut up," Big Man Mountain said.

I wasn't sure who he was talking to, me or the other guys, but we all went silent and the car cruised on and the wind was choked thick with the smell of damp earth. Sort that fills a grave.

Car lights swung in behind us, and for an instant they gave me an unreasonable hope. Then the lights moved to the side and the dark shape of the car passed us.

On we drove, into an even deeper wooded blackness where the trees dipped low and the vines hung loose, dripping down and scraping across the car like the wet hair of a drowned corpse, and finally there was just this little dirt driveway in a small clearing, and in the clearing was a shack. I reckoned it was some old hunting shack, probably abandoned, or owned by an out-of-towner, and Big Man and his buddies had taken it over. We parked and the two guys in the back helped me get out by encouraging me with a couple of sharp blows to the ribs.

I stood out there in the night, the moon leaking weak light through the trees like spoiled cheese dripping through a grater, and took in the smell of everything: rich earth, the rankness of swampy water, the stench of dead fish. Frogs bleated. A night bird cried. I could hear my heartbeat.

I figured these were to be the last things I would ever smell or hear, so I did my best to enjoy them. In an odd way I felt extremely alive.

I wondered if my body would ever be found. I wondered how long Brett would miss me. I wondered if animals would gnaw my bones. I wondered if Leonard would discover who did it, and if so I wondered how horribly they would die. I sort of hoped Leonard didn't find out. The idea of him spending the rest of his life in prison did not appeal to me.

Pock Face took the key from Big Man Mountain, opened the trunk of the car, took out a foam ice chest, and carried it toward the shack. Big Man Mountain pointed the beam of his flashlight at the door, and the black guy opened the door with a key and we went inside.

There was an old gas-powered generator in one corner of the room, and Big Man Mountain gave the flashlight to Pock Face and he held it while Big Man fired up the generator and turned on the light.

The light was a low-wattage bare bulb dangling on a frayed black wire, and in the light, dust motes rode about the starkness of the room like frenzied insects. Near the generator was a table, and on the table was a car battery, some cables, a stained brown pillow, and a large metal bowl. The windows were boarded over. The back door had a flap lock on it with a padlock through it.

Beneath the bulb was a wooden chair. They sat me in that and produced some cord and tied my ankles to the chair. From that position I could see there was a ball bat by the door, leaning against the frame. It was stained all over. I had an idea what with.

Big Man came over, squatted down in front of the chair, and took a long look at me. His beard was jet-black and well groomed. His brown eyes were almost friendly, reminded me of a puppy that wanted a pat on the head. His voice turned soft, almost feminine. He carefully unwrapped a breath mint and placed it gently on his tongue. "You got scared eyes," he said.

"You bet," I said. In fact, they were starting to water.

"You and your nigger, you got stuff stirred up," he said.

I glanced at the black guy. No help there. He wasn't outraged and ready to change sides. *Nigger* was just a word to him. Fact was, he seemed kind of bored, like this was a job he did a lot and didn't have feelings about one way or another, long as the paycheck showed up.

I glanced at Pock Face. He had his finger in his nostril, chasing a wily snot ball.

"You shouldn't go around askin' questions like you're askin'," Big Man said. "It could make some people look bad, know what I'm sayin'?"

"King Arthur?" I said.

"Well, let's just say it could make some people look bad," he said.

"Could I just apologize?" I asked.

"I don't think so," Big Man said. "Know what's in the ice chest?"

"Ice?"

"Right. But no beer. No soda pop. No fish. Just ice. Ever had your balls packed in ice, Collins?"

"No. It sounds kinky, but I'd really rather not. Especially if you're doing the packing."

Big Man turned to the black guy. "Get the chest over here, Booger."

"I ain't handling his bobs," said Booger. "You want his meat packed, you pack it."

"Git the ice chest, shithead," Big Man said.

Shithead didn't look happy about it, but he went over and got the ice chest and set it by the chair. He opened the lid. I glanced inside. Crushed ice.

Big Man said, "What I do here is I take the ice, put some in a metal bowl, and we drop your pants, and we set the bowl in the chair, and put your ass on that pillow over there, and we drop your oranges in that bowl, and guess what?"

"My balls get cold?"

"Real cold. That normally might even numb the pain. But the thing is, they also get wet. You take a little electricity, hit on them wet spots, and let me tell you—there ain't nothing like it. Know where I learned this little trick?"

"Your mom?" I said.

He grinned at me. "Guess."

"I don't want to guess."

"Yeah, but I want you to," Big Man said. "Unless you're ready to get started."

"Charm school," I said. "You learned it in charm school."

Big Man shook his head. "Professional wrestling."

"No shit?"

"No shit."

"Listen," I said, "I haven't got anything against you. I don't even know you, or these other gentlemen. You don't even have to drive me home. Just let me go."

"I'd like to," Big Man said. "I don't like my work, but it is my work, and I'm good at it, and I made a vow a long time ago, once I start a job I finish it, and I do what I'm going to do as well as I can, even if I don't like it."

"Is this going to be like a warning?" I asked.

Big Man shook his head. "Not to you. To the nigger, yes. We'd have got him first, it would have been like a warning to you. Know what I'm sayin'?"

"Maybe you could get someone me and Leonard don't even know and make it like a warning to the both of us," I said.

"Very funny," Big Man said. "It could be that woman you been bangin'."

"You sonofabitch."

"You want we should trade you for her?"

"Do your worst, asshole."

"Oh, you don't know my worst, gallant little man. Let me tell you, they put me out of professional wrestling 'cause I didn't like to lose, even when I was supposed to. I liked to give people permanent injuries. Wrenched neck. Dislocated elbow. Knee. Rupture. Little mementoes. Got so no one wanted to wrestle Big Man Mountain."

"It was probably the odor."

"Trying to provoke me, aren't you? You're thinking maybe I'll just finish you off. But no. You got to go the distance, you don't tell me what I want to know. Back when I wrestled, had a little thing I did where I took a battery with a crank into the ring with me, hooked cables to my ears and pretended to fire myself up a bit. You know, crank it while it was hooked to my ears. One time, I fucked up. Battery was charged and I did it for real. Knocked me on my ass. I sort of liked it. A little jolt, it perks you up, you get used to it. Sort of like shock therapy. Which, by the way, I've had."

"Get on with it," Booger said.

"Shut up, Booger," Big Man said. "I'm talking to Mr. Collins. You know, Collins, I know a lot about you. I been following you around. Having you followed. I know when you eat. When you shit. When you beat off. I know you're throwing a pound of round to that little nurse. I'm thinkin', all this gets through, you're nothing but a greasy rag, I might could pay her a visit."

"Leonard will kill you."

"The nigger? I don't think so, Collins. I think I will kill him."

"Whatever," Booger said.

"Mountain," said Pock Face, "I ain't ate yet. Can't we get this shit over with? I want to grab a burger."

"Get the ball bat," Big Man said. "Warm up a little."

Pock Face got the bat and started swinging it through the air. He banged it hard on the floor a couple of times, smashed it into the wall once. While this was going on, Big Man kept talking in that slow sweet voice of his.

"So, this shock business, if you're used to it, you can take a little voltage. You're not, hurts. I'm gonna hook your balls up, give you a few leaps to the meat, then I'm gonna ask some questions. Things about what you know and what you've done about it. Now I got to be honest here. You aren't going to make it, Collins. Don't try to imagine you are. You're gonna die. The boys here, they're good. They can make you suffer a long time. The faggot, Raul, you know about him. He made it hard on himself. I wouldn't have thought it, you know. A fruit with balls, but he had them. Literally. They were big mothers when we put them in the ice."

"Weren't so big later," Booger said.

"That's right," Big Man said. "That ice, the electricity. It doesn't do a man's *cojones* good, Collins. But you see, you tell us what we need to know, no voltage. Just a good shot to the bean with the bat. Puts you right out, if it don't kill you. Couple more, gone for good. You only feel the first one. And not much 'cause you get nailed hard. No more worries. Try to be the tough guy, hold out, we got to give you some business. Hear what I'm tryin' to tell you, Collins? Answer me, man."

"I hear," I said.

"Good. So we got no hearin' problems here. Now here's your first question, and I beg you to consider before you answer. Where's the video?"

"What video?"

Big Man hung his head. "All right. Booger, take down his pants."

"You take down his pants," Booger said.

Big Man, who had been kneeling, came up suddenly and slapped Booger behind the head, pulling him into his other hand, which took hold of Booger's throat.

"You big black dick!" Big Man said. "I told you to take down his pants. Now do it."

He pushed Booger to the floor. Booger unfastened my belt and tugged at my pants and underwear, pulled them down to my knees. Pock Face handed him the pillow. Booger shoved me up and put it under my ass. He sat the bowl up next to me and scooped out a handful of ice with his hands and put it in the bowl and then he pushed the bowl under me so that my testicles hung into it. At first it was a cold jolt, but almost immediately I started to numb. I tried to shake myself loose, but Booger held the bowl. Pock Face came up behind me and slipped a rope over me and tied me more firmly to the chair.

Big Man said, "You aren't gonna believe the kind of trip you're gonna take. Over there into Pain City, my man. But, I'm gonna give you another chance to take the Ball Bat Highway on out of here. Last thing you'll hear is the wind from that bat. Then it's all over."

"I swing it just right," Pock Face said, "you won't hardly hear that."

"There you are," Big Man said. "Now, once again. And I want you to come right at me with the answer when I ask this. Where is the video?"

"You're supposed to know so fuckin' much about me, why don't you know where the video is?"

"Okay," Big Man said. "Maybe I don't know as much as I said. Maybe I know a lot less, but I'm here to learn, Collins. Where is it?"

"Go to hell."

"Kinney," Big Man said to Pock Face, "hook up the battery, bring it over here. Couple shots from Reddy Kilowatt, this fucker's gonna sing like a mockingbird."

Pock Face set to work.

"I ain't gonna keep hold of this bowl now," Booger said.

" 'Course not, you moron," Big Man said. "You done this before."

"Naw, I did the bat last time," Booger said. "I like the bat."

"Everybody likes the bat," Big Man said. "Except, of course, the man in this chair. There's been a couple others in this chair, Collins, you know that?"

I wanted to say something smart, something strong. But I couldn't.

"You look a little nervous, Collins. Want to say about the video?"

My mouth was so dry I could hardly speak. "No."

"Man, what's the deal?" Big Man said. "It ain't nothin' to you. You're gonna die anyway. We don't get it from you, we got to go after the nigger. Maybe the nurse."

"She doesn't know anything," I said.

"I got to be the judge of that, Collins. I think you're an honest man. Really. I get those kind of vibes from you, but still, you see, I'm a professional. I might have to bring her out here. But I promise you this, Collins. I do, we'll make it nice for her. And since she ain't got no balls to drop in the ice, we might make it nice for her a lot of times. So many times it ain't so nice. And maybe it's not nice for her any time, but if it's nice for us, we got to keep it up till maybe she tells us something."

"She doesn't know a goddamn thing."

"Come on, Collins. Save her some trouble. Spare your nigger's balls. Tell us about the video."

"The police have it."

Big Man shook his head. "No they don't."

"Yes they do."

"Nope."

"Yes."

"Nope. They don't have it, Collins. I know that. You have it, or you know where it is."

Pock Face dropped two cables into the bowl. Booger let go of the bowl quick. Pock Face gripped the handle on the generator.

Big Man moved very close to me. He said. "We hit the crank, you get the juice, I can tell you now, you're most likely gonna shit yourself. If not this shot, the next one. Save the humiliation. Take the bat. We'll tidy you up a bit afterwards, pull your pants up, dump you in your nigger's yard. That way, you don't rot somewhere."

"I don't think you'd do that," I said.

"Use the bat?"

"Clean me up and dump me where I'd be found."

"You might be right," Big Man said, "but you could go out without all that pain. All right, Collins. The moment of truth. One last time, then Kinney, he's got to hit the crank, and then we got to start breakin' some things too. Where is the video?"

"What video?"

"Hit it, Kinney."

And Kinney did and the world went black and then white and then it threw colors all around and I felt my body jump like frog legs on a griddle, then I heard a scream, a loud, horrible scream, like a woman in fear, but the scream was mine. The room was blood-red, then black, and out of the blackness Big Man's face floated and hung above me like a moon made of gangrene flesh surrounded by hair and the sweet smell of a breath mint.

"How was that?" Big Man asked.

It took a while for me to get my breath. "Invigorating," I said.

"Oh," Big Man said. "You liked that, huh?"

Again, some time passed. I said, "I prefer it as a one-time experience."

"I bet. We got to do it again, Collins. Unless you want to tell me something I want to know. I'll say this for you, you let a fart like the clap of creation, but you didn't shit yourself. But let me tell you this. Booger, he knows better than to stand behind that chair. Shit has a way of flyin' out from the back there and sprayin'. Those stains on the pillow, what you think that is?"

"Olive oil?"

"Shit. A little blood."

"You might as well finish me," I said. "You aren't going to get anything from me, because I don't know anything."

"He might be tellin' the truth," Booger said.

"Yeah," Big Man said. "He might. But things still got to come out the same. How's about we give him another boost?"

I already felt as if I were going to pass out. I pulled up all my reserves, which were mostly AWOL, and steeled myself.

There was an explosion and the walls of the shack vibrated and the floor jumped and the lightbulb above me rocked and I realized it wasn't my balls and brain dealing with electricity. It was a real explosion, outside the shack.

Big Man bent down, snapped a revolver out of an ankle holster, leaped for the door, jerked it open. The night was bright orange and yellow with flecks of red. I could see the '64 Impala. It was blazing, sending up gasoline and oil to the great motor gods of the heavens.

A sound behind me. A *wham!* Followed by another. Then another. Booger leaped and got hold of the ball bat, and Pock Face jerked back from where he was kneeling. The wires on the battery jumped out of the bowl, and the bowl turned over and the ice ran under my ass. Pock Face bumped my chair and I went over sideways. Pock's head knocked against the lightbulb, sent it swinging.

Then it all happened in the alternating light and shadow of the swaying bulb.

Big Man popped a shot from his little ankle gun. It made a bright burst in the shadows. The bulb swung back and there was a blast from a shotgun.

Pock Face, aka Kinney, hurtled over my chair, crashed to the floor next to me. Some of the dark jelly that was now his face slapped against my cheek and chin. The blood was so hot it stung.

Big Man bellowed, bolted through the open door as another blast from the shotgun ripped into the air where he had been standing. Fragments of the wall and door frame leaped toward me.

Shadow.

A tall man, the one with the shotgun, stumped past me, and as the light swung back and finally came to rest, I saw his shotgun stock swing out, catch Booger upside the head with a sound like someone popping loose the vacuum-packed lid of a jar.

Booger took the blow with a grunt and a spray of teeth. He swung the bat, but the man holding the shotgun used his weapon to block it, brought the barrel around in a short arc and hit Booger in the face. Booger did a kind of backwards hop, hit the table, knocked it flat, fell down on top of it.

The man with the shotgun kicked his boot into Booger's balls. Booger screamed and the man fit the shotgun into Booger's mouth. He said, "Good night, ass-lick," and fired.

Booger's head sort of went away.

I lay very still. The man with the shotgun squatted down and looked at me. He was a lean-faced dude wearing a stained white cowboy hat, old boots, blue jeans, and a faded western shirt decorated with little green flowers. I realized the face belonged to the man in the yellow Pontiac.

"Your ass is hangin' out, friend," he said.

"I'm also tied to a chair."

"I see that."

"You planning on shooting me, too?"

"Well, you are kinda gift-wrapped . . . But no."

The cowboy took a large knife from his jeans pocket, cut the cord on my feet and around my chest, then he got behind me and went to work on the wire, twisting it free.

I wobbled as I tried to stand. The cowboy put the knife away with one quick movement, took my arm and helped me. I pulled up my pants and fastened them. I said, "Man, I don't know what to say . . . Did you have to kill them?"

"How about 'Howdy'? And yeah, I guess I did. I started to just yell time-out, but decided that wasn't a good idea. I'm Jim Bob Luke."

"Hap Collins," I said.

"I know who you are," he said. "I followed them out here, then drove past, you know, to stay cool, so they wouldn't know I was following them, but the sonofabitches sort of lost me for a time or I'd have been here sooner."

"I'm just glad you showed up. Not that I understand why. What about Big Man?"

"Oh, I ain't worried. I been watchin' the doors."

"Confident, aren't you?"

"I invented the goddamn word. Now, why don't you use your shirtsleeve and wipe them brains off your face, and let's skedaddle before ole big un comes back."

"I thought you were confident."

"I am. But I ain't stupid."

# 20

Jim Bob Luke led me out through the back way, over the door he had kicked down. We went quickly into the woods. He moved well in the woods, and we went along like that and found a spot where we could look through the foliage, back at the shack and the raging fire of the Impala, but there wasn't any sign of Big Man Mountain.

"Hated to burn a classic car like that," Jim Bob said. "I started to just kick the door down and come in blazin', but I like a little edge. You any good with guns?"

"I don't like them, but I'm good with them."

"Good. I got another one here, and it ain't no peashooter. It's a forty-five automatic."

He gave it to me. We sat there and watched the car burn. The fire wasn't so high now and it licked around the frame of the Impala like the devil's tongue licking the bones of an animal.

"Ole big un is out there somewhere," Jim Bob said. "I'm tryin' to decide I want to hunt him down or not."

"He has a gun."

"I know. He shot at me with it. He's a shitty shot. Couldn't hit a circus elephant in the ass with a trick stool. But out here in the dark, and this being his stomping grounds, maybe I ought not. How you feelin'?"

"Queasy."

"Can you buck up?"

"Yeah."

"Come on."

We moved deeper into the woods, along the edge of a swampy creek, then finally out of the trees into a clearing. We climbed under a barbed-wire fence and onto the grass next to the road. The yellow Pontiac was parked there, in the grass. It sat on four flat tires.

"Well," Jim Bob said, looking around. "Looks like ole big un got here ahead of us."

"Think he's watching us?"

"Could be."

Jim Bob reached in his back pocket, took out a penlight and flashed it around. He found tracks in the soft dirt of the road. He said, "Motherfucker's got some feet on him, don't he?"

"I'll say."

"And look here."

Jim Bob put the penlight's glow on the side of his car. There was a deep scrape along the side.

"He just had to do that, didn't he?" Jim Bob said. "Well, the scraped paint don't stop me, and I got me four spares in the trunk, so fuck him. I used to be a goddamn Boy Scout. I came prepared."

I hurt something awful downstairs in the ball department, but I changed the tires while Jim Bob kept guard with the shotgun. "Why'd he just do the tires?" I said. "Why not screw something else up?"

"I think we interrupted him," Jim Bob said. "And he didn't want any part of this shotgun."

I changed the tires as fast as I could, constantly expecting a shot in the back. But Big Man Mountain didn't come out of the woods with his little ankle gun blazing. He didn't offer to help me with the lug bolts. A Saint Bernard didn't bring me a keg.

When all four spares were on, Jim Bob put the flats in the trunk along with the jack and drove us out of there. I couldn't hold out any longer. The pain was too much. The activity had made it worse. I passed out on the car seat.

When I awoke, Jim Bob had my feet and Leonard had my arms. I looked up at Leonard. He said, "Take it easy, brother. You all right now."

"Funny," I said. "I don't feel all right."

I closed my eyes and they carried me away and put me on a cloud and the cloud was comfortable, except for a fire built between my legs, but I couldn't move to get away from the fire; no matter how hard I tried it followed me, and finally I slept, fire or no fire, and in my dream heads kept exploding, and two rabid squirrels, one with a pocked face, the other one black with a shaved head, bit me repeated on the balls, while another squirrel, very plump with oversized feet and a beard and devil's horns, turned a crank on a battery that threw sparks.

# 21

When I awoke it was early morning, still dark. There were strands of light in the darkness outside, but the strands seemed to be suffering against the night, as if blackness had decided to push the light back and hold it down until it stopped breathing.

And maybe it just seemed that way because I had witnessed two men killed and hadn't had any breakfast and my balls felt as if someone had borrowed them during the night for a game of Ping-Pong and had put them back in reverse.

I went into Leonard's kitchen, saw Jim Bob sitting at the table with Leonard. They were drinking beer. Jim Bob had his hat cocked back on his head, his legs resting on a chair.

"Breakfast of champions," I said.

"There you have it," Jim Bob said. "Pour these suds on

193

a bowl of cornflakes, you get all the vitamins you need for a day."

I got a glass and the milk jug out of the fridge and sat at the table. I poured milk in my glass. Even doing that made my balls hurt.

Leonard said, "Jim Bob here's been tellin' me about last night. Just started telling me some other stuff. Actually, now that I think about it, I been tellin' him stuff, and I don't know why."

"I'm charmin'," Jim Bob said.

"Yeah, and I could be fuckin' up, talkin' like that," Leonard said. "I don't even know you."

Jim Bob grinned. "Like I said. I'm charmin'."

"You saved my man's life, here," Leonard said. "That gives you some points. But it don't give you the game. Know what I'm sayin'?"

"I think I'm pickin' up the important parts," Jim Bob said.

"Way I see it," I said, "I could use lots of explanation. And let me throw in a tip, Jim Bob. Don't try and follow people in a yellow Pontiac. It's conspicuous."

"Hell," Jim Bob said. "I know that. I wasn't all that worried you saw me or not. Not later on. I followed you lots you didn't see me, yellow Pontiac or not. Actually, my preferred toolin' vehicle is a red fifties Cadillac I call the Red Bitch, but right now it's in the shop. Or to be more exact, it's being rebuilt from the tires up. I fucked that baby up big-time. Ran it into a brick wall tryin' to run over a sonofabitch tried to kill me."

"You're quick to take people out, aren't you?" I said.

"Wooo," Jim Bob said. "Now that he's at the house all safe and sound with his balls in his drawers, he don't want to like no killin's. Let me tell you something,

Collins. Wasn't for me, you'd have charcoal briquets for nuts right now. You think I could have gone in there last night and them boys would have just challenged me to a paper-rock-scissors contest?"

"Ole Hap here," Leonard said, "he swats a fly, he's gonna brood on it for a couple days, maybe put out a little sugar on a dog turd for the relatives."

"I'm just saying two men are dead. I'm not saying I'm against you saving my life or protecting your own. It had to be done, but I'm not proud of the fact."

"Hell, I'm proud," Jim Bob said. "Only thing I regret about drizzly shits like that is I can't kill them three or four times apiece."

"How do you know about us?" I asked.

"He's a private detective," Leonard said. "He also knows Charlie."

"That certainly helps with the detective work, doesn't it?" I said.

"That's a fact," Jim Bob said. "But I done told Leonard some of this stuff."

"How about you go over it a little more?" I said.

Jim Bob upended his beer. "You got any more of this piss?"

"Fridge," Leonard said.

Jim Bob got up, found himself a beer, sat down. He twisted off the top and took a deep jolt. He sounded like a pig sucking on a nursing bottle.

When he had slogged about half the beer down, he sat the bottle on the table, wiped his mouth with the back of his hand, said, "I reckon I can give you the short sporty version."

"I get the feeling nothing you say is going to be short," I said.

Jim Bob grinned at me. "You got a point there. I won't kid you, I like to hear myself talk, 'cause I'm so goddamn interestin'."

"Then make me interested," I said.

"Whoa, goddamn it, hold off," Jim Bob said. "Incoming."

Jim Bob lifted his hip and let a fart fly.

"I been saving that one," he said.

"It was nice of you to share it with us," Leonard said.

"Yeah, well, sniff deep and you can have a Mexican dinner secondhand," Jim Bob said.

"Don't you get a little tired working so hard to be folksy?" I said.

"Naw," Jim Bob said. "I figure it's kind of an edge. People don't know what you're really thinking. They think you're just a shallow good ole boy."

"But you aren't?" I said.

Jim Bob gave me a dazzling smile. "Naw, Collins, I ain't. But you can believe what you want."

"Jim Bob's here because of a kid named Custer Stevens," Leonard said.

"That's right," Jim Bob said. "His parents live in Houston. I have my office over in Pasadena, Texas. Or I call it an office. It's a little pig farm I own. These days you got to shoot the bad guys and raise your own meat, 'cause the pay for private detective work stinks."

"You're drifting again," I said.

"So I am," Jim Bob said. "Well, this Stevens, his boy come down here to go to the university. Damnedest thing was they sent him here to get him out of the big city, thought he'd be nice and safe here. Neither one of 'em knew Custer liked to suck dicks. Anyway, Stevens had a chum down here named Richard Dane. Few years back I did some work for ole Dane, and Dane recommended me to Stevens."

"You get around, don't you?" I said.

"I certainly do," Jim Bob said. "There ain't hardly a town in East Texas I ain't worked in one way or another. There's people all over the place got problems, and I'm a problem solver."

"You left out what this Dane recommended you to do," Leonard said.

"Well, this boy, Custer, he come down here and got in with boys liked to do the brown-eye express, and pretty soon he's hanging out in the park shoppin' for goober. He meets a guy, and this guy takes him into the middle of the park, then a bunch of guys jump out, beat him up, knock Custer's teeth out, make him do a circle suck and a goober jerk for about fifteen minutes."

"And they put it on film," I said.

"Exactly. Custer decides to phone his parents about the fact he's a Hershey highway kinda guy, tells them what happened. They get all bent out of shape about his sexual preference, but when they drive down to see him, see the beatin' he's took, hear about the video, they forget all that shit and do the right thing. They go to the police. They talk to the chief. He gives 'em a line of shit, but they can tell pretty quick-like he don't give a fuck about a fag and they get vibes he thinks the whole thing serves the boy right.

"To shorten it up, the boy leaves school, goes home, and they wait for justice. And wait. And wait. Chief ain't do'n dick. He's shufflin' some papers. Now, Richard Dane comes in. He's in contact with Stevens, and he's the one recommended the boy go to college here in the first place, so Dane, he feels guilty. He tells Stevens I done some work for him once came out satisfactory, and he might want to hire me to snoop around. Stevens hires me. I know Charlie on the department from a little job a year back. I call him, drive down to visit. Charlie helps where he can, but it ain't much. He tells me about the other beatings in the park. All of them swept under the rug by the chief, so I start poking my nose around and this fella McKnee keeps comin' up."

"Horse," I said.

"That's the one," Jim Bob said. "I check out the park, this guy's always around. There's gay action, this guy's around. You wouldn't believe how many propositions I got from goober grabbers while I was doin' this."

"You don't hear me propositionin' you," Leonard said.

"Yeah, well, it was just the good-lookin' ones," Jim Bob said. "I was flattered, but I don't swing that way. But hell, I played the game a little. There was even one with a fat ass and a funny hat I might have had a fantasy or two about."

"Cut the shit," Leonard said. "Get on with it."

"I'm doin' this for a while, then this Raul shows up. He's with Horse. I start seein' him around. It don't mean nothin' until I go to the park one night with my standard queer duds on—"

"What are standard queer duds?" Leonard said. "Do I look like I got on standard queer duds?"

"Well, I don't know what you got on underneath," Jim Bob said.

"You're startin' to fuck with me," Leonard said. "I don't like it."

"Like it or don't like it," Jim Bob said. "There's a way most of them fellas dress. I ain't puttin' 'em down for it, but they dress a certain way, 'specially if they're tryin' to get their cable up a butt. I dressed way I seen them dress. And it worked. So there."

Leonard leaned back in his chair with his arms crossed. He looked as if he could eat ground glass and chew nails.

Jim Bob said, "I'm tryin' to connect with these fucks beat up Custer Stevens, so I'm roamin' the park day and night, and one night this fella, a good-sized fella, comes up to me and makes with the come-on.

"I'm thinkin', now, if this guy just wants to play and I lead him on, I'm gonna feel kinda silly when it gets to the part where I'm supposed to swing my rope, but I play along, and this guy leads me to a spot, and these guys come out of the bushes on me. I had to give a couple of them an attitude adjustment with my blackjack."

Jim Bob suddenly produced the blackjack from his back pocket and slapped it into his palm. "Couple of shots from this and it's lights out and a headache in the mornin'. Them fuckers bolted. When they did, I seen there was someone else runnin', some fuck in the bushes. I chased after him. He had a video camera. I was closin' on him when this guy—one led me into ambush in the first place—caught up with me and jumped me. It was the fella I shot to hell last night. White guy with the moon craters. I wrestled that fuck all over the park, got him in a step-over-toe hold, and cranked on that baby a while."

Jim Bob replaced his blackjack, sucked more beer, continued.

"By this time his buddies, ones weren't unconscious, got their shit together, and one of them had a gun, and I hadn't brought mine, and I knew that was my cue to go to the house. So I darted, and they let me dart. I made it to my car, and what do I see as I'm jettin' away from the park? The guy with the video camera, and he's gettin' on the back of this Harley, and ole Horse is drivin', and you got one guess who this video man was."

"Raul," Leonard said.

"On the nosey," Jim Bob said. "They were videotapin' this shit for their pleasure. Or, to be more precise, for money."

"Raul was the cameraman?" I said.

"You betcha," Jim Bob said.

I watched Leonard's face do a series of moves, then settle.

I turned back to Jim Bob. "Did you know these tapes were going underground to video stores?"

"Having encountered similar things before," Jim Bob said, "I sort of put it together. And it didn't take a genius to figure the folks I had my little tadoo with in the park were the ones beat the Stevens kid up and that Horse and Raul were connected. I followed them. And later I followed them some more. Sometimes one, sometimes both."

"I guess all that watchin' got you connected to me and Hap," Leonard said.

"Yeah," Jim Bob said. "And I found out Raul went out to King Arthur's place to cut hair, and later to his plant. And then all this shit starts comin' down, and I get to puttin' it all together, tryin' to make a case I can give the cops, and guess what. I lose track a bit, next thing I know Horse gets his head blown off and Raul disappears."

"And what did our intrepid investigator deduce from all this?" I asked.

"I figured Leonard done 'em both in. I figured I had to follow that part of the story too, you know, construct the whole picture. So I come here and I see you come out of the house, Hap. I been spot-checkin' you two ever since. You got good taste in nurses, Hap."

"Leave her out of this," I said.

"Nothing raw meant," Jim Bob said.

"Charlie knew all this?" Leonard asked.

"Nope," Jim Bob said. "I didn't keep Charlie informed. I got the original info from him, then I was on my own. I didn't even know he knew you two until after Horse bought his ticket. I seen him talkin' to you then. And I talked to him yesterday some."

"When did you decide I wasn't the killer?" Leonard asked.

"When the cops decided you weren't," Jim Bob said.

"But still you followed?" I said.

"That's right," Jim Bob said. "I didn't know exactly what I was followin', but I was followin'. I was checkin' other leads too. You guys weren't the only ones. You're lucky I was followin' last night."

"And why were you?" I asked.

"I thought it was time you and me met, talked," Jim Bob said. "I realized we were after the same thing—folks behind all this shit. I thought I'd talk to you, then Leonard. I was on my way to your place when Big Man Mountain passed me in the Impala and I seen you in the back. And you didn't look like you were on your way to the skatin' rink. I turned around, followed, and you know the rest."

"Bottom line," Leonard said. "What's this all about?"

"What do you figure?" Jim Bob said. "I've showed you mine, now show me yours."

Leonard looked at me. I nodded. Leonard said, "We figure King Arthur has some thugs who are stealin' grease, and Horse gets in with these thugs as an undercover cop.

He takes some secret video of King Arthur's men stealing grease and they want it back. Then there's this other video of the stuff like happened to your client in the park. I guess Horse and Raul found out about that business by accident, then dealt themselves in. Even started helping make the videos. Christ! I thought I knew Raul."

"Shit," I said, "that's the whole story right there, isn't it? Horse started out investigating, then got in on a better end of the business. Grease-napping was the sort of thing he'd turn in, but this other thing, the video business, he could make some real money there. He dove in and went to work for the bad guys. They said anything, he could turn them in and just say he was workin' undercover, playin' them along. He had them over a barrel."

"In summation," Leonard said, "we ended up with a couple videotapes and a notebook full of coded stuff."

"All right," Jim Bob said. "That's interesting. It may not mean what you think, though."

"How's that?" I asked.

"Look here," Jim Bob said. "You got to see things through. You take flyin' saucers, for instance."

"Flyin' saucers?" Leonard said.

"Yeah," Jim Bob said, "for instance. Guy goes out at night, sees somethin' in the sky he don't recognize, he starts talkin' about UFOs. And he's right. He did see an Unidentified Flying Object, but that's all he saw. UFO doesn't mean flyin' saucer, spacecraft. It means somethin' unidentified. But way most people think is they see something they don't know, next thing is they're sayin' they saw a flyin' saucer, when in fact they don't know what they saw. Might be a flyin' saucer, might be God moon'n' us, but they don't know. It's a jump they've made."

"You're sayin' we're jumpin' conclusions?" I said.

"I'm sayin' you could be," Jim Bob said. "Or rather I'm sayin' you could just have part of the story. Know what else it could be?"

Leonard sounded solemn as a reverend preaching his mother's funeral. "Could be Raul and Horse Dick decided to blackmail King Arthur about the videos he was makin'. Ones they helped make."

"Bingo," Jim Bob said.

"No shit!" I said.

"No shit," Jim Bob said. "Horse still has the undercover connection, King can't say anything to the cops 'cause he'll get nailed, and he can't really do anything legal to Horse, 'cause Horse can do what you said, claim it was all part of his undercover sting."

Leonard said, "I figure Raul and Horse decided to mail that package to my mailbox. Thought they were safe long as they had that. But they were wrong. Whoever they were blackmailing decided to eliminate the blackmailers, take the pressure off, then all they had to do was find the blackmail items."

"That's right," Jim Bob said. "They snooped around. Didn't come up with the business, decided you guys had a connection, took a flyer and toted Hap out to the woods for a few bouts with a battery and a ball bat."

"And they still don't have what they want," Leonard said.

"But they still want it," I said.

Jim Bob nodded and sipped the rest of his beer. "That's about the size of it," he said.

# 22

I managed a shower to give myself some perk, put back on my clothes, and Jim Bob drove me out to my house. Leonard rode with us. Leonard had armed himself with a little .38 revolver that he wore in a clamshell holster. He had his shirttail out, as usual, so the little pistol was not visible unless you were looking for it.

Jim Bob, equipped with his twelve-gauge, opened the front door and led the way inside. Leonard went in the back, I went after Jim Bob.

The place was empty. The back door had been jimmied and the door was completely off the hinges. That was how they had gotten in after parking the Impala out back.

I hadn't noticed it the other night, probably because my concentration was mostly on Big Man's knee in my face, but the house had been tossed from one end to the other.

"Maybe they know about my old place too," Leonard said. "We ought to get over there."

We went. Inside, his house looked the same. No footprints in the dust. Everything in its place. Leonard pulled the couch from the wall and reached up in the rip and removed the metal container. He opened it. The video and the King Arthur Chili pad were there. He had brought the video we bought from the store in Houston, and he added that to the box and took it with him.

We drove back to my place and Leonard and Jim Bob helped me set the door back on the hinges. We found the hinge pins they had knocked out lying in the backyard. We shoved those back in. The door hung a little crooked, and when it closed it bulged some at the lock, but at least it closed.

I went in the bedroom, opened my nightstand drawer. My .38 revolver was still there, along with a box of shells. I changed into a clean shirt and pants, got the revolver out of the drawer and made sure there wasn't a load under the hammer. I put the .38 in my waistband, took a handful of shells, poured them into my pants pocket. It's a good thing I was out of grenades, because I wouldn't have known where to wear them.

We talked a little about this and that, and Jim Bob gave us the number of the Holiday Inn where he was staying. He drove off, and Leonard took the videos and the notebook out of the box and stuffed them in a couple of plastic bags and put them back in the metal file box. He got my shovel and went into the woods while I straightened the house. He was going to the Robin Hood tree, to bury the file box. Good idea.

About an hour later he came back and helped me finish straightening up the living room. While we worked, I said, "How'd it go?"

"The ground was hard," he said.

We finished up and I made some coffee. Leonard and I sat down at the kitchen table with our cups. I said, "What do you think?"

Leonard shook his head. "I don't know. I think it's like I said, like what Jim Bob thinks. Raul and Horse Dick tried to blackmail King Arthur and lost their lives for it."

"Blackmail," I said. "That seems kind of intense. I always thought Raul was, as you say, a little shallow, but blackmail?"

"I look back on things, I think maybe it's his style. It's not something you really see close-up, or want to see, but now I feel like a fool. One of the things hardest to figure in life, and you may have been the one told me this, but there's this person you meet who seems intelligent, you know, has a common awareness of things, but when you get right down to it, they've got no real depth. They're less than what you see. I was beginning to realize that about Raul. Not that it helped much."

"Does it change how you feel about him?"

"Things changed the minute he started hanging out with Horse Dick. I started to understand things about him I didn't like. Worse, I got to understand some things about myself. Like maybe I'm not quite the tough guy I thought I was. I still love the guy, but it's mostly in memory. I got to say this, though, he was a hell of a sight tougher than I imagined. That's a side of him I didn't know."

"You mean the business with the battery? The ball bat?"
Leonard nodded. "Yeah."

206

"Could be he was just tryin' to hang on to life," I said. "Knew he told where stuff was, it was all over. Person will take a lot of pain to live as long as they can. It isn't necessarily brave, it's desperate. Guy like Raul, he might have thought no matter how much pain he went through, eventually they were gonna let him go. You know, like when you're a kid in the school yard and the bully holds you down and roughs you up, but you figure at some point he's got to quit."

"Hell, Hap. Let's just say he had guts."

"All right," I said. "He had guts. But knowing what you know now, can you let it go? It's not really our place, this judge-and-jury business."

"Don't forget executioner."

"I was trying to skip that part."

"Way I see it, you take Raul out of the equation, these fucks have screwed my house up, they've tried to torture and kill my best friend—"

"Wasn't no try about it. You ought to see my balls."

"No, thanks. You wouldn't look at my tick, so I'm not looking at your wounds. . . . What I think is, take 'em out. The law's got itself all balled up, so we got to do it. Charlie, he can only do so much. King Arthur, he's a man with money and thugs. He does what he wants, unless we get rid of him."

"Too much for me."

"After what they did to you?"

"I don't want to be like them, Leonard. I keep telling you that."

"Trust me. You aren't like them."

I sipped my coffee, studied the sky through the kitchen window. I said, "What about Jim Bob?"

"I think he's a dick, but I trust him."

"He's a friend of Charlie's. Charlie sees something in him, guess we got to give him the benefit of the doubt."

"He's full of himself, though."

"There's that," I said. "But let me tell you, he can do what he says he can do. You should have seen him take those two guys out, and ole Big Man, he knew the fucker wasn't kiddin'. He beat a retreat right off. He'd been about a fraction slower, you could have strained strawberries through him. And I tell you, Big Man, he isn't a shrinking violet. He told me how when he was wrestling he used to charge himself up with a shot from a generator and a battery."

"Don't believe everything you hear," Leonard said. "Wrestlers, they're showmen."

"Hey, I believe him. You haven't been face to face with the guy. He's some kind of seriously sincere scary, babe. That's what I'm tryin' to tell you. What I think is we ought to turn over the videos and the notebook to Charlie. He does the best he can, and we're out of it."

"I know how his best will turn out," Leonard said.

"He's a good man," I said.

"Yeah," Leonard said, "but without Hanson around, and the chief having his dick in more holes than we can imagine, it'll get buried. I don't want it to get buried."

"Shit," I said. "I can't believe how fucked up I am."

"What?" Leonard said.

"I'm sittin' here like I'm on holiday, and Big Man, he threatened Brett. Come on, let's get over to the hospital."

I drove us there and we went inside and up the elevator to the floor where Brett worked. I talked to a guy in a white jacket pushing a food cart, but he didn't know Brett from Eisenhower.

We went to the nurses' station and I asked a pretty black nurse if she knew Brett, and she did, and she pointed down the hall. A big heavy black nurse, who must have been head of operations, caught the tail end of our conversation and gave me a dirty look. I tried my charming smile on her. She didn't seem to like it much. She touched her nurse's hat as if it might have a razor edge and that she might whip it off at any moment and throw it at me.

I knew it wasn't wise to mess around Brett's job like this, put her on the spot, but I had to talk to her. Had to tell her what kind of bad position I had put her in. As usual, just knowing me was causing someone I cared about pain.

I looked around as we went down the hall, nervous as hell, half expecting Big Man to come out of a sickroom with a battery and generator under one arm, a ball bat under the other.

At the end of the corridor I saw Brett come out of a room, look in my direction, double-take, smile, then walk toward us.

"That her?" Leonard said.

"Yeah," I said.

"Looks your type," he said.

"What's that supposed to mean?"

But there wasn't time for him to answer. Brett was in front of us. I could tell she was looking over my shoulder, back at the nurses' station.

She said, "Hap. Good to see you. But I'm working right now."

"I know," I said. "This is Leonard Pine."

She smiled at Leonard. "I've heard a lot about you."

"Nice to meet you," Leonard said.

209

"Really," Brett said. "I can't visit. Old Lady Elmore runs a tight ship."

"That the fat lady looks like her feet hurt?" Leonard said.

Brett grinned. "That's her. And her feet probably do hurt. Mine do."

"Brett," I said. "I don't mean to bother you. This is kind of an emergency."

"Emergency?" she said.

"No one's hurt," I said. "Well, not much. But inadvertently I may have got you into some deep shit."

"I don't get it," she said.

"I know," I said. "Can you get off?"

"I . . . I don't know," she said. "If I can get Patsy to take over for me. But she won't like it. I was just on vacation."

"What about Ella?" I said.

"I wouldn't ask her right now," Brett said. "I'm just glad she and I have started talkin' again. She's finally thinkin' about leavin' that shit Kevin."

"Good," I said. "But you got to get off. Really. I wouldn't do this if it wasn't important."

"Okay," Brett said. "Okay. But will you go down to the lobby and wait?"

We sat in Brett's living room, Brett and I on the couch, Leonard in a chair across the way. I explained all that had happened, told her about Jim Bob and our conclusions.

"My God," she said. "I certainly know how to pick my men."

"I'm sorry," I said. "I never thought it would come to something like this."

"This wrestler?" Brett said. "He threatened me?"

"He knew about you," I said. "He may have been talking out of the side of his mouth, but after what happened to Raul, and me, I got to be worried about you."

Brett sat for a moment. She looked at me. She looked at Leonard. She went into the bedroom and shut the door.

Leonard said, "Sorry, Hap."

"Yeah."

The bedroom door opened. Brett came out with a holster containing a .38—.38's were certainly popular in my circles.

"Let him come," Brett said. "I like you, Hap. You got your warts, but so do I. You didn't bring this on yourself. Let the fucker come. I'll shoot him so full of holes he'll think he's a tennis net. I done burned one fucker's head, guess I can put a bullet in another one's."

I thought, goddamn, if this ain't true love, I don't know what is.

# 23

"They're a little slow," I said, "and I'd keep my conversation down to stuff like, 'Bathroom's over there,' 'Coca-Cola's in the fridge,' and 'Do you want that bucket of chicken crispy or original recipe?' "

We were in Brett's living room, me and her, and we were looking out the window at Leonard, who had just arrived in my truck with Leon and Clinton. You could see them clearly beneath the bright streetlight.

Leon and Clinton were two black twins in their thirties with heads like bowling balls and bodies like the columns that hold up the British Museum of Natural History.

They were friends of Leonard's. He met them after whipping their asses. They had given Raul a hard time at a convenience store, and Leonard, who was considerably smaller, heard about it, hunted them down, and wiped the floor with them. Him beating them like that had nothing to do with their toughness; they were tough. But Leonard was tougher. Better trained. And smarter. 'Course, bless their hearts, a snapshot of a human brain was smarter than they were.

Since that time, they had been there for Leonard when he needed them. He needed them now, for me.

They got out of the truck and stood around in Brett's yard. Leon, also known as Scum Eye because he had some kind of condition that'd made his eye mat over, picked up a rock in the yard and threw it and hit Clinton in the back. Clinton, pissed, looked around for a rock, found one, and threw it at Leon.

Leon, quicker than he looked, ducked and the rock struck something out of our sight that made Leonard, Clinton and Leon wince.

"Shit," I said.

"Christ," Brett said. "Are them fellas housebroken?"

"Barely, but they're all right," I said. "Anybody fucks with you, they'll take them apart and reassemble them so that they don't match up."

"They getting paid for this?" Brett asked.

"We're slippin' 'em some bills," I said. "They'd do it for nothing, but they haven't got jobs. Got laid off at the aluminum-chair factory sometime back, and they haven't worked since. All the brain surgeon jobs are taken. But they're all right."

"They look a little scary?"

"You ought to see Big Man Mountain."

Brett gave me a grim look.

"Sorry," I said. "But that's the reality. These guys, they can take care of themselves, and they'll take care of you."

213

"I can't go to work with these fellas hanging on my neck," Brett said.

"I know. What we're gonna do, we're gonna put Clinton here. He's gonna stay in the house while you're at work. That way, no one's comin' in to wait for you. You get home, need something, he goes with you if Leonard and I aren't around. Okay?"

"Okay. What about work?"

"Leon will be there. I don't know he needs to follow you around. He'll just be around. Sittin' in the waiting room, the parkin' lot, kinda watchin' out. I don't know we can do better than that if you're going to insist on workin'."

"Like I said, landlord won't fuck me for the rent."

"Yeah, well, he's a fool. You got your pistol?"

"Pistol-packin' mama," she said, reached down, and pulled up her nurse's uniform. The gun was strapped to a holster around her thigh.

"Would you like me to check and see that garter holster is too tight?"

"That's all right," she said, lowering her hem.

"You know how to use that?" I said. "Having it is one thing, using it is another."

"Hell, I'm certified to carry it. I took the course."

The course was for the new law passed in Texas where you could legally carry a concealed handgun after taking instruction in laws and marksmanship.

"My guess," she said, "is I'm the only one of us legal. And I could shoot before I was legal. And you can take that in any manner you want. I got a buck knife in my purse too. It isn't legal. But I'll tell you, that little honey, legal or not, will cut your fuckin' nuts off with a wisp of a blade."

214

"I'd rather not talk about nut injury right now," I said.

"Sorry . . . That business gonna cut down on our activity?"

"Not even if I have to tie them in a sling."

Leonard and the twins came inside. Leonard introduced them. Clinton, who did most of the talking, said, "How're ya doin'?"

"Fine," Brett said. "Well, not really. There's someone might want to hurt me."

"He ain't gonna hurt nothin'," Clinton said. "We tie that motherfucka in some fuckin' knots is what we do."

"And he don't like knots, we shoot him some," Leon said, reaching under his sweatshirt, producing a large, greasy .45 automatic.

"Yeah," Clinton said, "like till our guns run out of bullets."

"Then we gonna reload," Leon said.

"Good," Brett said. "That's what I want to hear."

"That don't stop him," Clinton said, "we reload again."

"We get the idea," I said.

Brett turned to me. "What about you and Leonard?"

"I figure we'll do what the old Southern guerrilla fighters used to do in the War Between the States."

"And what was that?" Brett asked.

"Cuss niggers?" Leonard said.

"No," I said.

"Lynch niggers?" Leonard said.

"Shut up, Leonard," I said. "We're going to quit waiting. We're going to take it to them."

"Goddamn," Leonard said. "Now I'm inspired."

Brett went back to work, Leon in tow. We left Clinton at the house with instructions not to eat Brett out of house and home, try and spare some furniture, and to piss in the toilet with the lid up.

A little research gave us the location of King Arthur's place, and next morning we drove out there. It was on a vast acreage of mostly red clay, because a bulldozer was pushing down trees when we got there, making it that way.

We parked alongside the road and watched from the truck, over a barbed-wire fence. Watched the dozer work. It was knocking down hills of dirt that I figured were Indian mounds. They had the look of mounds, and in traditional East Texas manner, they were being pushed flat for progress.

Fuck the Indians. Fuck the pottery. Fuck the heritage. Fuck the ground. Fuck the trees. Let's get this shit flat, mud red and nasty, bring in that double wide.

Which was exactly what had been done.

Several of them.

From where we sat we had a good view because there wasn't any trees, just some stumps, and this big dozer knocking those annoying mounds flat. The property was all red clay for acres and acres, except for a patch of costal bermuda in one corner, and some steroid-fed cows and a big, red, metal barn, and, I swear, four double-wide mobile homes. Two long, two wide, linked.

"Well, what we gonna do, brother?" Leonard said. "Charge in, beat the piss out of him?"

"No, that's more your style. I'm going to wait. We're going to follow. We're going to isolate. Then, we're going to talk."

Jim Bob's yellow Pontiac pulled up behind us and he got out and walked around to my side of the truck. I had the window down and he took off his cowboy hat and stuck his head in.

"I hope you fucks ain't sneakin' around," he said, " 'cause you ain't sneaky."

"We figure we're all right," I said.

"I'm surprised you fellas have lived as long as you have," he said. "You got charmed lives, that's what I think."

"Clean livin'," Leonard said.

"Guess that's it," Jim Bob said.

"How did you know we were here?" I asked.

"I followed you from the nurse's house."

"Why are *you* still sneaking around?" Leonard said.

"Habit, I reckon."

"When in hell do you sleep?" I asked.

"When I've got the time," Jim Bob said. "As for other matters, like this King Arthur fella, maybe I can help you out, since I done been through all this some time ago. King Arthur, he don't leave the place till after noon. Fact is, about one-fifteen every day, Monday through Friday. He drives over to the plant, goes in through a special back entrance. By five o'clock, he's back out at the car, and he goes home. 'Course, I ought to mention that when he goes and comes from work, he goes with some guys look like they'd twist the heads off parakeets and suck the neck stumps for entertainment."

"You know everything, don't you?"

"Damn near it," Jim Bob said. "What's your plan?"

"Actually," I said, "we have a simple plan. Two plans. I want to talk to King Arthur, but what I figure is, we'll follow Leonard's plan."

"Which is?" Jim Bob asked.

"We're going to beat the old fart up till he comes through with a confession."

"Yeah," Leonard said. "And we're gonna beat up his companions too."

"King Arthur ain't that old," Jim Bob said. "About my age. And he looks to me like he can handle himself. As for you beatin' the companions up, Leonard, I hope you've had your Malto-Meal."

"Well, what would you do?" I asked.

"I'd beat the fuckers up," Jim Bob said.

We left the dozer to its work, followed Jim Bob back to the Holiday Inn. We had coffee in the cafeteria and Jim Bob told us some things about King Arthur.

"You know that King Arthur used to be a chili cook-off king, and that's what catapulted his recipe to stardom, so to speak? Only thing is, they found ole King was payin' judges off to vote for him. Didn't matter it was some little local thing, or a big tadoo. He took winnin' serious-like, right down to money and young pussy for the judges. Took to callin' himself King Arthur. Started the chili business, and it skyrocketed. Didn't hurt he was also into every goddamn dirty deal in East Texas, from runnin' whores to makin' sure black folks who owned stores paid a little kickback. They didn't, their businesses had a way of attractin' fires."

Jim Bob talked about King Arthur for a while, depressing me. Then somehow he and Leonard veered off into politics.

While they generally agreed on issues, I went into the lobby, used the pay phone to call Brett's house.

She and Clinton had just watched a late-morning talk show.

"This was a rerun about people who stole stuff out of stores to give as wedding gifts," Brett said. "Whole family. Had 'em on television talkin' about it, like they're some kind of celebrities."

"These days they are."

"Bunch of white-trash thieves gettin' their fifteen minutes. And funnier yet, or sadder yet, while they're on the show, host gets a call from the hotel where these skunks are stayin', and they've taken the towels and sheets and ripped the hair dryer off the wall. They found all the stuff in their luggage backstage, and now they're in trouble again. I got access to all these channels, and this is the shit on them. It's scary."

"You watched it," I said.

"Clinton made me."

"Hell, Clinton likes game shows," I said.

"All right," she said, "you caught me. . . . How's things?"

"Right now they aren't happening. But they will. We have a plan."

"What?"

"We're gonna beat up King Arthur and his goons."

"That's well thought out."

"We might even steal his chili recipe."

"Make him eat it," she said.

"Say what?"

"You had any of that stuff? I don't know it could be a whole lot worse to put shit in your mouth."

"Trust me," I said. "It would."

"All right, you win," she said. "But not by much. You're kidding about beating King up, aren't you? Not that I mind, I just don't know that'll be such a good idea."

"I reckon we'll do what we do when we come to it, " I said.

219

"It's good to know I got you fellas setting up a complicated sting," Brett said.

"Yeah. Must be comforting. Take it easy, baby."

"You too, hon."

I rang off, joined Jim Bob and Leonard. They were talking about muzzle velocity in rifles.

I had another cup of coffee, listened till they wore down and we went to Jim Bob's room.

We watched television and jawed until noon, then headed for King Arthur's.

# 24

Jim Bob drove my truck with the three of us crowded in it. We had Jim Bob's shiny black twelve-gauge pump on the floorboard. I could smell the gun oil as we drove. I kept pushing my hand against my shirt, so I could feel the .38 beneath it in my waistband. Leonard was fumbling with the radio, trying to pick up a country station.

I had been in a lot of encounters, more than anyone had a right to believe. I had grown up in a rough town and fought dozens of fights until I graduated high school. Most of them were simple, not life-or-death battles, but a couple or three had been heavy-duty. During the sixties I had grown my hair long, and there was plenty of redneck opposition to that, so I was on the line daily, arguing or fighting with someone.

I had worked a number of blue-collar jobs, and the

length of my hair had been an issue. More fights. I didn't pick fights, and tried diplomacy first, but I was still too quick to use my fists, and though I don't like to admit it, there was a time when I had enjoyed it. I didn't lose my temper easy, but once I did, it was savage, and afterwards I felt a strange hollowness that made me feel dirty and inferior to people around me.

Once, late at night, Leonard and I discussed our physical encounters. Not only those that had happened to us together, but individual events. It was a strange moment, a mix of brag and fact, shame and pride, remorse mixed with euphoria.

And here I was again, on my way to what would most likely turn into a confrontation, and perhaps more than a couple of punches. We weren't carrying our guns to plunk at cans. My stomach boiled. My head throbbed. Yet, at the same time, I felt disconnected from my body; seized by a combination of fear and anticipation.

We parked behind a closed-up fireworks shack down the road from King Arthur's red clay nightmare, got out of the car and sat on the hood so we could watch when he drove by.

Jim Bob said he knew the car, so his eyes were the ones on the highway. While we waited, he told us some funny stories and some bad jokes, then said, "All right, get in the truck."

We looked and saw a big silver Lincoln with dark windows cruising down the highway. A moment later we were behind it, hauling as fast as my little pickup would go.

"Driver usually turns here," Jim Bob said.

Jim Bob was right. The car veered to the right, headed

down a blacktop road that I knew would meet Old Pine Road, and finally onto the highway that would lead to King Arthur's chili works.

Jim Bob gunned the truck and started around. The Lincoln tried to be helpful, pulled hard right, but Jim Bob pulled hard right too. Next thing I knew, he was nosing my truck into the side of the Lincoln. Sparks flew up. Paint flecks flicked by the window.

"Hey," I said.

Jim Bob paid no attention. He rammed hard with the pickup and the Lincoln began to veer. I realized it was starting to veer near the great oak where Horse Dick and Raul's bodies had been found.

Irony or accident? I had to remember to ask Jim Bob, provided I didn't end up with the dashboard in my teeth, the motor sticking out of my chest.

The Lincoln sailed onto the grass beside the road. The driver fought the wheel, missed the tree, but went over the edge of the incline, down the hill, clattered and bumped and slid into the weeds and slid again, this time sideways into the trees at the bottom. The Lincoln hit the trees with a solid whack and a crunch, and the sunlight caught taillight fragments flying into the air.

I could see all this because Jim Bob had driven the pickup after them. He hadn't let off a bit. We bumped and bopped, striking our heads on the roof, lurching toward the dash, and finally we skidded sideways to a stop just before the hill got really steep and dropped off toward the trees where our road partners had collided with a patch of wilderness.

Jim Bob jerked the door open, grabbed the shotgun, and yelled, "Showtime!"

Leonard and I got out quick. I slid in the grass but managed to keep my footing and get my gun drawn without shooting myself. We hurried down the hill toward the Lincoln.

The driver, a fat man in a black suit, and two other water buffaloes in black suits were staggering out of the car. One of them, the guy from the backseat, had his gun, a nine millimeter, drawn. The car door was open behind him, and I could see King Arthur sitting in the backseat, or at least I assumed it was King Arthur. I had seen his likeness on cans of his chili. Way he was sitting there, you would have thought he was waiting on a bus.

The man with the drawn gun lifted it and Jim Bob fired the shotgun, sprayed dirt in front of the guy.

Jim Bob said, "Mine's bigger than yours. Toss it!"

The man tossed the gun.

The other two—and one of them was on the far side of the car, having exited from the front passenger side—had their hands in their coats, and Leonard and I pointed our guns at them. Jim Bob said, "You guys lose the hardware before it gets you hurt."

They looked at one another, eased their weapons out of their coats and dropped them.

Jim Bob said, "You, on the other side there, mosey on around here where I can see you good and make sure you ain't got a bazooka in your sock."

The man, who was large with hair so thin and gray on the sides he looked completely bald at first glance, came around slow-like, his teeth, wet from saliva, shining like greased piano keys in the sunlight.

King Arthur, wearing a white Stetson, a gray cowboy suit with gray boots decorated with red chili peppers, slid out of the Lincoln on our side, stood and looked at us. He was about five-ten, a solid one-eighty, had a lined brown face with a anteater nose. He had a cleft chin deep enough to hide a dried pea in, and shit-ass eyes.

King reached inside his jacket, slowly pulled out a pack of cigarettes, showed them to us, lipped one, put the pack back, and nodded toward one of the buffaloes.

The one that had been in the backseat with King looked at us, slowly reached in his pants pocket, produced a lighter, and lit King's cigarette.

"Driver's ed, boys?" King Arthur said.

"Let's cut through the crap," Leonard said. "You know who we are?"

"Yeah, I do," King Arthur said, puffing on his cigarette. "Troublemakers. And look what you've done to my car."

"I don't think you'll be reportin' it," Jim Bob said. "Might toss a little too much light on you."

King Arthur smiled. "You thought that was the case, you'd have gone to the police. How come you didn't? You been puttin' your shitty noses in my business for a while now."

"So you do know us?" I said.

"I know all kinds of shit," King Arthur said. "You're all connected to them queers got killed."

"Here's the deal," I said. "We're gonna put it to you straight. We're out to cause you some grief. But right now, this is more personal. Three of your goons—and if you're missing a couple you might check a cabin in the woods—broke into my house, sacked it, roughed me

225

up, took me out to this shack, and a guy workin' for you, one Big Man Mountain—"

"The wrestler?" King Arthur said.

"You know who," I said. "This Mountain, he hooked a cable and battery and a little hand-cranked generator up to my balls, and gave me a few volts. Fortunately I'm still here, thanks to some help."

"Don't mention it," Jim Bob said.

"What I'm here to tell you," I said, "is very simple. We could kill you right now, and I think that would most likely be a good idea, but it's not my style."

"It's my style, though," Jim Bob said, "so keep in mind, King, things could change at a moment's notice."

I gave King Arthur a look hard enough to drive a nail. I said, "I'm going to tell you straight out we're going to nab your ass. You can count on it. Legal-like, if possible. But let me make this clear, and I suggest you open your eyes wide and put on your glasses and use binoculars so you can see what the fuck I'm making clear. You screw around me or Jim Bob or my brother Leonard, my girlfriend—and you know who she is because Big Man Mountain did—I will kill you."

"If I don't do it first," Leonard said.

"Don't forget me," Jim Bob said.

"This is your one and only warning," I said.

"You boys got me wrong," King said.

"Yeah," I said. "You're an innocent fella. That's why you have three bodyguards."

King nodded. "All right. I ain't so innocent, but I got bodyguards mostly because I can. I like the looks of it. And now and then, I get a little trouble. I got some deals goin' here and there outside the chili, but I ain't never had to shoot nobody. Or have nobody shot. 'Course, with you boys, I might make an exception. I don't get it. All this over some fuckin' grease?" King Arthur dropped his cigarette in the grass, put a boot heel to it. "Over some faggot cop took a video of my grease operation? You boys takin' over where he left off? That it, huh? How much you want?"

"We don't want anything other than what I just said," I told him, lowering my gun.

King Arthur said, "You think I killed those queers, don't you? Over some grease they filmed? I tried to pay them off, but I didn't kill them."

"Tell it to a lie detector," I said.

"I would," King Arthur said. "Listen up, you three. You think you're tough guys, but you ain't so tough. You don't know shit. I might have given those boys a rough time, but I wouldn't have killed them over grease. Chance of a murder rap isn't worth it. Not over two queers with a video of my boys stealing some grease."

"Big Man was on that video," I said. "You tryin' to act like you don't know him? And as for not killing, he was certainly in a killing mood the other night."

"I know him," King Arthur said, putting a fresh cigarette in his mouth. He turned to the buffalo beside him. "Dick Head, give me a light." The same big man who had lit his cigarette before produced the lighter again and lit this one. King Arthur took a puff. "But he doesn't work for me anymore. He went off on his own. As for those two guys you say were killed, I don't know them. And that can get you in trouble, boys, authorities found out about it."

"Go on and tell 'em," Jim Bob said.

King Arthur shook his head. "Naw. I don't give shit. They ain't none of mine. Let me tell you goober-doodles something. This grease business, so I got caught with my shorts down and my dick in a pig. It don't matter. It's profitable enough if I get caught and pay some fines, I can go back and start doing it a week later. I was even willin' to pay off the queers, even if they were a little greedy. I always kinda like to see a cop go bad. It justifies my belief in human nature, and that Horse, he was a real loser. The other faggot, I think he might have been the brains behind things. I don't know. I don't give a shit. They turned up dead and that didn't hurt my feelin's any. And yeah, I know who you three are. I got my contacts. You been nosin' around a lot. I know the nigger here is a dick sucker and a pervert too."

"Ixnay on the iggernay and the ervertpay," I said.

"Yeah," Leonard said, "I don't like it."

"Yeah," King Arthur said, "well, sorry. But you dick-licks are barkin' up the wrong tree. You got the video, I'll slip you some serious bucks to have it back, way I was doin' the queer boys, but to tell the truth, I don't get it back, I don't care. It don't matter to me. I'll deal with the consequences as they come along. I done played the game all I'm gonna play it."

"Thing is," Jim Bob said, "it ain't the grease we're talkin' about."

For the first time since he had crawled out of the Lincoln, I saw a look of puzzlement on King's face, or maybe it was concern, or perhaps a bowl of his chili had just backed up on him.

"Then what in hell is this all about?" King Arthur said.

"Another video," Leonard said.

228

"Of what?" King Arthur said. "You got two videos of my men stealing grease, it's no worse than one in my book. Look here, I do a little illegal business here and there, just to keep me in clean panties and corsages, but so what?"

"What about videos of LaBorde Park?" I asked.

"Say what?" King Arthur asked.

"What about a coded notebook with alphabetically hidden phone numbers of video stores?" I asked.

King Arthur blinked. "I don't know what the fuck you boys been drinkin', but it's fucked up what brains you might have. I don't know nothin' about no other videos or notebooks or video stores. That's what Bissinggame was sayin' y'all said. I figured he'd misunderstood you."

"What about a notebook from your plant?" I asked. "A King Arthur notebook?"

"Those things are everywhere," King said. "Listen here, boys. I got to get this car out of the ditch." King turned to the man beside him. "Get me the phone?"

Just as the man started to move, Jim Bob said, "Let's hold the phone."

The big man looked at King. King nodded. King said, "You got something to say, say it clear, or get on with it. Shoot us or let me get this car out of the ditch. I got a full day ahead of me. What's it gonna be?"

"All right," I said. "Get the phone. But before I go, King, let me come back to what I said in the first place. Stay away from me and my friends."

"Gladly," King said.

The big man got the phone out of the car and gave it to King. King started to dial as if we weren't there.

Jim Bob said, "You boys take it easy till we're gone. Just leave your guns on the ground."

We went up the hill backwards, our guns pointing at them. Jim Bob eased the truck back onto Old Pine Road.

As we cruised along, I said, "Well, we sure scared him."

"Yeah," Jim Bob said. "King was so nervous, he'd had a cot and a pillow, he might have taken him a little nap."

# 25

We went to Leonard's house, called the cop shop and asked for Charlie. He was out, but the dispatcher promised to shoot a message to him. Five minutes later, he called back and I answered.

"What's up?" he asked.

"We need to see you," I said. "Me, Leonard, and Jim Bob."

"All right. I'll be there pretty pronto-like."

"You don't sound as cheery as you're tryin' to sound," I said.

"Actually, I'm having a bittersweet day. But for the moment, I'd rather not talk about it. I'll tell you the sweet part when I get over there, though."

"What about the bitter?" I asked.

"I don't know yet," he said. "See you."

\*   \*   \*

We were sitting on Leonard's front porch in the swing seat when Charlie drove up. It was a sticky day with the sun bright as God's eyes and the sky a milky blue. The air smelled of mowed yards and perspiration. The scent of gun oil was still on my hands.

Charlie got out of his car and lumbered up the walk toward the porch. He didn't look good. Tired. Hair uncombed. No porkpie hat. His clothes were wrinkled and shiny-looking, as if he hadn't changed them in days. He smiled weakly, shook hands with all of us. He and Jim Bob exchanged some greetings.

Charlie sat down on the edge of the porch, got out a cigarette and lit it. He took a deep drag that turned about a quarter of the cigarette to ash. He held the smoke, and then let it out slowly through his nose and sighed as if he had just laid down for a good long nap.

"What you boys got?" he asked.

"We ain't sure," Jim Bob said. Then he told Charlie what had gone on, including running King off the road and us pulling guns on him. He left out Big Man Mountain and the two thugs he'd shot to death. He ended with: "King call in any charges?"

"Not that I know of," Charlie said. "But this running people off the road, it ain't good, pardner."

"I didn't think he'd call in," Jim Bob said.

"King could still be innocent," I said.

"I think we got our man," Jim Bob said. "What's the odds of two tapes and a notebook with King Arthur Chili on it being unrelated?"

"I don't know," I said. "King seemed pretty confident to me. He wasn't worried about the grease business, and he actually looked surprised when we brought up the other video, the notebook."

"I've seen some good liars," Leonard said.

"I damn near don't see nothing but liars," Charlie said. "Got so I think everyone's a liar. I find someone who isn't, I stick to them. I wasn't that way, all three of you goons would be under the jailhouse already."

"Any thoughts on any of this?" I asked Charlie.

"I don't know," Charlie said. "King has been in some shit, though most of it slides off of him, but murder . . . I wouldn't put it past him, but so far he's avoided that little bugaboo. He's got him a bunch of little rackets, but he gets caught, he usually squirms out of it. And he's got money. And lawyers. And he's got the chief, who I'm sure gets a pretty good chunk of pocket change from King himself." Charlie paused and smiled. "Thinking of the chief makes me think of Hanson. And my good news."

"You ain't gonna say what I think you are, are you?" Leonard said.

Charlie nodded. "Yeah. He came out of the coma."

"I'll be goddamn," I said.

"I talked to his wife," Charlie said. "She said the doctors think he's okay, just addled. He'll be down awhile, have to have some physical therapy later, but they say he seems all right. Confused some."

"I would be," I said. "Last thing he remembers is sliding into a tree, then he wakes up at his ex-wife's house with tubes in him. That would be disconcerting. You seen him yet?"

"Not yet," Charlie said. "I got to give it some time. They're holding back visitin', 'cept for the immediate family."

"Far as I'm concerned," Leonard said, "you are part of the immediate family."

"Well," Charlie said, "the immediate family doesn't see it that way. I don't think they like cops much. That's the whole beef between him and his wife. 'Course, now that I think about it, I don't like cops much either."

"I don't know Hanson well," Jim Bob said. "Met him a couple of times on business-related affairs here, mostly heard about his reputation. He used to be on the cop force in Houston a few years back. He busted a big case or two there. That's all I know, but what I do know of him, he seems like a good man."

"Good as they get," Charlie said.

"He's going to be all right?" I said. "I mean, really all right?"

"You mean in the head?" Charlie said.

"Yeah," I said.

"They think so."

"Well, I'll be goddamn," I said. "I figured he was ruined for life."

"You can't underestimate that fella," Charlie said. "He always comes back. And tougher than he was before. Now, what is it you want from me?"

"I think we got our answer when King didn't call in," Jim Bob said.

"King doesn't want trouble for the grease racket, doesn't want to direct attention to himself, but that doesn't mean he's in on this gay-bashin' video business," I said. "He could be tellin' the truth."

"King Arthur don't know from truth," Charlie said. "He used to be a used-car salesman."

"Well," Leonard said, "there's a strike against him."

"Amen," Jim Bob said.

"And he did some bible-thumpin' too," Charlie said.

"Way I remember it," Jim Bob said, "bible-thumpin' is like an automatic two strikes."

"With an extra penalty," Leonard said.

"Looks to me like there isn't anything I can add here," Charlie said. "I can harass King if you want to give me the videotape on the grease stealin'. He might readily cop to that part. We could maybe nail him on that."

"I like the idea of puttin' him in for the worst of it," Leonard said.

Jim Bob nodded. "Me too."

I nodded as well. "Can you give us a little more space?"

"Hell," Charlie said. "I haven't give you dudes anything but space. But, yeah. A little. Y'all got a beer?"

"Aren't you on duty?" I said.

"Yeah," Charlie said, "but I'll take my badge off and close my eyes while I drink."

"That'll work," Leonard said. "Let's go inside."


Charlie actually had three beers and kept going out on the front porch to smoke cigarettes. On his last trip to the porch I joined him, said, "Tell me the bitter."

He looked off at the heavens, which had changed. The sun had fallen behind some darkening clouds and the sky itself had lost its milky blue look and had clabbered. Everything was still.

"Tornado weather," Charlie said.

"The bitter?" I said.

Charlie took a deep drag on his smoke, said, "All right. You know, all this stuff 'tween me and Amy about cigarettes? The sex?"

"Sure."

"It ain't the cigarettes."

"What is it?"

"She just don't want to make love to me. She's foolin' around."

"You got proof, or you feeling paranoid?"

"Proof."

"I'm sorry," I said.

"Yeah. Me too."

"You're absolutely sure?"

"Yep."

"What you going to do?"

"I don't know yet. Somethin'."

"Nothing stupid, I hope?"

"You mean like shoot them?"

"Like that, yeah."

"Naw, that ain't my speed, bud. I might even could forgive her, you know."

"You confronted her?"

"Not yet . . . Hap, I got to tell you, this whole cop business—I've about had it."

"That's the beer talkin'," I said.

"Naw, it ain't the beer," Charlie said. "It's me. Listen, you guys told me about King Arthur, but there's stuff you haven't told me. I'd do that now."

I gave him the short version of Big Man Mountain and the ball-stimulator incident.

"You tellin' me Jim Bob killed those two bastards right out?" Charlie said.

"Looked dead to me."

"Guess I gotta find some reason to check that cabin out."

"He was just tryin' to protect me, Charlie. He burst in there like he did to keep me from going the way Raul went. He didn't have a choice but to shoot them."

"He came there to shoot 'em, Hap, you know that. That 'lectricity, it make your pecker stand out?"

"I tell you about how my life was threatened, I nearly died, and you want to know that?"

"Well, yeah."

"I think it made it curl up," I said. "Actually, I wasn't thinking about which direction it was going. It hurt too bad. What do you know about Big Man?"

"He's had him some arrests," Charlie said. "Quit wrestlin'—rather, they threw him out—a while ago. He's been in some shitty business. He worked for King a while. Word is they split early. Big Man didn't like takin' orders way King gave 'em. It wasn't a conflict in morals, it was two assholes bumpin' together and not likin' it. Story on Big Man is he starts a job, he finishes it. But when he finished for King last time, he didn't sign on again. Who knows, maybe he's had a change of heart. Or a need for money."

"So you really don't know if he's working for King?"

"Not last time I heard," Charlie said, lighting a cigarette. "But things change, man. Look at Hanson. Christ, my marriage."

"You know the guy?"

"Yeah, and I hate to say it. It's so goddamn insultin'. It's our goddamn insurance agent. Anybody would fuck an insurance agent, they got to be low. Sonofabitch don't buy at Kmart or Wal-Mart. Them suits he wears, they're tailor-made. Got him a razor cut. And you know what?"

"What?"

"Motherfucker smokes. And he's gettin' her pussy, and he smokes. Fuckin' cigars, no less. Now ain't that some shit?"

I smiled, and Charlie tried to smile, but it wasn't working.

"Tornado weather," Charlie said.

"You said that."

"Warnings are out. Been out all day. Things scare me to death. Can't stand the thought of them. You think I ought to let Amy go?"

"You're asking me about women?" I said. "You got to be desperate."

"You're right," Charlie said. "I forgot, you're like a number-one fuck-up in that department."

"Things are kind of better, now," I said. I told him about Brett, and about how Big Man had threatened her, what we were doin' about it.

"You could be fixin' yourself up for worse business," Charlie said.

"You going to put a twenty-four-hour guard on her house for me?" I asked.

"You know I can't," Charlie said. "More I pay attention to you guys, even tryin' to help, just makes it worse. Past business has made it so the chief would just as soon throw you boys to the dogs."

"Brett isn't part of that."

"I know. But the chief isn't going to let me put a twenty-four-hour guard on anybody. I do, I got to tell him why. Then I got to tell him Jim Bob blew two guys away, and that connects to you and Leonard. Fact is, I ought to do something about Jim Bob zeroin' them guys, but it just ain't in me, man. I don't give a shit. The one with the pock face, I know who he is. He's done everything from robbery to murder to fuckin' little girls. One of them his own eleven-year-old daughter. If you can call givin' sperm to an egg makin' you a father. Hard for me to lose much sleep on that sonofabitch it's him. It ain't him, it's one just like him. I don't know the black guy, but I figure he's a member of the same platoon. I got some off-duty time comin' up, though. I can help you watch your girlfriend then. Next week, all week."

"Charlie, I was you, I'd use that time to talk to my wife. I don't know much, but could be she's not getting what she wants at home, and I'm not talkin' about sex."

"Could be lots of things, Hap. And I don't know what any of them are. I think maybe I got to confront her. She's in love with this guy, not me, then she ought to go on. I want her to go on. But it has to do with me, I ain't doin' somethin' just right and can start doin' it way she needs, we might can work stuff out."

"I certainly hope so," I said.

" 'Course, she could just be an asshole."

"There is that."

Leonard came out on the porch. "What you guys doin'? Come back in. Have a beer."

"No, thanks," Charlie said. "Got to go. Good luck to both you fellas. And be careful, I'd hate to have to arrest you."

When Charlie was gone, Jim Bob came out on the porch to join us. He sat down on the swing and started moving it with his foot. He said, "Way I see it, boys, we're kind of at an impasse."

"How's that?" Leonard said.

"I think this chili fuck is responsible for the beating my client took. This connects with them other two gettin' killed, Horse and Raul, but that isn't strictly my business, though I'm willin' to make it my business. But, Hap, you don't feel confident chili dude's the man. Leonard, you think it's him, but I can see you fadin' a bit."

"Fadin'?" Leonard said.

"You got your doubts," Jim Bob said, "or rather you know Hap's got his and you're runnin' on his track."

"I think for myself," Leonard said.

"I never doubted that," Jim Bob said, "but you think a way fits in with how Hap feels. He's the same with you. I can respect that. It's stupid. But I can respect it."

"This leading up to something?" Leonard asked.

"Yeah, it's leading up to me goin' back to the hotel, takin' a bath, jerkin' off, watchin' a little TV, a good night's sleep, and tomorrow I'm back down to business. I'm gonna stay on chili man's ass until I get what I'm lookin' for."

"And if it isn't him?" I asked.

"It's him, all right," Jim Bob said. He stood up, set the beer bottle on the porch railing, went down to his car and drove away.

# 26

I lay in a tub of warm soapy water with my arm around Brett. She lay with her head against my shoulder. We had been lying like that for some time. Enough that the water was starting to cool.

Outside I could hear rain beating on the roof of the house. In the living room I knew Leonard, Clinton, and Leon were watching television, probably thinking about what we were doing in the bedroom, thinking all sorts of wild things, and of course, they were right.

We had bucked like colts, squirmed like snakes, rolled like seals, and done some cheap, disgusting things that had made us happy.

After a while the water cooled and so did we. We got out of the tub, dried each other, lay on the bed, kissed and fondled, and one thing led to another and we were at it again. Afterwards, we lay there in each other's arms and talked. I said, "I'm beginning to feel guilty. You and me in here having fun, and the boys having to watch television."

"Shit," Brett said. "There's this special on poisonous toad frogs in the Amazon tonight. How in hell could they be envious of us, knowin' that's comin' on?"

"You know, you're right."

"They finish that, we're still busy, they can switch over and watch the life of that shit O.J. Simpson on *Biography*. Sounds to me they got a pretty full evenin'."

"You're right again."

" 'Course, I have to go to work, so it doesn't matter much. We got to quit fuckin' sometime. 'Course, I'm not tryin' to say it has to be right now. You want to see you can lower the bald man into the canyon one more time?"

"Absolutely," I said.

We tried to make love again, but this time we weren't as successful. Oh, all right—I wasn't as successful. The bald man was tuckered out. We laughed about it, kissed, got dressed, went into the living room.

Leon was asleep on the couch. Clinton was lying on a pallet, his head propped up on pillows. Leonard was sitting on a chair drinking a Coca-Cola. They were watching an old detective show.

"Lazy, rainy day," I said.

"Man, ya'll must have been playin' Monopoly," Leonard said. "Long as y'all were in there, you had to be."

"Monopoly?" Clinton said. "I like that game. We could play to pass time."

"I was kidding," Leonard said.

"I do have a Monopoly game," Brett said. She went to the closet and dragged it out.

"I don't know," I said. "You get to playin' that, you might could get distracted too easy."

"Naw," Leonard said. "It's okay. It's not that engrossing."

I went to the window, pushed back the curtain, and looked out. It was rainy and dark and the day was dying on top of it. I could see lightning shimmering against distant clouds.

Soon Brett would be heading to work, Leon and his .45 with her. Me, I had a late job interview at the LaBorde Fowl Processing Plant for a night watchman job. My application had yielded some interest in the way of a postcard. I had called and a night foreman named George Waggoner had set up an interview.

I turned to Leonard. "What are your plans, Leonard?"

"Me and Clinton gonna play a little Monopoly, I think. Then I'll go pick up some grub. I might stay the night, Brett don't mind."

" 'Course not," Brett said. "It's good to know you'll be here when I come home."

"In the mornin' I'm supposed to meet Jim Bob at my place, and so are you, Hap."

"What for?"

"I called him earlier, see if he'd had any luck."

"Well?" I said.

"He said he had some things comin' together, he'd know better tomorrow, so we're gonna meet in the morning. Nine o'clock, my place."

"Good enough," I said.

"You fellas think this wrestler really means to hurt me?" Brett asked.

"I don't think so," I said. "I'm just being cautious. For a while."

"How long?" Brett said.

"I don't know."

"And you really haven't any idea if he means to hurt me or not, do you?"

"No."

"You can count on one thing, though," Leonard said. "It ain't gonna happen. He ain't gonna hurt nobody."

Brett smiled at him. "Thanks."

Leonard nodded.

Brett looked at me. "You got that interview."

"I know," I said. "I'm about to leave. . . . Didn't you tell me to remind you to call Ella?"

"That's right," Brett said. "I thought I'd check on her. She called yesterday. She's made up her mind to leave that thug Kevin."

"I'm glad," I said.

"Me too," Brett said. "I'm going to call, try and give her the moral support. 'Course, if he's there, that won't be easy. He sleeps a lot, though."

"He work?"

"Some kind of shift where he's on a few days, off a few days. He's off right now."

I gave Brett a kiss, told everyone so long, drove to the chicken-processing plant to check on the night watchman's job.

"This is a costly operation," Waggoner said.

"Yes, sir," I said. "I understand."

"There's all manner of expensive equipment here. We even have the occasional business spies. People trying to sneak in here and get our secrets. That's going to get worse, Collins."

"You've actually had spies?" I asked.

"Couple of niggers hired by our competition, and I won't even show the company the respect of saying their name."

"What did these spies do?"

"They took photographs of our equipment."

"No shit."

"And of our chickens."

"Doesn't one chicken look like another?"

"Not when they're raised the way we raise them. We slap the juice to them, Collins. We got the biggest, fattest chickens you ever seen. Big fat juicy drumsticks. That's 'cause they don't walk on 'em. Can't. Our chickens can't walk. We've bred them that way."

"Hope you haven't just given me one of your secrets."

"No. That one's out. Darn animal-rights people been all over our rear ends about that one. Let me tell you, Collins, we're the envy of every chicken-processing plant in East Texas. Possibly Oklahoma and Louisiana as well. You can even throw in Arkansas if you want."

"Why not," I said.

"What's that?"

"I said why not throw in Arkansas."

"Is that some kind of remark, Mr. Collins?"

"You said we could throw in Arkansas. I'm saying it's okay with me."

Shit, I thought, don't do it to yourself, Hap. Waggoner is an officious, fat, rednecked prick in an expensive suit with a tie that doesn't match, but hold back, baby. You need the work.

Waggoner studied me to see if I was being humorous. I could tell this was a guy didn't like humorous. He saw humorous, he'd shoot it and fuck it in the ass and bury it in the chicken shit at the plant. That's how he felt about humorous.

"We need a man who is willin' to put his life on the line, if need be," Waggoner said.

"For chickens?" I said.

"For the business, Mr. Collins. And yes, chickens. We take this business very serious, and I need a man who is serious."

"I think I can be serious about chickens," I said.

"No thinking to it, you are or you aren't."

"I can do the job, Mr. Waggoner. I can keep people out. I can patrol the area. And I don't think there's really that big a threat to the chickens or your industry from industrial spies, but I see one of those sonofabitches, I'll be on him like stink on shit."

"I'd prefer you not use that language, Mr. Collins."

"All right," I said.

"I'm a churchgoing man myself."

"Which church?"

"Methodist."

"Dancing Baptist."

"What's that?"

"That's what they call Methodist. Dancing Baptist. You know, they're allowed to dance. Baptist aren't supposed to. Sometimes, they call Methodist Baptist that can read."

"I'm not sure I care for that sort of thing, Mr. Collins."

"It's a joke, Mr. Waggoner. I'm a little nervous. I'm tryin' to warm us up."

"Well, you're not. I don't care for humor in job interviews."

"Sure you're not a Baptist?"

"What?"

"Never mind."

"You know, we got some other jobs here might be better for you. Chicken reproduction, for one."

"Come again."

"Chicken reproduction. We need people to help us stud chickens."

"I'm not sure I like the sound of that. How would I stud a chicken?"

"I think you're tryin' to be humorous again, Mr. Collins."

"I don't think so."

"Obviously, you would be required to stimulate the roosters and preserve their sperm."

"You're kiddin'?"

"I am not."

"You're sayin' you'd want me to jack a rooster off into a test tube?"

"Something like that."

"You really do that?"

"Have you heard of such a thing for bulls? Horses?"

"Well, yeah. That's bad enough, but you want to offer me a job jacking off chickens? You got to be out of your mind, man."

"People do it."

"Not me. I came to see about a night watchman job."

Waggoner took my application, opened a drawer, and slipped it inside. "I believe that'll be all the questions I need to ask, Mr. Collins. Something comes up, you fit the qualifications, I'll give you a call."

"You're not going to call me, are you?"

"No."

"I didn't think so. That being the case, let me tell you something. I think your fuckin' chickens are second-rate.

I wouldn't wipe my ass on your chickens, let alone jack one of the sonofabitches off."

"Good night, Mr. Collins."

I drove home, sat around in my kitchen with a glass of milk and a Moon Pie, nibbled at it, felt blue. I couldn't even get a job at the goddamn chicken plant being a night watchman. All they had for me was a position jerking a rooster's dick. It didn't get much worse than that.

I looked through my old record albums, my audiotapes, and the handful of CDs I owned. 'Course, I didn't own a CD player, so I just sort of pretended I could play those if I wanted to.

Finally I found a tape Leonard had given me. It was Junior Brown. Junior Brown played an instrument of his own devising, a cross between a guitar and steel. He sounded like Ernest Tubb singing to music played by Chet Atkins, Jimi Hendrix, and a honkie-tonk drunk.

I listened to that a while. Took a shower. Went to bed. Looked at the ceiling. Squirmed in the covers. Listened to the rain outside. I kept checking my .38 on the nightstand.

I tried to figure if Jim Bob was right, and this King Arthur was the mastermind. He seemed the most logical, but Big Man hadn't said he was behind it. He hadn't asked for videos. He had asked for *a* video and the book.

I churned all of this around for a while, got up, turned on the box fan, put a chair under the back doorknob to reinforce the lock. I put a chair under the front doorknob. I checked all the windows to make sure they were locked. I wanted them open to let in the cool, wet wind, but I was afraid. I kept visualizing Big Man Mountain slipping through one of the windows, that goddamn battery and crank generator under his arm.

I wished I had a vicious dog. I wished I was at Brett's place, in bed with her, holding her close. I wished I'd win the lottery. I sort of wished I'd gotten the job at the chicken plant, even if I had to jack off roosters. I wished I was a thousand miles away.

I felt as if I had just closed my eyes, then morning light was in my face and I got up.

It was early yet. Brett was not off work. I decided to dress and drive over to the hospital, catch her as she came out, see if she wanted to go somewhere for breakfast.

The day had cleared, the air was almost sparkly, and the birds were out in force, singing various operas. The streets were shiny-slick with water and there were few cars moving about.

As I drove off the highway and into the parking lot, I saw a cop car. There were medical personnel rushing about. My stomach sank. I parked and leaped out. I started walking very fast toward the sirens, the lights, the commotion. Another cop car whipped into the lot and whirled over there. People were coming out of the hospital, across the way, from houses nearby.

I walked even faster, but now a crowd had sprung up, most of them from the hospital staff. I grabbed a guy by the elbow.

"What happened?"

"I don't know," he said.

Another man standing next to him said, "Some guy shotgunned some people in a car. Big guy. He shotgunned them. I talked to a guy saw it happen. The cops got the guy saw it over there, talking to him."

I pushed through the crowd, got cussed, kept pushing. I made my way to the forefront. I could see Brett's car. The windshield was blown away. There was glass all over the place. They were lifting a man onto a stretcher. Even from a distance, I could see it was Leon. Big bad Leon. Minus the top of his head.

Oh, Jesus.

They covered him quickly.

On the driver's side of the car they were lifting someone else out. A woman in a nurse's uniform. Suddenly I was right there. Looking down on a woman's body. Her entire face was gone. Hell, her head was practically vaporized.

Shotgunned.

Both of them shotgunned.

I put my hand against a car and held myself up. A cop grabbed my elbow. "Hap," he said.

I turned. It was Jake, a cop I knew a little. "Did you get the guy did it?" I asked.

Jake shook his head. "No, we got a pretty good description, but we didn't get him. We will. You all right, man?"

"Yeah."

"Jesus, Hap. You know these people?"

"Yeah. I got to go."

"You're all right?"

I ignored him.

"I might need to talk to you," he yelled after me.

I shoved through the crowd and back to my car. I started it up. I drove away from there, nearly ran a half dozen people off the road. I drove over to Leonard's. He wasn't there. He'd be at Brett's, waiting for her to come home. Waiting for me to stop by.

I used my key and got the door open. I went to Leonard's closet, pulled his twelve-gauge out of there. I got the box of shells off the top shelf. My hands trembled as I pushed them into the loading chamber and put a handful in my front pants pocket.

I had been sleeping while Brett was murdered in the hospital parking lot. Sweet, beautiful, foul-mouthed Brett.

Brett and Leon.

I had been sleeping.

I had been stupid.

How could I think having a watch on her would matter? Not even Leon could handle Big Man Mountain. I could see it now. Mountain had merely waited until Brett got off work; then, as a punishment to me, he had shot her to death. Leon would have tried to stop him, but it didn't matter. Big Man had shot them both, fast as he could pump a shotgun.

Leonard and Jim Bob had been right. I should have gone savage. I should have gone wild. Had I done that in the first place, gotten rid of Big Man Mountain's employers, Brett and Leon would still be alive.

I was climbing in my truck with the shotgun when Jim Bob pulled into the drive. That's right. Nine o'clock, me and him and Leonard were supposed to meet. I'd have to take a rain check.

"Hey, Hap, where you goin'?" Jim Bob yelled.

I didn't answer. I backed out, drove very fast along the street toward the main highway, and when I reached it I drove even faster, toward King Arthur's place.

# 27

The world grew smaller as I drove, the exterior of the truck becoming nonexistent. I didn't remember the road at all. Just the world growing smaller, smaller, until it was nothing more than the cab of that truck, then my space on the seat, then the inside of my head. I drove with one hand on the wheel, the other on the shotgun stock, touching it as tenderly as a lonely man might touch his privates in the dark.

Thinking and wondering, how come the horrors happen to me and those I care about? What the hell have I done? Who's throwing the dice?

Well, this one time, I was going to throw the dice. I was going to throw them right down King Arthur's throat.

The driveway to King Arthur's trailers was blocked by a metal gate. I got out of the truck with the shotgun, climbed over the gate, and started walking briskly toward the trailers.

As I neared the trailers, a huge rottweiler appeared. It barked at me once, started to run toward me in that menacing manner dogs have. I lifted the shotgun, shot it in the head. It did a flip, splattered and slid on the red clay and lay there, one back leg flexing.

"Sorry," I said. "Nothing personal."

I walked faster, and now I was at the front of the closest trailer's door. One of the goons who had been in King's car that day jerked open the door, a nine in his hand. I was close, real close. I swung the shotgun stock up and connected with his chin. He straightened up and went backwards and lay on the floor, showing all the enthusiasm of a bearskin rug. I climbed over him, picked up the nine, tossed it backwards out the open door behind me.

I came along the hall, striding fast, and another one of the guards presented himself. I lifted the shotgun. He leaped aside as I fired and the blast took out a chunk of the trailer's back wall. I heard him making a rustling, scuttling noise somewhere out of sight, then I heard the back door open and slam, and I knew that big bad motherfucker wasn't so bad after all, that he was running fast now, and if nothing got in his way, he ought to make the edge of the goddamn Atlantic Ocean by midnight.

"King!" I yelled. "King!"

I picked a door to my left, blasted it with the shotgun. It flew open, and I was inside, and there was King, lying in bed, Bissinggame beside him. They sat up quickly. Both were nude. Bissinggame had a peach-colored leisure suit draped over a chair. On the chair were jockey shorts, peach socks, and white shoes.

King had his hat on the nightstand beside him and he had his hand in the nightstand drawer, reaching for something.

"I thought you hated queers," I said.

I shot the nightstand. It exploded. A lamp crashed. A .45 that had been in a drawer, before it became kindling, clattered to the floor. King jerked back a bleeding handful of wood splinters.

"Goddamn," he said.

"I just been to the hospital," I said. "My girlfriend. And a friend of mine. They've been shotgunned to death by your man, Big Man Mountain."

"He's not my man," King said, and he was as calm as a man about to order lunch in a restaurant.

"Jesus!" Bissinggame said. "I'm not queer. I'm churchgoing. He makes me do this."

"Big Man is your man," I said. "He's always been your man. I can't believe I listened to you. I want you to know, you sorry cocksucking asslicking piece of pig shit, what I'm gonna do. I'm gonna blow your ass away. Bissinggame, you want out of here, go now!"

Bissinggame slid out from under the covers, reached for his underwear on the chair.

"Go naked, or die naked," I said.

"I'm gone," Bissinggame said, and he came around the edge of the bed. Then I saw his eyes go wide, and I knew someone was behind me, but I didn't care. It didn't matter to me. Nothing mattered to me but that King would die. I jerked the shotgun to my shoulder and pulled the trigger.

I shot a big chunk of ceiling to pieces, and the pieces fluttered down all over the room. I wasn't sure how that happened, until I realized there was a black hand on the

254

barrel of the shotgun. I turned to fight, but the hand was Leonard's, and he pushed me and pulled the shotgun away from me and flung it in a corner.

Leonard pulled an automatic out from under his shirt and held it casually. "It ain't your style, brother," he said. "You ain't the one for it. Hell, you know that. I know that. Besides, you'll be doin' it for the wrong reasons and you'll feel bad about it in the morning."

"But I'll feel good now," I said.

There was a commotion in the hallway, a yell, a bunch of grunts, then a falling sound. Jim Bob came in holding his blackjack. He looked at me. "You gonna take a place, you got to secure it, Bub. There was another one in the house. Now there's two on the floor. Motherfucker tried some Tae Kwon Do kicks on me, only he ain't so good. Tae Kwon Do ain't so good no more. Fact is, it ain't been Tae Kwon Do for twenty years. It's been that tournament shit."

"Third man passed us in the yard, running," Leonard said. "I suppose you made a face at him, Hap."

I didn't answer. Leonard turned his attention to Bissinggame. "Goddamn, Bissinggame, you call that a dick? Put somethin' over that thing 'fore it makes me sick. Looks like a little old grub worm with pecans tied to its tail. Hell, get back in bed."

"He makes me do this," Bissinggame said. "He pays me a lot of money, so he makes me do this."

"Shut up," Leonard said. "You got a shit ring on your dick. Get back in bed."

Bissinggame got back in bed, pulled the covers over his hips. King sat up in bed. He didn't look any different than when I came in. Found nude with a man. A shotgun pointed at him. His car ran off the road. A bowl of chili. Everything was the same to him. He leaned over the side of the bed, picked up a pack of cigarettes and a lighter with his splinter-filled hand. He got out a cigarette, lit it and puffed it. Blood dripped off his hand onto his chest and onto the sheets. He said, "Now what? So you know I'm a lyin' sonofabitch. I fuck men. I fuck women. I'd fuck my goddamn dog, but I figure you killed it."

"I regret the dog," I said.

King grunted. "Bissinggame here, shit, he's a Baptist church deacon. Ever fuck a deacon, nigger?"

"Can't say that I have," Leonard said.

"Well, they give a whole new meaning to the word *tight-ass*," King said and laughed.

"King had Brett and Leon killed," I said. "Let me have the shotgun back, Leonard. I just want to do what you and Jim Bob wanted to do in the first place."

Leonard looked at me. "You go on outside," Leonard said. He went over and picked the shotgun up where it lay against the wall.

"You kill him instead of me, it ain't the same," I said.

"It's not your way, and you know it," Leonard said. "Go outside."

"You're wrong," I said. "I can kill him. I want to kill him. Let me have the shotgun."

I lunged for Leonard and the shotgun, but Jim Bob stepped in and hit me across the back of the hand with the blackjack. I went to my knees for a moment, eased slowly to my feet. The pain passed quickly.

Jim Bob grabbed my shirt collar, said, "Come with me, or the next one's upside your ear."

"He's going to kill him. I want to do it," I said.

Jim Bob jerked me around and I rabbit-shot him one in the ribs. Jim Bob bent. Leonard flicked out his left hand, caught me on the back of the head, and down I went.

Then Jim Bob twisted my wrist into a lock, used it as come-along, took me out of there.

Behind me I heard King say, "You gonna shoot, nigger, get it over with, otherwise I'm gonna get up and take a shower. Throw a little alcohol on this hand."

Out in the yard Jim Bob said, "You gotta calm down, Hap. You got to listen."

A shotgun blast went off inside the trailer.

"Jesus!" I said. "Fuck that sonofabitch!"

A moment later Leonard appeared in the doorway holding Bissinggame's leisure suit. He came down to where we were standing.

"You shouldn't have done it," I said.

"Oh, I don't intend to wear it," Leonard said.

"I don't mean the leisure suit, you idiot," I said. "You shouldn't have killed King. Now it's your neck. I wanted to take him out. I didn't care what happened to me. I wanted to see that smug sonofabitch's head go to pieces. I didn't want you in on this shit."

"I know," Leonard said. "But I didn't shoot anybody. I just shot another hole in the ceiling."

I stared at him. Leonard took one of my arms, Jim Bob the other. "For Christ sakes, you're letting him off scot-free," I said.

"He didn't do anything," Jim Bob said.

"You said it was him," I said. "You said he was behind it all."

"I thought he was," Jim Bob said. "Guess what, I think I could be wrong. And let me tell you, Hap. This bein' wrong—I find it disturbing. It ain't somethin' I'm used to."

# 28

Jim Bob drove my pickup with me on the passenger side. He parked it behind the fireworks stand not far from King's place. Leonard picked us up in his rental, took us back for Jim Bob's car.

I rode with Leonard as Jim Bob followed. We drove east, way out to a roadside park, pulled over. Jim Bob pulled in behind us. We gathered at a concrete picnic table. There was a cool wind blowing, but you could feel warmth creeping into the breeze. Another half hour to an hour the air would be sticky as Velcro.

"You know, I'm going to kill King anyway," I said.

"If you do," Jim Bob said, "make it a lot less obvious."

"You've made it harder now," I said. "He'll be expecting me. He'll maybe even call the cops."

Jim Bob shook his head. "Naw. He may act cool, but he ain't anxious the word gets around he brown-rings. It don't go with his image. That's what King is. Image. I'll say this for him, though. He ain't excitable."

"How the hell did you two know where I was going?"

"We can come to that in a moment," Leonard said. "Listen here, Hap. Leon is dead, but Brett isn't."

"Horseshit!" I said. "What the fuck they going to do? Give her a new head, pump a little blood in her heart, prop her up with a stick? Believe me, you asshole, she's dead."

"No," Leonard said. "Leon and Ella are dead."

I sat silently for a moment. I was looking at a brick barbecue cooker. Someone had stuffed it with trash. A crow lit on it, pecked at something between the bricks.

"I don't understand," I said.

"We been tryin' to tell you for a time," Jim Bob said. "But you won't shut up."

"My God," I said. "Brett is okay?"

"Right as rain," Jim Bob said.

"After you left Brett's," Leonard said, "she called Ella. Ella wanted to swap shifts with her this week."

"Oh, God," I said. "I forgot."

Leonard said, "Brett called, Ella answered, said she'd call back. She did, about twenty minutes later. She was at her mother's. She'd walked out of the trailer while Kevin was sleepin', walked down to a fillin' station and called a taxi. She called Brett from her mom's. Seems Ella finally decided she was gonna leave her husband, but she had to go to work in a couple hours and she didn't have any more money after the taxi. Leon drove Brett's car over there to give Ella a ride to work. They got to the hospital—"

"Big Man was waiting and thought Ella was Brett," I said.

"Nope," Leonard said. "Big Man didn't shoot anybody. It was Kevin. He didn't want her leavin'. He was waiting on Ella. He recognized Brett's car, saw Ella driving. He had his shotgun. He walked over and shot her, killed Leon, who I figure was trying to protect her."

"You know it was Kevin?" I said.

"Uh-huh," Leonard said. "He drove over to Brett's house, stood out in the front yard with a shotgun and a pistol and yelled obscenities and said he'd killed the bitch, et cetera. Somehow, he blamed Brett. Least that's what we were gettin' from his rantings. Before any of us could do anything about it. Shoot him. Call the law. He put the revolver against his eye and took the A-train."

"I'll be goddamn," I said.

"You'd killed King," Jim Bob said, "you'd have killed him for something he didn't order done."

"Thing is, cops were on this Kevin asshole pronto," Leonard said. "Someone at the hospital knew who he was, seen him do the deed, and told the cops. They didn't have any trouble spottin' his car, following him over to Brett's. They got there before the gunsmoke from Kevin's pistol cleared. We were standin' out in the yard when they showed up. One of the cops said he saw you at the hospital. Said you took out of there like a bat out of hell. I had a pretty good idea where you were going. I left Clinton with Brett and went after you."

"And me," Jim Bob said. "I was on my way to Leonard's house to tell you boys some new business. That look in your eyes and the shotgun told me you weren't just goin' for breakfast, so I followed. Met Leonard in King's yard. Now I'm learning some of the details for the first time."

"Poor Leon," I said. "Poor, poor Ella."

"Poor Clinton," Leonard said. "Fact is, I don't want to

leave him with Brett long. He's a messed-up man. Something came up, well, he might not be up to his usual standards."

"Leon wasn't up to his," I said.

"They aren't pros," Leonard said. "They're just a couple schmucks like us. Jim Bob's the only pro here."

We sat for a few minutes, studied the cars zipping by on the highway. I turned to Jim Bob, said, "You said you thought you might be wrong about King Arthur?"

"Could be," Jim Bob said. "I got to thinking you might be right, that I ought to follow all the leads, not make a snap judgment. I checked out this other fella, other name this Pierre gave you. Bill Cunningham."

"We didn't tell you that," I said.

"I'll come to that," Jim Bob said. "Cunningham's a lawyer. Nothing obviously funny about him. Fact is, I think he's clean."

"I thought you said he was a lawyer," Leonard said.

"You're right," Jim Bob said. "I lost my head."

"So you don't know anything more than you did know?" I said.

"You know how I got on to King in the first place?" Jim Bob asked. "I come to town, I look around, I connect with this Raul in the park, follow him around, finally over to this hair spot, Antone's. Raul gets killed, I go in there and ask around, pretend to be a Texas Ranger. Pierre, guy with the cartoon skunk voice, gave me a couple names. Same names you guys got."

"So?" I said.

"I get to thinking, what if you're right and chili man is just a low-rent crook, not into all this. I check out this Bill Cunningham, and nothin'. I get to thinkin' what could be

JOE R. LANSDALE

the source. You know, tryin' to go back to where the river starts instead of just jumpin' in and swimmin'."

"I don't follow you," I said.

"The source for your information about King was Pierre. The source of my information about King was Pierre. That don't mean nothin' by itself, but why not check this Pierre out? So I watch this Antone's. Being the astute sonofabitch I am, I notice bikers from next door like to wander in there, but ain't none of them come out with haircuts or dye jobs."

"The biker connection?" Leonard said.

"Bikers would show up at the rec hall over there, hang out a while, then go to Antone's, in the back way, come out with little packages, get on their wheels and ride away. Interesting, huh?"

"Very," Leonard said.

"That's number one," Jim Bob said. "Number two is I call a cop friend in Houston, someone can give me the information but can stay out of our business. This Pierre, it took some time to run him down on the computer, but his real name is Terry Wesley, and guess what? He's got a rap sheet longer than the pope's robes. Lot of it is pimpin' young boys. In Houston he used to meet buses, catch the kids had run off from home. He'd befriend them, pull them into the service. Had them hangin' around the goddamn Greyhound station hustlin' goobers. Anyway, Pierre got busted for pimpin' more than a couple times. Word was, he specialized in providin' the rough trade. You know, guy comes in, wants to butt-fuck him a boy, likes to slap him around a bit. This way, fucker gets some ass, feels like a tough guy too. You'd be surprised how much of that shit goes on."

"Sad thing is," Leonard said, "I ain't much surprised at anything anymore."

"Got one more card to play," Jim Bob said. "I followed one of the bikers carried a package out the back of the hair joint. He took a little road trip to Dallas. I followed. He delivered the package to a video store in Dallas. Got a little package back. My guess, a video for the store owner, money for Pierre, and a nice cut for the biker. Pierre, he's got these bikers jettin' all over East Texas. It's an easy, cheap way to deliver the shit. And another thing, they can dub this crap forever."

"And there's always new films," Leonard said.

"That's right," Jim Bob said. "It's not like they got to have a Francis Ford Coppola behind the lens."

"Could King and Pierre be together on all this?" I asked.

"I thought about that," Jim Bob said. "It's possible. But I don't think so. I think Pierre gave us King's name pretty easy. They were partners, he'd have held out."

"What gets me is it's gays doin' it to gays," I said.

"Welcome once again to the real world," Leonard said.

"I suggest we have a little talk with Pierre," Jim Bob said. "Pretend to have taken Raul and Horse's place as blackmailers, make him push a move. Then we gift-wrap him for the cops."

We went in Jim Bob's car to Antone's. Pierre wasn't there.

"Well, where is he?" I asked the lady in charge.

She was a heavyset blond lady whose hair looked as if it had been the recipient of many an experiment, the most recent being an incredible rat job that revealed pink patches of skull. She was badly made up with too much powder and lipstick, false eyelashes thick enough and long enough to support a transport plane. She was out-going and windy as hell; had a mouth like a leaf blower. No doubt she had given phone death to many a listener.

She said, "Well, I don't rightly know where that little Frenchy is. He kind of comes and goes, you know. I'm in charge most of the time. Name's Delores. Pierre has other things goin' on I don't know much about. Quite the little entrepreneur. Sometimes he's here all week, sometimes you don't see him for a week. I ain't seen him for days. I open up, do hair, teach some of the students how to do hair, then I go home. You smell them peroxide fumes all day, you get so you can't wait to get out of here. I go home and drink lots of goat's milk. It's supposed to help get rid of all kinds of toxins in the body, or at least that's what my herbal medicine man tells me. He's this Mex'kin lives on the other side of the railroad tracks. Hear him tell it, there ain't a goddamn thing that goat milk can't cure. 'Course, at four dollars a gallon, that shit ought to make you younger, tighten up your love sack, and put your cherry back in it. You boys want to leave a message?"

"He comes back," Jim Bob said, "just tell Pierre three fellows came by to extort some money out of him, but not to worry, we'll be back."

"That's a hell of a message," she said.

"Ain't it?" Leonard said.

"He got a home address?" Jim Bob asked.

"I can look it up," Delores said. "You know, I been workin' for that little French twist for a full year now, and he ain't never invited me or anyone here over to his house."

"Maybe he hangs his underwear on the doors," Leonard said.

"I hadn't thought of that," Delores said. "One thing I

can do without is lookin' at stains in drawers. My husband was terrible about that. I figure he wiped his butt, it was an accident, or his shorts got sucked up his crack. Way I figure, when he died, the undertaker had to use a hose and a putty knife to get him clean."

"Soul mates, huh?" Jim Bob said.

"Hell, only thing that bastard had any soulful connection with was *Championship Bowlin'*, a beer, and a bag of taco chips, which is what I figure killed him. I'd have known that, I'd have kept a bigger supply around."

We followed her into Pierre's office. She got out the phone book, flipped it open, found his name. "There it is," she said.

When we were outside in the parking lot, I said, "Gee, Jim Bob, right in the phone book. You're quite the detective."

"Go fuck yourself," Jim Bob said.

# 29

Pierre's house was easy to find. We drove over there and parked at the curb and sat for a moment.

"Are we waiting for Pierre to come out to the curb?" Leonard said.

"No," Jim Bob said. "We're gonna go up there and intimidate him."

"Intimidation is good," Leonard said.

"We don't push in," Jim Bob said. "We don't go past the door. We just intimidate. We put him in a position where he wants our asses dead."

"He already wants our asses dead," Leonard said.

"What we're gonna do is let him know we're on to him," Jim Bob said. "We're gonna make him so nervous his shit will be nervous. Then we'll leave. Let him think a while, see if he makes a play."

"If he doesn't?" Leonard asked.

"We'll come back on him like ass rash in a few days," Jim Bob said. "We'll keep it up until he's got to scratch."

We walked up the drive. It was a nice drive. The lawn was well clipped. There was a sprinkler system going, which, considering we'd just had a lot of rain, seemed wasteful. The garage was locked up tight. The houses on either side were nice and well dressed. Suburbia, U.S.A.

We went to the door. Jim Bob rang the bell.

We waited.

Jim Bob rang the bell again.

"Maybe the bell doesn't work," Leonard said, and he knocked.

We waited some more.

"You boys stand here," Jim Bob said, and he slipped around the side of the house.

Leonard said, "Watch that sonofabitch move? He's like a ghost."

"You think he moves good going around the side of a house, you ought to see him blow up a car, kick down a door, shoot two thugs to death, and run Big Man Mountain into the woods. Then take me out the back door with him. He may actually have been eating dinner while he was doin' that."

Few moments later Jim Bob came back. He said, "Back door is opened. Been jimmied."

"Uh-oh," I said.

"Yeah," Jim Bob said. "Uh-oh."

"What now?" Leonard asked.

"Well," Jim Bob said, "ain't nobody seems to be lookin', and since we don't need a search warrant . . ."

The back door had that distinctive Big Man Mountain look. It appeared a crowbar had been inserted, and with a heave, the door had been snapped free of its lock. Even with a crowbar, that took some muscle.

Jim Bob kicked the door with the toe of his boot; it swung open, and we slipped inside. The air-conditioning unit was humming nicely. It felt good. Sunlight crept through the cracks of the living room curtains. Place looked like a magazine shoot. Expensive furniture, carpet, and paintings.

Jim Bob knelt, pulled up his pants legs. He reached inside his boot, took out a little leather zippered case. He unzipped it. There was everything in that case but a change of clothes.

Jim Bob removed a small wad of plastic from it. He replaced the case and unfolded the plastic. The plastic was several paper-thin gloves. He gave us each a pair. We put them on. He said, "Let's look around."

I took the kitchen. There were food dishes on the table, some kind of leftover Chinese was my guess, but I couldn't tell for certain. What was left of it was long spoiled, gone black and full of flies that had come in through the cracked back door. There were two smeary plates on the table, two wineglasses, a half bottle of red wine. Flies skated over the greasy plate and sat around on the mouth of the bottle, making small talk, I presumed.

Jim Bob opened a bedroom door, peeked in. "This is sweet."

Leonard and I took a look. The decor had gone from *Better Homes and Gardens* to Elvis on drugs. It was a big bedroom with a round bed and a mirrored ceiling. The covers, crushed red velvet, were in a wad. There was a huge television set and a VCR. A glass bedside table with books on it. The books were photographs of nude men.

On the walls were paintings of nude men making love to one another.

We slid into the room and Jim Bob went around the bed and stopped and said, "This, however, isn't so sweet."

Leonard and I took a look. Some guy I had never seen before lay there, tiger-striped underwear pulled down to his knees. His arms were bent at the elbows, his hands pushing palms up, as if he had ended up that way trying to fend someone off.

He was long and lean and might have been in his thirties. He smelled bad and his gut was swollen. The air conditioning had kept him in pretty good shape and the stink was surprisingly minimal. There was a small, but well-defined hole in his forehead. Not a designer move, this hole. It didn't go with the gold earring or the toupee that had blown off his noggin and onto the wall like a kitten tossed from a speeding car. A puddle of blood pooled under his head. I figured you rolled him over, you'd find an exit hole about the size of the national debt.

"I think we can safely declare that whoever this fucker is, he's dead," Jim Bob said.

"Any idea who he is?" I said.

"One of Pierre's boyfriends," Leonard said.

The bathroom door was partially open. I went over there and gave the door a shove. "Oh, shit," I said.

Flies rose up angrily, buzzed about, then found their footing again. Unlike the body on the bedroom floor, this job had taken some time. Pierre—I assumed it was Pierre from the general build and greasy hair—was naked, his knees on the floor in a pudding of dried blood. He was bent over and leaning into the tub. His hands were tied behind his back with blood-splattered zebra-striped underwear.

There was something long, thin, and dark shoved up his ass, and what had once been his face was a swath of dark ruin and happy flies. His head nodded toward the tub as if bowing in reverence. There was blood on the wall, inside the tub, all around the body. There were footprints in the blood, and there was a towel on the floor where the man who had made the footprints had wiped the blood off his shoes.

Way Pierre was arranged, it was obvious that whoever had shoved whatever up his ass had sat on the commode to do their work. Nice and comfy, easy to get to Pierre's blow hole. Behind the commode on the wall was a plaque that said READING ROOM.

On the floor next to the commode lay a heavy tenderizing mallet, a gold cigarette lighter, a box cutter, and a pair of tin snips.

I eased in a little closer. Jim Bob and Leonard looked over my shoulder. The stink in there was more intense than in the bedroom. I put my hand over my mouth and breathed shallow breaths. I glanced in the tub. There were some messy things in there. I thought I recognized a dick and balls, but how can one tell about these things when they're covered in gore and withered from a few days of disconnection? It could have been a blackened and withered banana and two dried grapes, for all I could tell. There were teeth in there too, some gums and jawbone attached. There was also a hole in the tub where a bullet had gone through the back of Pierre's head and out the front and into the ceramic.

"I guess intimidation is out, huh?" Jim Bob said.

"Yeah," Leonard said. "I don't think we can beat this."

Jim Bob eased past me, lifted Pierre's head by the hair, squatted down and took a look at his face. "It's Pierre," he said, confirming what we already knew. "And he's had a dental job and a little tattoo work."

We leaned for a glance. Carved into his forehead with the box cutter was the word WELSHER. Below that, the tip of his nose was missing, and what had once been a mouth was just a gaping hole edged by bone and a tooth hanging by a strip of bloody skin.

"What's that in his ass?" Leonard asked.

"Barbed wire," Jim Bob said. "And you can be certain it wasn't no fencin' accident. I bet whoever stuck it up there didn't even grease it."

"You know who stuck it up there?" I said. "You see the size of those prints? Way that back door was opened?"

"Yeah," Jim Bob said. "Big Man Mountain."

"So maybe you're wrong a second time," Leonard said. "Looks like Big Man and Pierre weren't in cahoots."

"I think the word *welsher* carved into Pierre's head explains a few things," Jim Bob said.

"Explain them to us somewhere else," I said. "I've had about all this I can take."

We returned to the living room. The air was considerably better in there. Jim Bob said, "I think Pierre made some kind of financial arrangement with Big Man, and Pierre didn't deliver, and Big Man took it personal. Figure Pierre was in here with his fist up this guy's ass and Big Man came in and gave them a surprise party. A noise maker for the lover, and a bag of games for Pierre himself. I think toward the end there, it didn't have nothing to do with money. Big Man had a mission in mind, and it was supposed to end with Pierre dying slowly and

271

badly. And that's just the way it went. Let's finish look-ing."

We checked another bedroom. It was full of shelves, and on the shelves were rows and rows of videotapes. Jim Bob took a couple of them down, went back to the bedroom with the body and the VCR. Reluctantly, we fol-lowed. Jim Bob played a bit of each video.

"Jesus," Leonard said. "This shit is worse than the ones we got."

"Later stuff is my guess," Jim Bob said. "Fucks like this, they start out doin' a little rough stuff, then they build on it. Pretty soon, it's beyond a few bites and pinches and ass whippin's. It steps over into torture. You'll note, the park isn't the background for these. More seclusion. More time to make the kind of videos Pierre wanted to make, wanted to sell."

Jim Bob returned the videos to the shelves. We finished off our little escapade by looking in the garage. No car, but there was a motorcycle. It looked as if Big Man had traded out with Pierre, leaving his bike and taking Pierre's car.

We left out of there and drove away. It was a hot day now and the car's air conditioner was off, but I felt a chill anyway.

We stopped at a self-service gas station, threw away the gloves we'd used. I called the police department with a little tip about a house with two dead bodies in it. Before they could ask any questions, I hung up.

I went out to the car. Jim Bob had his hat pushed way back on his forehead and was pumping gas into his car's tank and Leonard was using Bissinggame's leisure-suit jacket to clean bugs off the windshield.

I leaned against the car. I kept hearing those damn flies

and smelling that stench, seeing that face that wasn't a face. Poor bastard. Worse yet, he hadn't even had the taste to wear decent jockey shorts. Who the fuck made them zebra-striped briefs anyway? There ought to be a law against that kind of shit. That and leisure suits.

Leonard trash-canned the suit, came over, leaned next to me. "You know, you dampen that material, it makes a pretty good swipe."

"Neat," I said.

"How you doin', man?"

"I don't know."

"Yeah, me neither," Leonard said. "Lot has changed in a short time. I don't know how I feel about anything. Poor old Leon."

"Yeah," I said.

"Clinton is gonna be seriously fucked up."

"Yeah."

"Poor Ella."

"Yep," Leonard said. "Poor Ella. Know what I think?"

"What?"

"I think the worst is over."

"You're talkin' about our lives," I said. "Seems to me you're being foolishly optimistic. Every time we turn around, we're openin' up a can of worms."

Leonard clapped me on the shoulder. "It's all right, man. We're both gonna be all right. Big Man had a falling-out with Pierre, took care of Pierre, so Pierre's no longer a problem. Big Man won't have any interest in us now. It's just a matter of time before the law runs him aground. Guy looks like that can't hide forever. As for King, well, we turn in the tapes to Charlie, and let Charlie sort stuff out. We've done all we can do."

"Reckon so," I said.

"You know, today's been different."

"That's an understatement."

"No, I mean it's been me keepin' you from goin' off half-cocked. Usually, it's the other way around."

"That's what's bothering me," I said. "I came within an inch of killing a man for no reason other than anger and suspicion. One squeeze of the trigger, I'd have been no better than Big Man, Pierre, or the rest."

"On your worst day, you're better than all of them," Leonard said. "You'd killed King, it wouldn't have hurt my feelin's."

"Leonard, sometimes you scare me."

Jim Bob went inside to pay for the gas.

I said, "He doesn't seem particularly perturbed, does he?"

"I have a feeling that weird fuck has seen more bodies and strange shit than we have, Hap."

"All I know is I feel like my life has been poisoned. I come home from a shitty job, get bit by a rabid squirrel, find out my insurance policy sucks the dog dick and my best friend is accused of murder."

Leonard nodded. "I know. One day I'm living with this guy I love, next thing I know he's run off with a grease ball, then Raul's killed, and I find out he was a grease ball himself. It's pretty disconcerting. I thought I could choose my men better than that."

"Considering my fuck-ups with women, I can't say much," I said.

"You're right," Leonard said. "You can't."

"I think Brett might be different. I want to believe she is. I want to believe I'm different. That I've changed. That I'm not quite so stupid."

"Well," Leonard said, "Brett strikes me as one hell of a lady. As for you, howsabout we not hope for too much?"

274

# 30

Couple days later, as reinforcement, I phoned Charlie and told him most of what I knew, holding very little back. The cops had already been to Pierre's and had found the videos. There were videos without face bars on them as well, so most of the people involved in the sorry business could be identified.

"I want to thank you and Leonard for the stuff you stuck in my mailbox, Hap."

"What stuff?"

Charlie laughed. "All right. Play it that way. But some helpful sonofabitch put two videos and a notebook full of coded phone numbers in there. One video is about grease, the other is about sex and violence."

"Does it help any?"

"Doesn't hurt. Fact is, this is one time where an entire ring of assholes is gonna get nailed. A few of the bikers involved won't get pinned, 'cause there ain't enough proof, but there's a string of video-store owners right now whose assholes are suckin' wind. I hate to give you any fuckin' credit, but you and Leonard can be proud of yourselves on this one."

"Yeah," I said, "but at what price?"

"At the price had to be paid," Charlie said. "You could have done better. You should have had the law in on it, but the law wasn't worth a shit on this one. You did all right, Hap. You and Leonard and Jim Bob. There's anyone ought to feel bad, it's the law."

"Long as you don't," I said. "Your hands were tied."

"I ought not to have let them been tied," Charlie said. "I don't know I'm thinkin' clear as I ought to be."

"Can you keep mention of me and Leonard out of this?"

"Yeah. We can use Jim Bob a little. He don't mind and it won't hurt him like it might hurt you. He was hired to do a job, you see, even if being a private detective don't exactly make everything he did legal."

"Maybe you could drop the two boys in the cabin," I said.

"We found them fellas," Charlie said. "One I thought I knew I did know. The other one's got a record long as the other. Scumbags, both. We're gonna blame it on Pierre. That way Jim Bob isn't put on the spot, and neither are you."

"Pierre wasn't the kind to do his own handiwork," I said.

"Maybe, but we're gonna make it look like he was."

"That's not very nice," I said.

"No," Charlie said, "and it ain't even legal."

"What about Jim Bob?" I said. "Haven't seen him since the day we found Pierre with a length of fence up his ass.

276

He didn't say 'bye or kiss my ass, he dropped us off and was gone."

"That's his way. Saw too many Lone Ranger movies when he was a kid. He's gone back to Pasadena. His job was finished. He can tell his client the stalk-and-rape ring is busted and he can go back to farmin' hogs and waitin' for the next job."

"What about Hanson?"

"I been over to see him, Hap. He's doin' pretty god-damn good. Amazing, actually. He gets better, I'll tell him all this shit. He'd want to know."

"What about Big Man Mountain?"

"Still hasn't turned up. He took off in Pierre's red Mercedes."

"That ought to show up."

"My guess is he dumped it right away, caught a bus to someplace hot and dry."

"Right now, Texas is hot and dry."

"Drier yet. Mexico."

"I don't know I should ask, but how about the wife?"

"We're separated, Hap. I think maybe it won't work out, know what I'm sayin'?"

"Yeah."

"She's seein' this fuckin' insurance guy kind of regular-like. Did I tell you he smokes?"

"Yeah."

"Sonofabitch," Charlie said.

"I hear that," I said.


Ella was buried the next day. I went to the funeral with Brett. Day after that, Leon was put down. Leonard and I got together, made a deal to pay for his funeral. Doing that tapped me out, but it didn't matter.

It was a hot day with a hot wind and the striped funeral tent rustled as the preacher talked a hot wind of his own. Leon got as good a sendoff as a launch party for the dead can be, considering, as is often the case, the minister who preached the sermon didn't know him from creamed corn.

Later, when me and Leonard and Brett walked with Clinton out to his car, he said, "Wouldn't none of that stuff preacher said about Leon true."

"It's just the way it's done," Brett said.

"Yeah," Clinton said, "well, they ought to do it some other kinda way. They made Leon all out to be this suit-type man. Shit, I'm gonna miss my bro."

"I'm sorry, Clinton," I said. "It's sort of my fault."

"More like mine since I asked you and Leon to help out," Leonard said.

"And mine," Brett said. "He was helping me."

"No, it ain't y'all no kind of way," Clinton said. "It's that sonofabitch killed him's fault. Me and Leon, we knew what we was gettin' into. You folks hang tough."

Clinton, trying to hold his head up and stay solid, climbed in his car and clattered away.

"I got to tell you," Brett said. "I first met those two, I thought they were just a couple of ignorant thugs. I think now they're better than most of the educated people I know."

"Leon and Clinton," Leonard said, "they invented grit. I'm gonna miss ole Scum Eye. He was a stand-up guy."

Brett took us both by the arms. "So are you two guys," she said. And with her holding our arms, we walked down to my pickup and drove away from the hot wind and the striped funeral tent, the headstones rising up sad and white and gray.

\* \* \*

Next few days weren't so bad. Things started to sort themselves out. I got a job at a club, bouncing. The pay wasn't much, but I figured I could do it for a week or two until I found something else. Only thing was, I didn't start for a couple of days, and I was dead broke.

Brett soothed that. She managed to take some time off from work, even if she didn't have it coming. We spent a lot of time together, at her place and mine, getting to know each other better, and from my end I certainly liked what I had come to know.

Brett coming out to my house changed the place. She couldn't stand the way I did things, so she did it her way, and I liked her way better. The dishes were cleaner and neater and the house smelled better. The gym-sock stink in the bathroom was gone and the mold was off the shower curtain.

'Course, Brett made me do all the work to get the place in shipshape condition, and she was one hell of a D.I. I figured next thing coming was I'd have little wooden plaques with slogans on them hanging over the kitchen sink and the bathroom shitter.

On a hot Sunday morning, two weeks after all hell had gone down, the sky began to darken and threaten rain. By eleven A.M. the heat was dissipating and the air turned cool. I got up and opened all the windows. In the distance, in the dark clouds, lighting bolts hopped and squirmed as if mating.

Brett and I had spent a large portion of the morning in bed, making love, and now we were in the kitchen. Brett was wearing one of my T-shirts, and she sure did it more justice than I could have, especially since that was all she was wearing. I liked to watch her move, leaning over the sink, messing with pots and pans, trying to find some-thing in the cabinet worth fixing for lunch.

I was in deck shoes, torn jeans and a black T-shirt so faded it looked the color of ancient cigarette ash. I washed my hands and surveyed the interior of the refrig-erator. It was as lonesome in there as Custer on the Little Big Horn.

"Hap," Brett said, "even I can't make a meal out of this stuff, and I can toast shit and bricks and make you happy. This calls for severe action. I'm gonna go to town and buy some grub."

"I'd offer you money, but I don't have any."

"Hell, I know that."

"I'll pay you back when I get my first check."

"You can buy me a meal."

Brett darted into the bedroom, pulled on a dress and shoes, bounced out of there with my truck keys. I stood on the porch and waved. She wasn't gone thirty seconds before I took notice of the sky. It had changed. The air was neither cool nor hot. I felt as if I was in the middle of a bowl, and the sky, which had gone green, was grad-ually descending on me. I knew the signs. Tornado.

I wished I had noticed before Brett drove away. Now there was nothing I could do but stand there in the eerie silence, wondering if it would happen, wondering if she would be okay. A car on the road is not a good place to be during a tornado.

I watched to see if a funnel might be forming. The clouds were nervous, though not as nervous as me. They rolled and twisted and at times I fancied I could see them dipping down like the bottom part of a blackened snow cone, but in the next moment it looked like nothing more than a wispy black cloud.

I decided to pour myself a cup of coffee, sit on the front porch and keep an eye on things. Weather turned sour and the sky skipped down, I was going to make a run for the bathroom and my tub, supposedly one of the safest places you could be during a tornado, if for no other reason than the plumbing is rooted deep into the ground. But of course there was really no safe place to be during a tornado, unless it was someplace where the tornado wasn't.

Before I got back to the front porch, the rain came, blowing hard, and there was a sudden blast of hail so ferocious I couldn't stay on the porch. Sitting there was like being a victim of a biblical stoning.

I rushed inside, shaking the rain off of me, listening to it blow at a slant under the porch and slam the wall. A chunk of ice literally the size of a baseball crashed through the window behind the couch, flew over it, slammed against the floor and bounced and hit a chair in the kitchen, thudded back into the living room, rolled to the middle of the floor.

I turned to look at the broken window. Rain and smaller chunks of hail were slamming against it now, and I heard another glass go in the bedroom. It was eerie, the wind blowing that way, pushing the hail straight before it. If this wasn't a tornado, it would damn sure do until the real thing showed up.

I was thinking about pouring another cup of coffee and nesting in the bathtub with a flashlight and a book and one ear cocked for wind. Anything to get my mind off the storm and Brett being in it. But I didn't do that. I guess it was people like me that waited until the last minute and were taken away by the wind. Instead I went to the side window of my living room and glanced out.

Trees were bending way too far, and I saw lightning leap out of the sky and smack one like an insolent teenager, knocking pine bark and needles a-flying.

When I turned around the back door jumped away from the wall with an explosion of busted lock, and I thought, goddamn, the twister's got me, but then I saw it was a human tornado.

Big Man Mountain. He came quickly into the room. He was wearing jeans and a filthy white T-shirt and his clod-hopper boots. He was soaked with rain and it ran off of him in great rivulets and pooled quickly at his feet. He looked like hell. He was pale as Casper the Ghost.

I thought about my gun, back in my bedroom in the nightstand drawer, and I started to run for it, but Big Man came through the open kitchen and into the living room at a rush. I braced myself to fight, but he leaped up and twisted and shot out both feet and hit me with a drop-kick that flung me across the room and into the front door with a sound like someone dropping a dead blow-fish on the dock. It hurt like a sonofabitch. I tried to get up but didn't have any wind in me. Big Man had hold of me and lifted me over his head as if I were a sack of flour, tossed me back onto the floor. I tried to curl my body and duck my chin, roll with the fall, but it still hurt like hell.

Next thing I knew, Big Man had me by the head and was yanking me around and whirling me onto the couch. I came to a sitting position and shot out my foot as he came at me, scored a good one on his chin. He went back and I came up and he swung and I went under and struck out with a knee that caught him in the thigh, and it was a good shot, right on that point in the thigh that makes you wish it was someone else's leg, even your mother's. I whipped my arm around and hammered him in the kidneys, slid in behind him, tried to grab him in a stranglehold. But this wasn't smart. That was his game.

Big Man grabbed my arm, bent forward suddenly, and I found myself flying. I landed on the couch again, face-down. I tried to get up but took a kick in the ass, right above the blow hole, right there on the tip of the spinal cord. I went out, and when I awoke I was in hell.

I was on the couch, sitting. My feet were tied with a twisted coat hanger and my wrists were bound behind my back with what I figured was the same. At my back the wind and small pellets of ice whirled through the broken glass and smacked the back of my head, neck, and shoulders. The couch was soaked with cold rain.

Big Man had pulled a chair up in front of the couch and he was looking at me. To his right he had placed another chair. On the chair, from my cabinets and closets, were a variety of items. Straightened coat hangers, a butcher knife, a corkscrew, pliers, and an ice pick. There was also a glass of water and a bottle of aspirin.

Big Man had taken his shirt off, and he was a massive hunk, with a big solid belly and a hairy chest and arms that looked like knotted ship cables. On his right lower arm was a large festered wound. His face was oily and covered with sweat beads the size of his own knuckles, which were considerably larger than diesel truck lug bolts. He was holding his head up with difficulty. His breathing was bad. His face had gone from pale to blue, but not as blue as his lips. His eyes were scummy around the edges and the whites were no longer whites, but reds. In his left hand he held a Swiss Army knife open to the spoon.

"I was thinking of your eyes," he said. "I thought they

might be a good place to start. But I'm having second thoughts. I say let you see what there is to see until the very last."

"There's no reason to do this, Big Man," I said. "It's all over. You did Pierre in yourself. What's the point?"

Big Man smiled at me. His teeth appeared not to have been cleaned in ages. They were yellow, with brown roots that were probably from chewing tobacco.

"The point is *completion*," Big Man said. "No one believes in completion anymore. I do. I finish what I start. I was paid to do you in, get a video and a book, and now I'm here to do just that. I could have done the nigger, but you worked out better. I been hiding in the woods. You're easier to get to here. You, the nigger, the cunt, it don't matter, long as I come up with what I set out to come up with. The book. The video."

"It's over, Big Man."

Big Man shook his head. "No. The other night was left undone, Mr. Collins, but as you can see, here we are again."

"You did your job, man. Pierre isn't here to pay you anymore. You're not obligated."

"He hired me. He didn't pay me. I had to extract some vengeance for that. I took a little money from him, a few items I could sell. Nothing that drastically exceeded what was owed me for the job I had done so far. He wanted to not pay me because I didn't get the video and the book. He wasn't giving me enough time. Jesus, you know, Collins, I feel like shit."

"Big Man. Listen. The notebook, the videos. The cops have them."

"You said that before."

"And I lied, but this time it's true. It's all over. I wasn't trying to blackmail anyone. That wasn't my purpose."

"Shut up. I got a headache. I'll do the talkin'."

"That looks like a bite," I said, nodding toward the wound on his arm.

"Fox. I was campin'. Livin' in the woods in Pierre's Mercedes. I got out to take a piss. Fox came at me. Leaped at me. Bit me. I strangled it. I never seen one do like that before."

"It was rabid, Big Man. You've been bitten by a rabid fox."

"No."

"Yes. A rabid squirrel bit me, so I should know!"

Big Man burst out laughing. "A rabid squirrel! What's your game, Mr. Collins?"

"Big Man, I don't have the video or the notebook. Your job is over."

"It's over when I say it's over. And if you don't have the video or the notebook, well, I'll know for sure after we try out a few of these instruments. A corkscrew twisted into the knee, just above the knee joint. You wouldn't be-lieve—"

"Yes, I would."

"Oh, no. Experiencing it is the only way to believe it. I've tried it on myself. It really hurts. Of course, I didn't go as deep into my flesh as I'm going to go into yours. I'm going to screw it right into your leg and through the muscle and nerves and into the bone. Then I'm going to do your triceps tendons. Now there's some pain, my man."

The house rattled. The rain slammed harder and harder.

Big Man took the aspirin bottle and unscrewed it and

shook several aspirin into his mouth. He picked up the glass of water, tried to sip it. He tossed it across the room, spat the aspirin in my lap.

"I can't swallow," he said. "Hell of a cold."

"It's the water. Hydrophobia. You have rabies, Big Man. You need a doctor. It may not be too late."

Big Man stood up violently, causing the chair he had been sitting in to fall backwards to the floor. "I do not have rabies. I startled a fox, that's all. You're not going to frighten me."

"I got bit by the squirrel, doctor told me a story about a boy got bit and died screaming in bed, gnashing his teeth. Finally his father smothered him. Whatever you do to me, it won't be half of what's going to happen to you. Call the doctor, Big Man. Get some help. This rabies stuff, it's got you half out of your mind. Maybe more."

"Oh, you think you're clever. Well, you aren't. I'm gonna start with the coat hanger." Big Man closed up the Swiss Army knife and jammed it in his pants pocket. He grabbed the straightened wire hanger off the chair. "What we're gonna do is, I'm gonna pull down your pants, Collins, then I'm going to insert this up your asshole slowly, twisting, pushing, and you are gonna talk like a sonofabitch. You're gonna—"

The front door came open suddenly, and standing in the doorway, soaked to the skin, was Brett. Water was running out of her hair and into her eyes, and she was scared-looking and talking as the door came open. "Truck ran off in a ditch. I—"

Then she saw Big Man.

"Come on in, honey," Big Man said. "You're just in time to see me screw this up your lover's ass. Maybe up the pee-hole in his dick. Fact is, that sounds better. I haven't tried that."

Brett's face went slack and her right hand smoothed the side of her thigh and dropped lower and took the hem of her dress. She lifted it, and I could see her panties, all wet and sticking to her like cobwebs, and I could see her beautiful legs. One of them had a belt around it with a holster strapped to it and a .38 in the holster. I had forgotten about that. She didn't go anywhere without it anymore.

She came up with the .38 and fired three times, so goddamn quick it was almost like one shot.

Big Man looked down at his chest. Three small red spots appeared on his filthy T-shirt. He looked at Brett, said, "You're first, split tail. Right up the cunt."

He stepped toward her, holding the coat hanger, which wobbled like a giant insect antennae. Brett fired twice more.

Big Man paused, as if he had been strolling and decided not to cross at a certain traffic light, but to go the other way. He stepped back once, turned around, started walking toward the back door. He fell and grabbed the counter that separated the living room from the kitchen and held himself up. Brett fired again, and Big Man reached behind him, fanned at his spine like he was trying to swat a wasp.

He kept his feet, went out the back door walking briskly, but not running.

"Brett," I said. "You all right?"

"I guess so," Brett said, stepping out of the doorway and into the house.

"There's pliers on the chair here. Get them, undo these coat hangers."

Brett got the pliers and started twisting my ankles and wrists free.

"That must have been Big Man," she said.

"In the flesh," I said. When I was free I rushed to the bedroom, came back with my shotgun, a flashlight, and my .38. I gave Brett the shotgun. "He comes back, cut down on him with this."

"You bet," she said. I kissed her. Her lips trembled, and so did mine.

I took my .38, went out the back way, into the rain and the dark and wind so stout it could have blown Jesus off the cross.

There was no trail to follow in the blasting rain, but I went the path of least resistance into the woods. It was the way he would have gone, hit like he was. I found an animal trail and went along that, and once in the glow of my flashlight I saw blood on the leafy ground, being washing away by the rain. Fast and hard as it was raining, that meant Big Man was a very short space ahead of me.

As I went, I heard limbs cracking under the stress of the wind, and the tops of trees nodded down and lashed above me like mad women wailing. I went along until the trees broke and there was a clearing where there had been a bit of forest fire, and next to the clearing was a dirt road, more of a trail really, and in the clearing was what had to be Pierre's red Mercedes. It had been lashed by limbs and splattered with mud, which had dried so hard even the rain wasn't knocking it off. The windshield was cracked in several places. It was easy to figure Big Man had been using it like a tank, driving down the wooded backroads and sometimes over no roads at all, trying to avoid the cops. Looking for me, trying to finish some mad mission made madder by the bite of a rabid animal.

I looked around and didn't see Big Man. I walked carefully around the Mercedes. On the other side the back door was open. I could see Big Man's feet sticking out through the opening.

I eased over there and looked in. Big Man lay on his back on the seat, looking at the roof with eyes wide open. He had the Swiss Army knife in his fist, and it was open to a small blade, and the blade was buried in his jugular. He had managed to start at the center of his throat and pull the blade all the way through the artery.

Somewhere in the back of his jumbled brain maybe he believed what I said about the rabies. Or the .38 slugs were too much. Or he was just tired. It was hard to say, and it didn't matter. He was dead. His blood ran down his neck and over his chest and puddled beneath his head on the leather seat, dripped off the side and onto the floorboard, where his jacket and dozens of candy-bar wrappers and soda cans lay.

I put the .38 in my belt. I got hold of his feet and bent his legs and pushed him all the way inside and closed the door.

I started back for the house and for Brett, ready to start yelling soon as I broke the woods, lest she shoot me with the shotgun.

But the wind picked up and trees began to crack and fall. All around me they fell, and I tried to maintain the flashlight, but lost it. I was knocked to the ground, then the rain stopped and the wind stopped and the sky lightened, but when I crawled out from under a clutch of small limbs and looked upwards through the trees, the sky was green.

Then there came a howl. I had heard it before, and my blood chilled.

Tornado.

I dropped to the ground in a little indentation and the trees began to whip, and directly to my right I could see an oak being pulled up by the roots. I tucked my face into the wet leaf mold and tried to become one with the earth, and all around came the howling and the lashing of rain, and there was a tugging at me, as if I might be pulled from the ground like a farmer jerking a turnip from the dirt, but I was low enough, and clinging to the earth like a goddamn lizard, and I held.

And the great storm raged and screamed around me and Mixmastered the forest, filled my nostrils with leaf mold and soil, and still it churned, and still I held, and after what seemed like the proverbial eternity the wind died down and there was a gentle breeze and a light rain and the air was filled with the aroma of damp earth and raw tree sap from twisted pines.

I stood up slowly. My pants were around my ankles and my shoes were gone and so was one sock. A vast expanse of the woods had been annihilated. I stood amongst twisted stumps and shattered limbs. My shirt fell forward, and I realized the storm had twisted the damn thing off my back. I tried to pull my pants up, but the backs of the legs and the seat of the pants were gone.

I pulled the shirt off and threw it down and stepped out of the ruin of my pants. Wearing my underwear and one sock, I started back for my house, but as I went I found that I could see a great distance now because the storm had taken away the natural barrier between me and my house, and where it ought to have been was only a bathtub and some bits of wreckage. Across the way, over the little dirt road and the barbed-wire fence and into the pasture there, I could see what was left of my house, sitting on the tip of its roof, the walls spread out and shattered like the staves of a barrel.

I tried to run but couldn't. There were limbs and stumps everywhere, and I was barefoot. I hopped and stumbled my way into the clearing that had been my backyard, tiptoed through the grass burrs that had grown up from me not mowing. I started yelling for Brett.

My stomach turned to acid. This was my life. Murder and storms and destruction, the loss of loved ones. I started to cry. I stumbled to where my house once stood and called for Brett as if I could scream her down from the heavens into which she had been blown, or perhaps call her up from beneath the sickening pile of lumber.

Then I heard, "Hap."

I turned. Rising out of the bathtub, which had held to the ground because of the deeply buried pipes, was Brett. She was holding the shotgun and her hair was cluttered with plaster and splinters.

I blundered over to her and she laid the shotgun beside the tub, stood up and hugged me. We both began to cry. I held her and held her, then I was in the tub with her, the two of us clinging to each other as if we were two parts of a whole.

We held like that for hours and hours, crying and kissing and not really talking, and finally the gentle rain stopped, and we lay there sopping wet in the cool tub, watching the light of the sky die out slowly and the night creep in. The stars poked at the velvety blackness, like the tips of pins being stabbed through dark fabric. The moon rose up then, quartered and weak, but lovely just the same.

There in the dampness, the tub our bed, the night our roof, overwhelmed with a strange sense of peace, we fell asleep, holding each other.